The Christmas

Presence

CAROL KINNEE

ISBN-978-0-9958515-3-5

ISBN-13: 978-0-9958515-0-4 (e-book)

*For Colin—thanks for
letting me sneak off to write*

and

Jean—thanks for the copy-edit

The Christmas
Presence

1

"The kid didn't see anything, Ang." Jake listened for a minute, and then said, "So don't back me on it. You weren't there, I was."

Jake held the phone away from his ear as the silence on the other end exploded.

"Look Ang—" He rolled his eyes and tried to cut through her string of words. "I am not going to wreck the future of some dumb jock who spends a night hanging with the wrong crowd." He listened for a moment and said, "Does this make you feel better? I, Jake Ryan, interviewed Chase Evans and found that he was unable to identify the shooter."

Ang carried on as if he hadn't spoken. Half-listening, Jake shoved his house key into the lock and pushed open the door. His partner Angelina was going ballistic on the other end of the phone. For Jake, the case of the kid in question was closed. Basketball superstar Chase Evans had hung out with the bad boys for one alcohol-fueled night. When the shooting went down, Evans was puking his guts out in an alley across the street. Sure the kid knew the shooter—what kid that age didn't—but five of the gangsters he was hanging out with had positively identified the guy. The way Jake saw it, there was no point wrecking the future of a straight "A" student looking at a full ride scholarship to university. The Evans kid had learned his lesson. He wouldn't be cruising the mean streets of inter-urban Toronto anytime soon. Besides, the kid deserved the chance to see there was more to life than Ross Park.

Jake listened to Ang run on for another minute.

"Alright already. Go to bed. It's one a.m.," he cut in.

Ang snorted and hung up. Jake knew that in the morning she would continue her rant as though he had never interrupted.

He sighed and stepped through the door of his townhouse. Inside it was warm and welcoming, a break from the cold wet outside. He shrugged out of his heavy woolen jacket and draped it over the back of a leather recliner. He'd deal with the fallout tomorrow. For now, he would take his own advice and grab some slumber.

***

"No . . . Don't . . . I can't . . ." Jake muttered and turned in his sleep.

A gust of wind churned through a gap in the window and rattled the venetian blinds. He groaned, rolling over in the sweat-drenched bed, his long limbs tangling in the rumpled sheets.

"Can't you see . . ? No!"

Awareness returned with the force of an icy bucket of water to the face. He lunged to a sitting position as the dream fled.

"What the . . ." Shadows, conjured by the trees outside the window, danced across the blank canvas of wall in front of him. His heart pounded as if he'd tried to outrun a suspect in a footrace. He kicked his feet free of the sheets, grimacing at the brush of damp linen on his skin. That one had been bad, the worst dream yet. He could feel the fire, smell the smoke. Groaning, he levered himself back against the headboard, shivering as cold air struck his sweat-slicked skin.

The nightmare still hovered over him, reaching into his conscious mind, winding his muscles into tightly woven knots. Jake listened to the silence, straining to hear the call of the dream's distant voice over the heavy thud of his heart.

Beyond the window, a growl of wind shook the branches of a stunted oak. Its wooden fingers rapped the glass. Jake jerked at the sound. Closing his eyes, he forced himself to relax. The storm was to blame for the dream. Somehow, he'd pulled the fury of the wind into his subconscious and let it shape the nightmare's direction.

Yeah. He snorted. If only it were that simple. He was desperate to find a nice rational excuse for waking. A twist of wind snaked through the open inch of window, catching the blinds and sucking them through the gap in the glass. Jake's heart rate ratcheted upwards.

Damn. Stop jumping at shadows.

"It's the wind, you fool," he muttered.

The dream's only meaning was the long-predicted ice storm had arrived. When he had fallen into bed with no other thought than sleep, he'd left the window open. Hell, he yawned. Fifteen-hour shifts screwed with your head. He barely remembered coming in the front door.

Murderers didn't respect the sleep patterns of the detectives working their cases. Last night's shift was a special pain. At least this time they caught the dirt bag that did the crime. As an added bonus, the victim wouldn't be missed; he was as sleazy as the killer was.

Jake lifted his head and listened to the howling wind. Tomorrow would be bad. If the storm lived up to predictions, it would smack Toronto harder than it had struck Winnipeg the day before. Warnings of heavy snow and power outages had already spurred a rush of grocery stockpiling and snow blower buying. At least it would put some of the bad guys on ice for a while. The crime rate always dropped during a snowstorm. What was the point of stealing a car if you ended up in a snowdrift?

He yawned again, his jaw cracking. His eyes were dry and gritty, a memento of the lack of sleep. Man, he was tired. He dragged his fingers through his hair, pushing the damp black waves from his eyes. A tiny tremor shook his left hand. He tightened it into a fist and scowled.

"Get it together," he muttered, propping his shoulders against the wooden headboard and cautiously sucking in a breath. His thoughts were a confused muddle of dream and reality.

Enough already. He groped for the switch on his bedside lamp, flipped it on, and blinked in the brightness. The numbers on the clock face chased away any hope of rest. Grumbling at the loss of another night's sleep, he swung his legs over the edge of the bed and grabbed a pair of sweat pants. Three o'clock in the morning, five mornings in a row. That was a record, but *why* was it happening? He rubbed his chin, and stubble scraped his palm.

Slowly he stood, pulling the faded pants over long muscular legs. The nightmare taunted him, replaying in slow-moving fragments offering glimpses of horror. Jake closed his eyes and willed the images from his head. Right. He was fooling himself; the nightmare wasn't going away. It would live on through the rest of the night, teasing his memory and coloring his every thought.

With a groan of disgust, he sat back down, breathing deeply, trying to pull air into his lungs. His throat burned. He'd been shouting, screaming in that soundless dream way. Goosebumps pebbled his arms. He leaned over, slammed the window shut, and turned to stare at the flickering light of the TV. He didn't remember turning it on.

The nightmare—it was so vivid—as if with his next breath his lungs would fill with choking smoke. The dream's sticky fingers clung to him, refusing to let go. Angered by his imagination's freefall, Jake stood and strode into the kitchen. He yanked open the door of the refrigerator and scowled at the pizza box and carton of orange juice inside. When had he last taken the time to shop—a week—two weeks? Resigned to the limited choices, he snatched the carton of juice and gulped the cold liquid straight from the spout. The tart citrus flavor drove the dryness from his mouth. Absently he swiped his hand over his lips and lifted the last piece of shriveled pepperoni pizza from the box.

"Three in the morning? What the hell does it mean?" His voice echoed in the stillness. He was too logical to believe that the dreams were random. There had to be a rational explanation; he just had to figure it out.

Okay. He chewed a mouthful of dry pizza and stared at the wall and its flickering shadows. The dream always began the same way—flames roaring in the rafters, acrid smoke choking him—he was searching for someone. His fingers tightened around the juice container as he saw the flames, felt the heat robbing him of breath. In the distance, a voice shouted his name. Jake blinked as a face floated before him. His mouth twisted into an expression that would have sent his snitch diving for cover. He knew that face—his ex-wife, Noelle. He hadn't seen her in ten years, *now* she was haunting his nights?

He blew out a gusty sigh and rolled his shoulders, trying to relax the tension that thought of Noelle brought. Marriage. What a fiasco . . . but that farce was ancient history. He took a restless turn around the kitchen. Why dream of Noelle now?

His partner Ang would say it was some sort of psychic connection. Ang saw mumbo jumbo everywhere. He snorted. Yeah right, what a crock. He'd seen some of the flakes offering the department their services as mediums. Maybe his aura was too gray or maybe like Scrooge, his diet was getting to him—too much pizza and not enough greens. Maybe the nightmares were a bit of bad pepperoni.

His fingers drummed the countertop as he stared at the clock. The numbers were branded in his brain. Why dream of Noelle now? He turned and paced another length of the kitchen. Were the dreams some sort of warning?

Enough already, he was starting to sound like Ang. He had to get some shuteye. It was tough enough doing the job when he slept. Right now, his temper was short, really short. If he didn't solve this dream thing, he'd find himself chatting about it and psychic connections with the Captain.

Yeah, that was all he needed. He was already on thin ice. Leaving the Evans kid's witness statement out of his report was probably a dumb move, but the kid's only crime was stupidity. He wouldn't be hanging out with the gangs again anytime soon. Witnessing a violent hit had a way of changing your perspective, especially if you were an "A" level basketball player going through a little rebellion. With so many witnesses, the statement of one terrified teen wouldn't make a difference.

Why Ang couldn't see that was a mystery. You would think someone who believed so much psychic mumbo jumbo would be more flexible, but instead, she insisted that it was a sign he was burning out. What did she know? As a fresh detective, she did everything by the book. A cop's job had more gray areas than that. Sometimes you had to be creative.

But then again, maybe she was right. Maybe he needed a break. Maybe he should take some holidays and get away from the job. Maybe he should leave work behind before he did something that got him suspended.

It would be Christmas soon. The weather in Landings, British Columbia beat Toronto's in winter. He'd go to Vancouver Island, look up the source of his nightmares, and settle his mind. It would give him a break from homicide, and maybe lay his personal ghost to rest. It was a long time since he visited the island. It might be interesting to see Noelle again—for old time sake—nothing else.

He yawned and stretched. The decision loosened some of the tension in his shoulders. Jake headed back to his rumpled bed, switching off the television as he passed. Tomorrow he would book a flight. His parents would love his company for a week or so. He turned out the light and climbed back into bed.

2

Noelle groaned and opened her eyes to the cacophony of bells. The hazy features of her dream lover wavered and fizzled, blinking out of existence, leaving behind the glowing numbers of the clock.

"No, no, no, not again," she moaned, slapping the snooze bar and sliding the alarm to off. Rolling over she collapsed against the pillows, draping one arm across her eyes, shutting out the glare of the over-sized numbers.

It wasn't fair. The dream was just getting to the good part. Her body still tingled—hot, restless, waiting for— what? She sat up and sighed. Waiting for Prince Charming to have his wicked way with her was what. Well, the fairy tale had just come to a bad end, and judging by the time, it wasn't her first slap of the snooze button. So much for using the Trans-Siberian Orchestra's *Carol of the Bells* as a wakeup call. She had slept through half the song, not stirring until the bells reached full crescendo.

Swearing, she flung the covers back and staggered out of bed, cringing as her toes met the icy hardwood. She fished her robe off the end of the bed and pulled it on, knotting the belt tightly around her waist as she stumbled out of the bedroom.

"Crap," she mumbled, catching her big toe on the edge of the door. She limped towards the kitchen.

"Coffee," she muttered. "Coffee will bring me back to life as well as a kiss from good old Prince Charming." She thought about that and shook her head. Maybe not, but it was all she had.

"Morning, Jackson," she called, greeting a sleepy black Labrador retriever stretched out by the back door.

The dog's inky tail waved in response.

"I'm running late," she told him as she dumped coffee and water into the coffee maker and pushed brew. "I'll shower and then out you go." She paused. "Maybe not. You can go out now. There's no time for accidents!"

Jackson stood, stretched, and offered up a hearty shake that sent his dog tags jingling. Noelle ruffled his ears and unlocked the back door, pulling it open to a gust of raindrop-laden wind. Jackson paused in the open doorway, turning reproachful eyes to her as the first droplets splattered his dark coat.

"Out," she said firmly.

The dog cast her a baleful look followed by a deep sigh and slunk down the steps to the grass. Noelle slammed the door and headed towards the bathroom, shedding her nightclothes on the way. Twisting on the taps, she stepped into the warm spray, sighing in pleasure as the hot water slicked her skin.

"Two extra minutes," she muttered, closing her eyes and leaning into the warmth. She could give herself that much. She would cut her coffee intake to one and skip reading the newspaper.

Under the mesmerizing spell of the hot water, her thoughts returned to her dream lover. If only that kind of passion existed outside of fairy tales. She shook her head and grabbed the shampoo bottle, massaging lavender-scented soap through her hair. She tilted her head back and icy water cascaded over her face. Gasping, she groped blindly for the taps, spinning them off and yanking open the shower curtain. Teeth chattering, she fumbled for a towel, swiped the soapy hair from her eyes and pulled another fleecy towel from the cupboard to wrap around her body.

"Okay, it's time to replace the hot water heater," she muttered. "Figures it would pack it in right before Christmas."

Gritting her teeth against the cold, she ducked her head under the tap and rinsed the rest of the suds from her hair. She scooped her robe from the floor, shrugged into it and then paused at the sound of muffled barking. Right—she closed her eyes. She hadn't covered the dirt pile in the back yard and Jackson had found it. She didn't have to look to know she was right. She groaned, ran the few steps to the kitchen, and peered out the window. Sure enough, Jackson had gone from digging to chasing seagulls. Mud caked his black coat in a chocolate glaze.

"Oh, Jackson, why? Why today?" she said. She grabbed a rag from under the kitchen sink and opened the back door. Jackson bounded up the wooden steps, his tail slashing the air.

"Not so fast." Noelle grabbed his collar and forced him to sit. She lifted his paws and wiped away the mud, rubbing his feet clean. Deglazing his coat came next. She scrubbed the mud from his sides, lecturing him as she worked. "When are you going to grow up? You're three. It's time you acted like a mature dog. It's the name, isn't it? I should have called you Angel or Rover. I knew Jackson had bad written all over it from the start."

Discarding the dirty rag in a bucket under the sink, she washed her hands and took a snowflake-covered coffee mug from the cupboard. Pouring a cup of coffee, she stirred in cream and sugar and headed down the hall to her bedroom. Jackson trailed behind her leaving faint muddy prints on the wooden floor.

Noelle set the cup on the edge of a carved antique dresser and opened the door to the closet. She chose a soft mauve-colored sweater and gray dress pants. Thanks to the abbreviated shower, she had time to gulp another cup of coffee and organize her thoughts before leaving for work.

The shock of the eye-opening blast of cold was leaving her, and the caffeine hit hadn't kicked in. She yawned and eyed the tangled sheets. Hard to believe she had slept there alone. Usually when she fell into bed, she didn't move until morning. Last night . . . she shook her head and grabbed the corner of the fluffy white duvet. Yeah, that was one heck of a dream. Someone had told her that dreams were a compilation of things that you heard or saw during the day. She hadn't had a date in a month and wasn't watching erotic movies, so where had that sizzling, hot fantasy come from? She lifted a couple of black filigree-patterned pillows from the worn steamer trunk at the foot of the bed and piled them against the high wooden headboard. That done, she flipped up the slats on the window shutters.

Dull grey light straggled into the room. She shivered. These cold wet days made it hard to muster the energy to climb out of bed, much less work up the enthusiasm to face the day, but, she consoled herself, it was the last day of work before Christmas holidays. Starting tomorrow she was free to sleep in and do whatever she wanted.

First though, she reminded herself, shaking off the reverie and stepping away from the window, she had to survive the next eight hours.

No more wasting time. She yanked the towel from her head, grabbed the hairdryer and scrunched and styled her wild curls into order. That done, she dropped the dryer onto the counter and reached for her cosmetics bag. A light touch of eye shadow, followed by a powdering of soft rose blush, and her make up regime was almost complete. She scanned her face in the mirror and nodded, satisfied with the results. The moss and gold hues of the shadows lent a smoky quality to her green eyes. She added a rim of chocolate brown liner and black mascara to her lashes, drained the last sip of coffee in her cup and offered Jackson a quick pat. Retracing her steps to the entry hall, she retrieved the newspaper from in front of the mail slot and carried it to the kitchen, scanning the headlines as she walked. "Politician implicated in local scandal," "Middle East Strife," "Convenience store gunman strikes again." She flipped the paper open and checked her horoscope.

"Chapter you thought closed may reopen. Be analytical. Avoid confrontation," she read to the dog.

"Does that mean that we reread chapter four, or that I should watch out for fights on the playground?"

She dropped the paper onto the glossy surface of the black granite countertop, filled Jackson's metal bowl with dry dog food and placed it in front of him. "There you go. Bon appétit!"

Propping her elbows on the counter, she stared out the window. Rain fell in a continuous curtain, washing the last leaves from the trees. Funny how the weather didn't affect the exuberance of the kids, she mused, watching a fat drop trail down the glass.

Christmas was a week away, and classroom spirits were far from gloomy. Her grade one students were bouncing off the walls. Santa was coming and the children wanted snow. They were convinced Santa's sleigh couldn't land without it. Noelle had tried reassuring them that Santa's sleigh was equipped with all-weather sleigh runners, and he knew how to cope with wet West coast weather, but yesterday the hum in the classroom had reached fever pitch. Keeping twenty-one little elves amused was becoming almost impossible.

Noelle's full lips pursed as she thought about the upcoming day. She understood the message that Christmas was over-commercialized, that not everyone celebrated the season, but did the parent council really think the kids would forget reindeer and short fat men in red plush in favor of a day at the farm? Farm day was a great idea—for May—but December? Noelle rolled her eyes. To her, it was carrying political correctness too far.

Shaking her head over an idea she felt doomed to disaster, she refilled her coffee cup and settled into a high-backed kitchen chair. Her cell phone rang, vibrating across the surface of the table. Noelle jerked at the sudden noise, banging her knee against the table leg. Her coffee cup rocked and tipped, spilling a milky wave into her lap.

"Damn!" She jumped up, banging her knee again as she tried to pull hot wool away from her skin.

"Hello!" she answered breathlessly.

"Noelle?"

"Yes."

"Great, I caught you before you left. It's Anne."

"Hi." Noelle said, blotting the coffee stain with a tea towel.

"Are you okay?"

"Aside from the fact that I just spilled a cup of coffee all over myself?" Noelle asked, tossing the towel into the sink.

"Oh no. I'm sorry. I won't keep you," Anne apologized. "Sue is sick, so we're out a rabbit."

"So what do we do?" Noelle pulled the damp cloth away from her legs, half-listening.

"Well I'd wear it, but I'm a bit too wide," Anne said wryly.

Noelle's attention snapped back to the call.

"You want *me* to wear the suit?" Pain crossed her face at the thought of the fluffy faux fur costume resting in the box at the edge of the counter.

"Well, since you have it, you might as well wear it. See you, Fluffy. I'll bring carrots and my version of the ears. They stand up better than yours do. Bye." Laughter cackled over the line ending the call.

Noelle dropped the phone onto the table and sighed. "I should have been a lawyer," she muttered. Instantly, she shook her head discarding the thought. The career switch she'd made ten years ago was the smartest thing she had ever done. Teaching to her was like carrots to a rabbit. She wouldn't change her decision for anything, even on a day like this.

"Well, Jackson," she said, looking at the dog lying at her feet. "Shall we go see what the well-dressed rabbit is wearing this season?"

The dog cocked his head quizzically.

Plucking the box from the counter, she retraced her steps to the bedroom and stripped off the coffee-soaked pants and sweater. Flipping the lid off the box, she eyed the dreaded rabbit suit. When she had volunteered to sew the costume, she hadn't expected to be stuck wearing it. Her nose wrinkled. Spending the day as a fluffy white rabbit was undignified, especially on the last day of class before Christmas. Santa hats, elf ears, even a Rudolph nose, but long white ears—no.

She ran a hand through her hair. Rabbits were cute and cuddly—a five-foot six-inch rabbit was nothing but a plush white wall. Mourning the loss of her dignity, she picked up the suit and stepped into it, twisting to reach the long zipper in the back. She pulled the hood up and faced the mirror. It was worse than she had expected. She looked like an over-stuffed rodent with good teeth.

"Great," she muttered, glaring at her reflection as she imagined smirking parents lining the hallways. Jackson gamboled into the room and came to a growling stop.

"No, Jackson! Down!" she yelled.

Too late. Jackson lunged, knocking her off her feet.

"Get off!" She pushed him away and scrambled up. "Bad dog. No, get down."

His woeful eyes locked on hers and he whined, as if apologizing for his mistake. She shook her head, trying to keep her frown, but gave in, stroking his head in forgiveness.

"I should have known you would turn out like this when I named you," she said.

The thought of the name's origins returned the frown to her face. She had named him Jackson after three glasses of wine with her friends egging her on. Naming the dog after her ex-husband had seemed a funny way of declaring herself free of the past, but things had not ended up that way. Instead, far too often, the dog's name conjured a picture of its namesake.

Noelle stopped mid-pat, the heat pooling in her cheeks. The face on last night's dream lover had an uncanny resemblance to her ex.

"Obviously," she said straightening, "I need a date. I'm having nightmares." Jake had been slipping into her subconscious at the oddest moments lately. She had run into his parents at the mall the week before. Maybe that was why. The Ryans were full of excitement over an upcoming Christmas cruise to Panama.

"Okay, Jackson," Noelle said, forcing her thoughts back to the present. "Let's get rolling. Jake Ryan is the last person on earth I should waste two seconds of thought on."

The doorbell rang.

She grabbed for the zipper on the suit and yanked. The fastener slid part way and snagged in the thick fur. She pulled harder, burying the zipper deeper. The bell rang again. She sighed in disgust. She had two options—keep wearing the bunny suit, or answer the door and beg help from whoever was there.

It's probably Anne dropping off the ears, she consoled herself, shuffling down the hall in the oversized bunny slippers.

She snuck a peak through the curtain at the figure outside. It wasn't Anne. The form on the other side of the curtain was big—over six-feet-tall—and broad shouldered. One of her brothers? She hesitated but visions of wearing the bunny suit on her drive to work forced her decision. Turning the deadbolt, she swung the door open.

Cobalt blue eyes met hers. Her heart bounced, stuttered, and returned to life at double time. The thick black hair and angular features of her dream lover sent a ball of fire snaking through her veins.

"Jake!" She plucked at the plush white fur, cursing Sue for getting sick and leaving her to wear the suit. The suit—she wanted to curl up and disappear. She had thought that if she ever saw Jake again, she would be looking sleek and sophisticated. He would be balding and overweight, perspiring in a scruffy suit. She was a fool. Ten years had added muscle to his already athletic body. Ten years had brought her dream lover to reality. She scrunched her eyes shut. She was in hell.

3

Jake lodged one hip against the low railing of the covered porch and ran his eyes over the furry figure in front of him. His look of surprise faded to amusement and a smile twitched across his lips.

"Is this where I say, "What's up, doc?" he asked. "Or, wrong season—Halloween is over?"

Not the best question to ask, but what the hell; it wasn't every day you got to see your ex-wife dressed in a bunny suit. So what if it weren't the type of bunny he wanted to see? It was still a bunny.

The full lips of said bunny compressed into a thin line. Jake could see the cost it took for her to meet his eyes. For a second, he felt sorry for her.

"Jake?"

She closed her eyes as if in pain. When she reopened them, he fell under the spell of their green magic.

"Why are you here?" she demanded.

The magic evaporated.

"What? No 'Hi Jake, how have you been? Me, I've changed jobs and hit the bunny trail.' Although," Jake said, studying the mismatched ears, "you might want to file an animal rights complaint about those ears."

Noelle's mouth flattened further as her eyes crystallized to green ice. "Funny. Now, why are you here?"

Jake's smirk slid. Okay, so maybe he hadn't thought things through. He had no excuse for knocking on her door at seven in the morning, but from the tomato red of her cheeks, she hadn't figured that out yet. Covertly he searched for a sign she was maybe a little bit glad to see him. There was none.

He had gotten out of bed to the suffocating sound of silence and escaped the empty house in search of company. Forty-five minutes of pretending to read the local paper while swilling coffee in McDonalds, had convinced him that this surprise visit was a good idea. His homecoming was a bust. Far from falling all over him in welcome, his parents had greeted his arrival in stunned silence. They were cruising the Panama Canal for their anniversary, a

Christmas vacation that they had planned for years. He arrived in time to drive them to the airport. Instead of hopping a plane back to Toronto, he had decided to stick around, look up old friends, ski a bit and take the much-needed time off. That plan hadn't worked out either. Everyone he met was happy to see him, but busy with the holidays. He'd spent last night alone, staring at an address book he had unearthed from a desk drawer while hunting for a deck of cards. That's when he had decided it was time to look Noelle up. The reason for the visit had sounded especially fine after a couple of festive double rum and eggnogs. In the dull light of day his logic was as thin as overstretched tinsel.

"Nice look, Noelle. Is that the new dress code in corporate law or are you a closet bunny?"

"Jake, why are you here?"

"I was in town for a few days and thought I'd look you up, see if you had my old CD collection." Oh God, had he said that? His cheeks began a slow burn. He hadn't felt this stupid since . . . since the last time he had seen Noelle. Yeah, recovering ancient CDs was a great reason to appear on her doorstep at seven o'clock in the morning.

"Are you going to ask me in?" He took a step forward. He could tell she was wavering. Abruptly she gave way, opening the door wider and gesturing him through. Jake brushed past her, raindrops from his jacket dripping onto the hardwood floor. He took off the jacket and draped it over the arm of an old pine rocking chair. The warmth of the room was welcome after the deep freeze outside. He had forgotten the damp cold of winter on the coast. Idly he glanced around the room, noting the old wood patinas and the jewel tones of the upholstery on the overstuffed furniture. The décor surprised him. Noelle had always seemed more of a chrome and glass kind of girl.

"Nice outfit," he said again, trying to provoke her. If he kept her on the defensive, she might not question his weak excuse.

"You know what Jake? I am glad to see you. The zipper on this suit is stuck. Since you're here, maybe you can help get it unstuck." As she spoke, Noelle yanked off the floppy-eared hood. A cascade of rich chocolate hair fell to her shoulders. She presented her back to him and waited.

He stared at the long curls. She had added streaks of gold since he had last seen her. He liked it. Her hair shimmered like rich silk begging to be touched. Carefully he collected a thick handful, resisting the urge to hold it to his face. A flood of memories assailed him. He pulled his thoughts back from the brink and jerked the rope of hair clear of the zipper. Noelle yelped.

"Ouch! Let me do it." She gathered her hair and held it away from her neck.

"Sorry. It was caught. Hold still. I think I just about have it. There."

The zipper parted abruptly. The suit opened to her waist revealing smooth white skin and the thin lace band of her thong. As his knuckles brushed her skin a jolt of awareness arced through him. Noelle moved away, dropping her hair over her back. She looked breathless.

"I'll go change. Thanks . . . I," she muttered and bolted. Somewhere down the hall a door slammed.

Jake leaned against the wall. What just happened? Absently he rubbed the knuckles of his right hand. He still felt a tingle of warmth.

***

In the safety of her room, Noelle raised a hand to her hot cheeks and glared at her flushed face in the mirror. Jake! His touch lingered on her skin. You aren't supposed to feel like this, she told herself. Breathe, damn it, think. She drew in a strangled breath. Why now? Be calm. But it's Jake . . . here . . . now. She grabbed a brush from the top of her dresser and gathered her hair into a messy bun, looping the hair tie around and around. Good. Take another breath. Of all the places and times, she had envisioned meeting him, she had never imagined anything like this. She had to be at school in an hour. What was she going to do about what was waiting in the other room?

Hurriedly she stepped out of the bunny suit and flung it onto the bed. She grabbed black jeans and a blue and white empire waist shirt from her closet and dressed hastily. What was she thinking letting Jake through the door? Was she nuts? She should have worn the bunny suit to school. Her fingers shook, slowing at the memory of the heat of his touch.

Flipping open her jewelry box, she dug out silver hoop earrings and a chunky chain, putting them on before glancing at her watch. Five minutes since she had fled the living room. With luck, her unwanted company was gone. She glared at the mirror, and then grabbed the evil bunny suit and swung open the door.

The living room was empty, the jacket gone from the chair. With a sigh of relief, she walked down the hall to find her luck still bad. Jake was standing by the counter, sipping a cup of coffee, watching Jackson.

"Good coffee. I grabbed a cup. Want one?" Without waiting for an answer, he reached into the cupboard and pulled out a red Santa mug. "Black?"

"No, cream . . ." She snatched the cup from him and banged it onto the counter. "You can't come in here, go through my cupboards and help yourself to my things."

"A little crabby this morning, eh? I guess you still need a couple of cups of coffee to wake up." Jake appeared unmoved by her words. He took another sip. "So what's with the bunny suit? I mean this is an improvement for sure, but that outfit had a certain charm."

Hot color flooded her cheeks. She tried another calming breath, mentally counting to ten.

Finally, she answered. "Jake, I need to get ready for work."

"Need to put together a few last-minute briefs? I guess you're not in court, since you're not dressed for it. Even here on the blasé West Coast, they dress more conservatively than that. Unless you're defending a Playboy bunny?" he asked, looking hopeful.

She decided the best course of action was to ignore him. She poured a coffee and stirred in cream. Taking a quick sip, she closed her eyes as the rich, full-bodied flavor bathed her tongue. Regretfully she settled the cup back on the counter, pulled open the fridge and grabbing the peanut butter, popped a slice of bread into the toaster. From the corner of her eye, she saw Jake add another piece of bread and top up his coffee. She glared at him, yanked open the cutlery drawer and grabbed a butter knife.

He quirked an eyebrow and flashed a challenging grin. "Threatening me?" He nodded in the direction of the knife.

"Not worth it. When you're done breakfast, maybe you can take yourself off, back to where you came from."

"I'm hurt. Aren't you a little glad to see me?"

"No," she lied. "Now if you'll move out of my way, I'll have my breakfast and go to school."

"School?"

"My job," she said.

His look of surprise might have been funny but she was too unsettled to enjoy it. Obviously, he didn't know about the change she had made ten years ago. The switch from law to education had been hard but she'd never looked back. The more time she spent in the classroom, the more she realized how much she would have hated corporate law.

"School?" he repeated, prodding her to continue.

"School," she said, buttering her toast, leaving his sitting in the toaster. "I teach grade one and today, I have a date to be a rabbit. So, if you don't mind, I'll get my things together and go."

She felt his gaze as she ate her toast and frowned over a pile of neatly stacked papers. She shoved the stack into her workbag feeling a twinge of resentment. It was hard to pretend indifference when what she wanted to do was stare back and catalogue the changes the years had brought. He looked like he had gotten past the bad times and moved on. She flipped through the animal pictures, barely recognizing the difference between a rabbit and a snarling wolf. Why now? Why did he have to show up on her doorstep looking like a model for *GQ*? She nibbled her bottom lip and paused over a picture of the backside of a baboon. She dropped it into the bag.

Unable to bear the silence she looked up and met his gaze. She looked away first, and crammed the rest of the pictures into the bag.

"Look Jake, it's been a long time. I have my life and you have yours. I dumped all your stuff at your parent's place ten years ago. Look there."

Jake leisurely finished his toast and popped another slice of bread into the toaster. He was pushing his luck but he couldn't drag himself away. He had thought coming here and seeing her would exorcise the dreams but this new

Noelle fascinated him. The magnetic pull of attraction was still there, stronger than ever. He had to leave so she could get to work but he needed to see her again.

Noelle zipped the bag shut and grabbed her jacket from a hook on the wall by the back door. She shrugged into the jacket and pointedly picked up the case. Scooping up the bunny suit, she gestured towards the door.

"If you don't mind, I have things to do."

"Sure, no problem. We can continue this conversation later," Jake said obligingly.

She stopped and slowly turned to face him. "No, Jake, we can't and we won't. This conversation is over. You should stay put on your side of the country and leave me alone."

Jake studied the ramrod posture and tight lips of the woman in front of him. Sorry Noelle, he said silently. Not going to happen. Now that he had seen her, he wanted to know more about this new Noelle. The toaster popped, breaking the taut silence. Grabbing the slice, Jake hurriedly spread peanut butter on it. He opened his mouth to take a bite but Noelle snatched it from his hand. She opened the door below the sink and tossed the toast into the garbage can.

"You didn't come here for breakfast. The door is there. Go now!"

Jake leisurely licked the crumbs from his fingers, smiling as Noelle's eyes followed the motion.

"Noelle you have to relax. Those little kids will pick up the tension in your aura."

He lifted his jacket from the chair and made his way down the hallway to the front door. He paused, one hand resting on the doorknob, his gaze lingering on her flushed face.

"It's been great seeing you. We'll have to do it again soon. Supper tonight, maybe?"

Noelle's hand curled into a fist. Jake hastily opened the door and stepped onto the porch. The door slammed behind him. He smiled at the heavy thud and fished his keys from his pocket, stepping off the sheltered porch into the rain. Glancing back at the house, he raised a hand in mocking salute and muttered, "See you soon, sweetheart. This trip may not be a bust after all."

4

First the hot water, and now Jake. What next? No. Noelle shook her head and shifted the car into second gear. Stop, she told herself firmly. Don't start thinking that bad things only happen in threes. This is nothing but a dumb coincidence. If she started expecting a third calamity, she would make herself crazy. Her fingers drummed the steering wheel in time with the blinking red of the taillights in front of her. Traffic on the four-lane highway stopped, crawled forward, and rolled to another halt. Grimacing, she wrapped her fingers around the wheel to stop their nervous tapping.

"Why," she muttered. "Why can't people drive in a straight line without hitting something?"

Ahead the red and blue strobe of police lights marked the cause of the slowdown. A refrain of flashing yellow signal lights joined the red brake lights. Noelle sighed and flipped on her turn signal, ready to merge into the right lane. Maybe the slow commute was a blessing? It let her work through the Jake thing. Jake, she sighed again and cranked up the speed of the windshield wipers in response to a heavy wave of raindrops.

The shock of seeing him crackled through her veins. Jake. She snorted in disgust. Once again, she had let him crawl under her skin and wind her up tighter than a wigged-out jack-in-the-box. Before she even backed out of the driveway, her teeth were clenched so tightly she would need a crowbar to pry them apart. Minutes into her commute, she had given way to muttering, venting the nervous energy running through her veins.

By the time she reached the school parking lot, she had compiled a list of Jake's faults. The list was ten-years-old but the faults were probably still the same. She yanked on the emergency brake and shut off the engine, taking a moment to breathe deeply before grabbing her briefcase and gathering up the ill-fated bunny suit. Forcing a grim smile in response to the wave of a passing parent, she made her way up the path to the school, oblivious to the puzzled gaze that followed her.

"Why?" she muttered. "He looks better than great and I'm wearing a giant bunny suit." Flags of red bathed her cheeks.

She stepped blindly into the center of a puddle and cursed as rainwater sloshed over her ankle boot. Even the weather had conspired against her.

A parent held the door for her as she entered the school. The warmth of the building chased away the chill of cold rain. She breathed in the scent of crayons and running shoes. It was time to concentrate on the day, not ancient history. If she wanted to cope effectively with twenty-five six-year-olds, she needed to be as tranquil as a summer pond. Teaching was like guerrilla warfare. You never knew when the next ambush would happen. Today's farm theme was uncharted territory. She had to focus on that, not reappearing ex-husbands.

"Hi, Ms. Ryan," a shrill voice shouted in greeting.

"Hi, Kenny. How are you?"

"Great! I got new runners. See?" The stocky little boy proudly lifted a mud-splattered runner.

"Those are nice," she said, dutifully admiring them. "I bet you walked to school."

"How did you know?" he said, his eyes widening at her magical powers of deduction.

"Kenny! Come on."

"Okay, bye."

Kenny dashed down the hall towards the gym.

"Walk, Kenny," Noelle called after him.

Kenny's pace slowed.

On days too wet for outside play, the children gathered in the gym where parent volunteers organized indoor games.

Noelle stepped through the staff room door into bedlam.

"Noelle, good you're here." A deep voice rumbled over the noise. "I need an honest opinion on my costume."

"Sure, Ed. I would be delighted to help…" Noelle's voice trailed off as she beheld the bizarre outfit Principal Ed Winston had donned. Ed had paired a pink rubber glove, its wrinkled fingers sticking up from his balding head, with a moth-eaten feather boa wrapped around his barrel chest. The red paper cup secured to his nose with an elastic band, made him look like a demented rooster.

"Well?" he asked.

"I'm, um . . . I'm in awe, Ed. I hope you didn't use glue to attach that glove."

Snickers greeted her comment. Ed's bald spot was a standing joke with the staff.

"Noelle, I'm wounded." His dancing brown eyes belied his saddened tone. "I expected that from one of these peons, but you . . ." Mournfully, he shook his head.

"We thought about it, but were afraid it would rip out what hair he has left," Marcella, the learning assistance aid chimed in.

"Of all the nerve," Ed muttered indignantly.

Everyone laughed. Noelle smiled. The staff was a good team. Ed was a fair hardworking principal, interested in his people and quick to lend a sympathetic ear.

"So, Noelle, I hear you are going to be our little Christmas bunny." Jack Howard, one of the grade five teachers, waggled lecherous eyebrows and twisted an imaginary mustache.

"No, Tom. I'm a rabbit, not a bunny. You're reading the wrong magazines."

The door opened and the short round form of Anne Roberts blew into the staff room. Anne's cheeks were rosy from the wind, her arms loaded with boxes. Noelle jumped up to help unload the pile.

"Wow, Anne, what is all this stuff? You look like Santa."

"Hah, these, I'll have you know," Anne said, setting the remaining pile precariously on the window ledge. "Are rabbit ears, a duck costume, and assorted school supplies."

"Ah, the bunny ears, excuse me, rabbit, I mean." Jack looked as if he were trying to suppress a grin.

"Anne, I have ears." Noelle shuddered at the memory of the flopping sticks.

"These are better. Presto!" Anne pulled the ears out of a box. "They're not as saggy."

"Okay, folks, it's show time," Ed cut in, glancing at his watch.

Noelle stepped into the staff washroom to change. Pulling on the outfit, she zipped it up, wincing at the memory of the last time she had worn it. The suit fit, but the legs, tailored to a taller form, flopped over the bunny flippers. Hastily, she rolled them higher and reached up to secure the ears to the hood. One ear stood proudly at attention, the other drooped No amount of straightening helped and she gave up in defeat, emerging from the washroom to find the farm animals multiplied to include a cat, a dog, and a pig.

Shaking her head, she said, "I guess I should be grateful that Sue wasn't going to be a cow."

"Looks good Noelle," Anne said, smiling.

Noelle craned her neck to check that she'd rolled the pant legs high enough she wouldn't step on them.

"Right, the kids will love it," she muttered.

"Okay troops," Ed announced, glancing at the clock. "Move out."

Noelle folded her clothes and placed them by her jacket. Grabbing her briefcase, she fluttered her fingers in farewell and headed towards her classroom. The room was unnaturally quiet; its small chairs tucked under short tables awaiting their occupants. Inside the tiny tables, pens and pencils nestled in their plastic boxes. Paper chains festooned the walls, while finger-painted Christmas trees covered the bulletin boards. Pictures of farm animals marched across a tack board in bright bold colors guaranteed to catch the eyes of the room's inhabitants. Noelle ducked under a low hanging paper snowflake and made her way to the front of the room.

Depositing her workbag on the desk, she opened it, and dropped her agenda onto its surface. With Christmas so near the children were short on attention. The staff may have agreed farm day was a good way to wrap up for Christmas holidays, but Noelle was reserving judgement. The bell rang putting an end to her thoughts as the room filled with wide-eyed, excited children confronted by a rabbit teacher.

***

"Wow," Noelle moaned, easing off a floppy bunny slipper to rub her aching foot. "Those kids are wired."

"I hear you," Anne said sympathetically, passing her a mug of coffee.

"Don't worry, Noelle," Tom said jovially. "Only four more hours."

The school secretary stuck her head in the door. "Phone call, Noelle."

"I wonder who that is." Noelle placed her cup on the ledge as a twinge of anxiety shot through her. She could count on one hand the times she had received calls at work. What new disaster had happened, she wondered, returning to her nervous superstition of bad things occurring in threes. Crossing the hall to the office, she shrugged off the bunny hood and picked up the phone.

"Hello, Ms. Ryan here. Can I help you?"

"Noelle?"

"Mom. What's up?" she asked.

"Brace yourself." Louise Hamilton replied grimly.

Foreboding settled in Noelle's stomach.

"What?" she asked tersely.

"Jake's in town."

Noelle let out the breath she was holding in a noisy exhale of relief. "I know. I had the pleasure of a visit this morning. How did you find out he was here?"

"He dropped by for coffee. His parents are away on a cruise. He came all this way to visit them, and now he's all alone . . . It was nice to see him." Louise's voice held a defensive edge.

Noelle's stomach muscles clenched and her foreboding doubled. "What did you do?"

Silence.

"Mom!" she said impatiently.

"You know, Noelle, I always liked Jake. I don't think he got a fair deal. I think he had the right to know."

"Mother." Noelle's voice held a note of warning.

"Okay." A long pause and then, "I invited him to dinner."

That wasn't so bad. Noelle would be too busy to make it.

Louise was still speaking. ". . . on your birthday."

"What?" Noelle's voice rose.

The secretary looked up from her computer.

Noelle lowered her voice. "You did what?"

". . . and I told him to come for Christmas if he found himself at a loss for something to do."

"I can't believe…"

The end of recess bell rang. Noelle hung up. Renee, the secretary studied her distracted expression.

"Bad news?" she queried.

"No, it's nothing," Noelle answered pulling open the office door.

The rest of the day passed in a blur. Noelle played her rabbit part, letting the children pat her ears, explaining what she ate and how she lived. The afternoon finally lurched to a close bringing the start of the holidays. She stood in the doorway chatting to parents and pupils, handing out small Christmas gifts of Santa-topped pencils and candy canes to her students. When the last of them disappeared through the door, Noelle leaned against the wall and surveyed the leftover mess. Bits of brightly colored construction paper, wool, and fluff covered the floor, remnants of the Christmas crafts the children had created. If Mr. Perkins, the Grinch janitor saw the mess, he would impound Santa's sleigh.

Noelle bent and began gathering the scraps of paper and lost crayons. The earlier conversation with her mother replayed in her head. Typical Jake, she thought sourly—

stage the return of the prodigal son and make Louise feel sorry for him. He had always had too much charm. If anyone knew that, it was Noelle. After what Jake had put her through, how could Louise invite him in for the fatted calf?

Noelle shoved her day planner into her workbag. How was she going to get rid of Jake? The bright spot was the invitation marked the final event in the triad of disaster. If Jake thought he could use Louise to maneuver himself anywhere near her, he was in for a surprise. A knock at the door made her look up.

A slinky cat leaned against the doorframe.

"I knocked but you were far away," the cat said. "What's so important you lose track of everything around you?"

Noelle studied her slinky visitor. Maria was a tall black-haired beauty, with a childhood spent acting and modeling. As the elected cat, she slipped sublimely into the role. Why not? Maria was a cat—a pussycat. Kids and parents adored her. She was a good friend too, but right now Maria and her uncanny intuition were the last things Noelle needed.

"My water heater blew up this morning." Noelle muttered forcing a laugh, hoping Maria would accept the excuse.

Maria eyes narrowed. "You know, Noelle, you're a ball of tension. You need to relax and I have just the thing to help you out. We'll go to the gym and have a nice long workout. No, better yet, let's go out for dinner. We can have a couple of glasses of wine and catch up on things." Maria smiled. Her resemblance to the contented cat that swallowed the poor dumb canary was almost too much for Noelle to bear.

Trapped, Noelle sank deeper into her chair. She hated the gym. Hiking, skiing, even tennis, anything, but the gym. Maria on the other hand loved the gym. She went three or four times a week and always tried to drag Noelle along. Usually Noelle wiggled out of it. The gym meant Zumba, Maria's newest obsession. Noelle couldn't master the moves. Everyone in the class would be mambo-*ing* left while she was salsa-*ing* right. Zumba brought out all Noelle's clumsy qualities for everyone to see. On the other hand, a cozy dinner with Maria could be a disaster.

A slow smile spread over Maria's face. She knew she had Noelle firmly cornered.

"I'll meet you there. I know that you have to go home and feed Jackson. The class is at six." Maria stood and turned to leave. "Don't forget, it's the one downtown."

Noelle grimaced and nodded. "Fine. I'll see you there."

"Bye." Maria left the classroom. Her voice drifted back to Noelle as she greeted someone in the hallway, male, Noelle decided, judging by Maria's purr.

Noelle checked the clock. If she left now, she could go home, feed Jackson, and settle her scrambled nerves. She groaned and buried her face in her hands. It wasn't fair. All she wanted was to hole up in her little house and lick her wounds. She still had to figure out what to do about Jake and the dinner invitation. Some birthday this was going to be. Inviting Jake was like asking the wolf to the three little pigs' party and saying, "What's for dinner?" She shook her head and stuffed a handful of notebooks into her briefcase.

Maybe Maria was right; it would do her good to get some exercise. She could vent her feelings in a healthy way. If she went home, she would wallow in misery, dredging up the anger and hurt of a decade ago. That wouldn't do her any good, especially if she had to sit and be civil to the source of all that angst at dinner. She grabbed her purse and bag, glanced around the now tidy room and turned out the lights. After a few last good-byes, she headed home.

5

Noelle blinked, leaned forward in the driver's seat, and tightened her death grip on the steering wheel. The weather channel had been bang on in their predictions, she thought sourly. The rain pummeling the car created lousy driving conditions at any time, but right now the arcs of water splashing over the windshield threatened to overwhelm the tattered wipers. Already cranked to high speed, the wipers smeared more than cleared the muddy sheets of water from the glass. Noelle braked sharply, cursed softly and peered through the triangular opening left by the wipers.

The car's right front tire dropped into a pothole sending a geyser of water up and over the sidewalk. Noelle winced and risked a glance at the bus stop bench. It was empty. A gust of wind pushed the car to the left as another wave of fat raindrops pounded the windows. If this kept up she would drown in the dash from her car to the front door. She brightened. That meant no Zumba and escape from seeing Jake again.

She rounded the final corner onto her street and pulled into her driveway, switching off the engine and slumping in the seat. Tension trickled from her limbs. West coast life meant avoiding much of the snow and sleet they faced back east, but true "wet coasters" knew winter brought wind and rain that flooded basements and brought down branches. She pushed open the car door and cringing under the onslaught of icy rain, bolted for the house.

The small porch offered her a tiny oasis from the elements. She shook the rain off her jacket and stabbed her key into the lock. The key jammed.

"Damn it," she swore, jiggling it until she heard a dull click. Ramming her shoulder into the door, she shoved it open, stepped inside, and slammed it behind her. Kicking off her boots, she braced herself for Jackson's arrival.

"Hi buddy, are you happy to see me?" she crooned, bending to stroke his head and hold him off at the same time. "You act like you haven't seen a soul all day. Let's go see what Mrs. Wallace left for you." She straightened. She was lucky to have a retired neighbor who loved dogs. Mrs.

Wallace visited twice a day to top up Jackson's food dish and let him out for a run.

Noelle hung up her soggy jacket and collected the mail from under the slot in the door. Sorting through the pile, she wandered into the kitchen contemplating the upcoming Zumba class. Going back out into the raging monsoon rated a two on her scale of things to avoid. Swimming the Amazon coated in fish oil would be number one. The temperature was hovering around zero, and the downpour alternating between sleet and rain. Snow could be imminent. She should call Maria and tell her about the useless windshield wipers. No, she should tell Maria that she had suddenly developed the plague. She shook her head discarding the idea. Maria would see through such a lame excuse. She'd appear on the doorstep with her ancient Grandma's chicken soup. Grandma's version might have been a cure, but Maria's soup, complete with instant noodles and tufts of tofu, was toxic sludge. It was probably more deadly than any sickness it might cure.

Noelle sighed. It was rotten luck having such a caring friend. She tossed the mail onto the table and eyed the coffee cups on the counter. Unable to stop herself, she reached out and traced her finger over the rim of the mug Jake had used. A lump formed in her throat. Abruptly, she opened the dishwasher, dropped the offending cup onto the rack and set about scouring the kitchen, intent on obliterating any trace of Jake's presence.

Finally, incapacitated by the scent of lemon-fresh spray bleach, she was satisfied she had removed all traces of Jake Ryan. She grabbed a yogurt from the fridge and spoon in hand, wandered down the hall to find clean yoga pants. It was easier to go to Zumba than lie to Maria. She might even sweat off some of the tension tying her muscles in knots.

After changing, she picked up her keys and purse and headed out into the rain. Brightly colored lights decorated the downtown lampposts creating blurry pools of red and green on the wet pavement. She turned the corner into old town and felt the thump of cobblestones beneath the tires. This time a week ago, the street was three deep in umbrella-bearing shoppers lined up to watch the Christmas parade.

Noelle had skipped the parade in favor of staying home and having a hot bath. Face it, she was bored and restless before Jake showed up. She'd convinced herself that it was a stage. It would pass. Next year she would check out the parade and shop until midnight like the rest of the town.

The light turned red, leaving her idling next to the display window of the town's largest store. Winslow's had set up their traditional miniature village. Noelle studied the scene with its tiny skaters and strolling carolers, and smiled at the sight of the ugly garden gnome looming over the town. Score one for the hardware shop across the road. They'd gained first blood in the annual decorating war.

Tomorrow's paper would carry a full-page write up on how the rival business had sabotaged the venerable old store's display. The truth was the garden gnome saw guerilla action on both sides of the street. Neither store admitted to sneaking the gnome into the other's displays, but every year, there was a new battle.

Noelle pulled into the parking lot behind the fitness center and cut the engine. Grabbing her purse, she locked the car and hurried inside to find Maria stretching in preparation for the class.

"You made it!" Maria looked surprised.

"I said I'd come." Noelle tried to hide the defensive note in her voice behind a bright smile.

Maria studied Noelle's flushed cheeks and raised an eyebrow.

"I see," she said mildly.

Noelle yanked off her jacket and dropped it against the wall before bending to retie her shoelaces. She studiously avoided Maria's gaze.

"Something wrong?" Maria asked.

"Shh, I'm seeking my inner center of energy," Noelle said.

"Are you still mad about that hot yoga class?" Maria asked, starting to laugh.

The arrival of the instructor saved Noelle from replying.

***

Noelle groaned and sagged onto the bench in front of the bay of battered lockers. Unable to come up with an excuse to cut and run, she had followed Maria into the change room.

"That was amazing." Maria dropped onto the bench beside her. "That is what I love about Zumba. You feel so energized afterwards."

"Hmph," Noelle answered weakly.

The mirror at the end of the wall showed just how energized Noelle felt. Her sweat-soaked hair straggled loose from its ponytail holder and her bright red cheeks made her look as perky as a boiled tomato.

"I've never seen you work so hard at keeping up. Amazing." Maria shook her head in mock awe. "What gives?"

"Nothing." Noelle scowled. "I'm glad I gave you a few laughs. Now go take your shower and leave me to die alone."

Maria opened her locker and grabbed her bag. She cast a last smirk Noelle's way and glided towards the showers.

Noelle glared at the row of lockers. As much as she hated to admit it, Maria was right. She had pushed herself hard, concentrating on keeping up, hoping to find some Zen-like state of exercise-induced coma. She'd found only sweat. She batted a trickle out of her eyes. Now she not only lacked inner peace, but tomorrow she would have to pay the price demanded by her groaning muscles.

She forced herself up, wincing at the jelly-like consistency of her legs. Thank God she was on holidays. She wouldn't have to drag herself out of bed in the morning. She ran her fingers through her wet ponytail. Right now, she didn't care how she looked. She wanted to go home, lick her wounds and bury her sorrows in junk food.

Maria reappeared looking as if she hadn't spent the last hour sweating in an overheated room. Noelle hated her.

"You ready?" Maria asked.

"No, I, um, I'm not going out for dinner. I'm tired. End of school and all that," Noelle mumbled.

"Noelle, what's going on?"

"I don't want to talk about it, okay? I'll call you later." Tears burned Noelle's eyes. She would not break down in front of Maria. Blindly she groped for her jacket and waving a vague hand in farewell, bolted, leaving Maria staring after her.

6

Noelle ducked out the back entrance of the fitness center, running for her car as though Santa's evil elves were on her trail. She had to get away, to be alone so she could figure out what to do about Jake.

Why now? What right did he have to show up ten years after he had walked away without a backward look? No, a little voice protested. He hadn't. He'd tried to see her, but she had suffered the miscarriage and frozen him out before he even knew he was an expectant father. There was no way he could get past the barriers she had thrown in his way. With the gauntlet of three older brothers in place, Jake hadn't had a chance of breaking through.

"Grow up, Noelle," she muttered. "The past is the past."

So why did he have to come back? She was happy! Was she, mocked the tiny voice.

The heavy rain had chased away the last of the shoppers and the streets were empty, the stores closed for the night. At the corner of Main and Second, the lights on the community Christmas tree twinkled through the drizzle on the windshield. Down the block, the familiar logo of a convenience store beckoned. She gave in to temptation, pulled into the empty parking lot, and eased her aching body from the car. She would drown her misery in junk food.

"Hey," the clerk at the till muttered, glancing up as she entered the store.

Noelle nodded, smiling briefly.

Having fulfilled the requirements of his job, the clerk— Denny—according to the peeling nametag on his blue and white t-shirt, returned to his newspaper.

Left alone, Noelle wandered the aisles eying the bags of chips stacked on the shelves. Ketchup... she shuddered. Dill pickle . . . she rolled her eyes. Smoky barbeque . . . she grabbed a bag off the rack, turned and spied a stand holding paperbacks. Maybe a little distraction was what she needed? She curled her lip at the romance titles, choosing instead a blood and guts thriller. She didn't have the heart for a steamy romance novel. She smiled weakly at the corny pun and limped back to the checkout.

Denny reluctantly pushed aside his hockey scores, accepted her visa card and swiped it through the machine. "Is that it?" he asked.

"Oh, wait," Noelle said remembering the cola slush she had promised herself. "I wanted a drink, too."

"Yeah, whatever," Denny nodded in disinterest, cancelling the transaction and returning to the sports page. He left the Visa card on the counter.

Shaking her head in amusement, Noelle retraced her steps to the back of the store.

"Hey, the banana-grape freezer isn't working, so don't use that one," Denny called after her.

Banana-grape? Who picked these flavors? Who drank them? The counter hosting the drink freezers needed a cleanup. Lime green, purple, and brown syrups puddled the surface, dripping down the front of the metal cabinet. Noelle grimaced and stepped over a pond of sticky grape syrup. Judging from the mess, Denny didn't spend much time away from his chair. At the front of the store a soft chime signaled another customer. Maybe this new client would get him up off his butt? She returned to the slushy machine.

What size cup? It had to be big enough to deliver the right amount of brain freeze and small enough she could feel virtuous about having withstood the temptation to give in to gluttony. She skipped the mega size, stuck a large cup under the spout and turned the handle. Air blasted through the dispenser blowing frothy liquid into the cup. Noelle jumped back, brushing splattered drops of cola from her jacket.

"Hey . . ." she stopped, hearing the murmur of voices from the front of the store. The clerk was busy. She craned her neck to see if she could catch his eye, but a rack of magazines blocked her view of the storefront.

"Look I'm telling you how it is."

Noelle shivered. Something about the voice made the hairs on the back of her neck rise. Uneasy she stepped closer to the magazine rack, hiding in its shadow as she angled her eyes to the security mirror above.

"There's fifty bucks in the till. Take it!" Denny said. His voice was thin and shaky.

"Don't screw with me. Find more!" the other voice exploded.

Noelle watched in horror as the man at the counter lunged and grabbed Denny by the neck of his t-shirt. Denny choked. His arms flailed as the larger man dragged him across the counter.

"You little shit. Get me the money!" the man shouted, shoving the clerk backwards, sending him sprawling against the opposite counter.

"The money!" he repeated.

Denny staggered up. His hands shook as he fumbled to open the cash drawer. Fear made Noelle's hands clumsy as she fought to ease her cell phone from her purse.

"You're not moving fast enough."

She flinched at the whip of raw anger in the voice. The phone dropped from her hand and clattered to the floor. Falling to her knees, she fumbled for it blindly, her eyes locked on the mirror above. The thief's arm rose and stretched towards the clerk. He took a step nearer the counter.

Denny fell back. Hands waving, his voice high and cracking, he whimpered, "That's all there is."

"Sorry, wrong answer." The other man laughed.

The flat coldness in the voice chilled her. Noelle peered between the shelves, the phone forgotten at her feet. The thief vaulted the counter and grabbed the clerk, slamming him against the wall.

"Open the till or I shoot you," he ordered. His forearm flattened Denny's neck against the wall. He rested the gun's muzzle on Denny's left temple.

Noelle's legs turned boneless. She sank to the ground and raised the phone.

The cash drawer released with a dull ding. Denny cowered as far from the other man as he could get.

"That's more like it. Now give me one of those bags," the thief ordered. Denny was too slow. The thief shoved him aside and tore a bag from the rack. He rifled through the cash drawer, shoving money into the plastic bag. Dropping the bag onto the counter, he swept the change and everything else on its surface into the bag. Loose coins and packages of mints rained onto the floor.

Noelle pushed the last one on her phone, almost sobbing in relief when she heard the voice of the 911 dispatcher. She opened her mouth to speak and realized the man at the front of the store might hear. Carefully she placed the phone on the ground and slid it under the shelf, not daring to answer the voice on the other end.

At the front of the store the frightened clerk looked up. His face was a blurry circle in the mirror. He lunged towards the alarm button. The thief turned at the sudden motion. The alarm screamed as the revolver boomed.

Noelle's gasp vanished in the echo of the shot. Denny sagged against the counter, red blossoming through his shirt. The gunman shoved him aside and kicked him in the stomach. He snatched up the bag and grabbed a handful of cigarette packages from the shelf behind the counter.

"Stupid, *manno*. You shouldn't have done that," he said to the downed clerk. He turned and ran his eyes over the store aisles, his gaze sliding past Noelle's hiding spot. For a moment, she looked straight at him. The shooter hopped the counter and pushed through the door.

Noelle snatched up her phone and scrambled to her feet. Her legs barely held her weight as she staggered to the front of the store. What if he came back? Had he seen her? She stumbled to Denny's side and bent over him. His face was still and white against the grey of the floor tiles, his blood pooling in a bright puddle of red beneath him as his chest heaved irregularly under her hands. The sound of his breathing was harsh and strident; the sweet coppery scent of his blood filled the air.

His mouth moved soundlessly. Noelle bent over him, gingerly touching his shoulder . . . so much blood. She fought off a wave of dizziness.

"Can you hear me?" she called sharply.

He moaned. His eyelids fluttered open and he stared blankly at her.

Noelle lifted her cell, but before she said a word, the pulsing red and blue lights of a police car filled the room. Two officers climbed from the car. They hung back studying the entrance before cautiously proceeding to the door. Noelle dropped the phone and shot to her feet.

"Call an ambulance. A man's been shot," she called.

Wary, the police entered, their eyes sweeping the aisles. In unspoken agreement one headed to the back, the other crossed to the wounded man at the front. The officer was calling for an ambulance when his partner reappeared.

"It's clear," the officer said tersely holstering his revolver.

Noelle's head snapped up from where she knelt beside the injured man. "He took off when the alarm went," she said. Her voice was distant and fuzzy.

"Hey, are you okay?" a far-off voice asked.

A firm hand pushed her head down, making her sit.

"Take a few deep breaths. That's right—in and out. It'll pass—just give it a minute."

She gulped in a deep lungful of air. The mist receded.

"I'm okay," she whispered.

More sirens. The door banged open as police and paramedics entered. Grimly the paramedics went to work, one inserting a breathing tube into Denny's throat, while the other started intravenous fluids. Noelle watched dumbly. A gentle tug on her arm pulled her back to reality. She glanced up to find a man squatting beside her, quietly studying her face. He was dressed casually, his hair damp from the falling rain. His grey eyes met hers calmly as he gently grasped her elbow.

"Miss . . ?"

"Ryan." She filled in the unspoken question, "Noelle."

"Hi, Noelle. I'm Detective Ryerson. I want to ask you a few questions." He smiled reassuringly. "He's in good hands. Why don't you come outside? It's crowded in here." He led her through the door, grabbing a blanket from the ambulance and draping it around her shoulders as they passed.

The parking lot was crammed with emergency vehicles. The pulsing lights lent a surreal feel to the scene.

Detective Ryerson opened the back door of a police cruiser.

"Have a seat," he said.

She slid gratefully into the back of the car and pulled the blanket tighter around her neck. Leaning her head back, she closed her eyes, trying to blot out the horror of the last few minutes.

"Okay, I'm ready," she said shakily.

"I know this is hard for you, but try and bear with me, okay?" At her nod, Ryerson continued. "Were you in the store when it was robbed?"

"Yes." Noelle shuddered, a wave of nausea passing through her at the thought of the junk food she had planned to buy.

"Did you see the gunman?"

She nodded.

"Can you describe him?"

"I was down the aisle from the cashier, so mostly, I saw his back. In the . . . in the end, I saw his face for a second," she said.

Detective Ryerson looked disappointed. "Did he have any distinguishing marks—tattoos, mustache . . . anything you can remember?"

"He had on dark clothing . . . oh, and a toque. He had a mustache. I don't remember anything else. I was at the back of the store. Wait, he had an accent." *Stupid, manno.* She shivered.

The detective asked more questions, walking her through what had happened; making her remember each tiny detail until she shook her head in frustration. That's it," she said, shrugging helplessly.

"Okay," he said. "Write down anything else you remember. I'll need your name, telephone number, and address. Here's my card." His grey eyes watched her. "Do you have any questions?"

"You'll get him, right? His face will be on the store security tapes, won't it?" Noelle asked.

Ryerson shrugged. "We'll talk more tomorrow. If you remember anything before then, I want you to call me." He tapped the card in her hand to reinforce his instructions.

Mechanically, Noelle provided the information he'd requested. She wanted to go home.

"How are you getting home?" he asked.

"That's my car." She pointed to her Honda Civic hemmed in by emergency vehicles.

"You think you can drive or do you want a ride?"

"I'm fine." She jumped to her feet. The sick shaky feeling had passed. She wanted to get away from here.

The doors of the store opened and the paramedics wheeled the stretcher out. The blanketed form was still, the faces of the paramedics set and grim.

"Will Denny be okay?" she asked, gesturing at the swaddled form on the gurney.

"Did you know him?" Ryerson asked.

"No," Noelle shook her head. "That's his name. It was on his name tag."

"We'll have to wait and see," Ryerson said. The detective's troubled eyes met hers. "We'll let you know. For your own safety, you should refrain from discussing this."

"Am I in danger?" she asked, stunned at the thought.

"We'll be in touch in the morning," he said avoiding the question. He walked her to her car. The ambulance pulled out of the parking lot, siren blaring. More police arrived. They entered the building carrying cases. One was unwrapping yellow tape—securing the crime scene—she realized in horror. She shuddered and yanked her keys from her jacket pocket.

"You sure you're up to driving?" Detective Ryerson asked.

At her nod, he stepped back. She felt his eyes on her as she climbed into her car. Carefully she backed around the police cars and pulled out of the parking lot.

The detective sighed and headed back inside for what promised to be a long night. It seemed the Cobra had added another robbery to his trophy list and this time, he was upping his game.

7

Noelle closed her eyes and sank deeper into the bath. The aroma of frankincense and cinnamon rose up, mingling with the sharp tang of eucalyptus from the candles burning on the window ledge. Now when she closed her eyes, she didn't smell the coppery scent of blood. Before that odor had colored every breath she took. She sighed and reopened her eyes. Face it, as long as her mind kept replaying the graphic events of the night, relaxation wasn't going to happen.

She groaned and levered herself up. Water streamed from her shoulders as she leaned forward to lift the wine glass from the edge of the bath. Here's to forgetting, she toasted, swallowing a gulp of merlot. She had eked out enough hot water for one last bath, enough to soak the ache from her muscles. The wine had done its part, making those same muscles loose and relaxed. With luck the combination would let her sleep.

Sighing again, she pulled a towel off the rack, dried quickly and wrapped herself in a fleecy bathrobe. She had been a block from the shooting when the shakes set in. She'd picked the parking lot of a wine store as the handiest place to stop. There she had waited out the worst of the tremors before going into the store and picking out a bottle of wine. The fact that she could pretend normalcy and make small talk with the clerk meant she was fine. She was safe.

She pulled the knot on her robe tighter, thinking about her visit to the shop. She had paid cash. She hadn't been able to find her Visa. She'd used it at the convenience store. Was the card still sitting on the checkout counter? Would the store put through the charges, even if she didn't actually buy anything? She would check in the morning. Nice, Noelle—worrying about ten dollars' worth of junk food when the clerk lay in a hospital bed fighting for his life.

The candles flickered and guttered in their fragrant pools of wax. She leaned forward, blew them out, and wandered restlessly into the living room, perching on the arm of an easy chair. She needed to put the events of the night into some sort of order. Tomorrow Detective Ryerson would call and ask if she remembered anything. It would be nice to say, "Oh yeah, the guy was five feet ten, brown eyes, black hair, with a rose tattoo saying "Mom" on his left forearm.

But it wasn't that easy. When she tried to picture his face, she saw darkness. So much for thinking his image indelibly inked in her brain. *Did* he have a mustache? She shrugged. A beard? He'd had a black toque—she stared into the fireplace flames—a toque like the ones that Special Forces guys wore. Okay, she sighed. That was a start. What else? A memory floated just out of reach. *Stupid, manno.* She draped the towel over the back of the chair. *Manno*— an accent? He had shouted at the clerk. Okay, start again. This time, go slow. Put it in order. His clothes were dark. He had a toque pulled low over a broad brow. *Stupid manno.* Yes—an accent. Spanish? French?

Frustrated, she grabbed the TV remote and switched on the news.

"Fat lot of good I am," she muttered, dropping into the chair to watch.

Jackson ambled over. He rested his head on her knee and sighed. His eyes closed in bliss as she scratched behind his ears. He settled at her feet, his back to the fireplace. Jackson didn't like the cold any more than she did.

The scene on the TV was the parking lot of the convenience store. A reporter began the lead-in to the story. Behind his umbrella yards of yellow tape held back a huddle of curious onlookers. Noelle turned up the volume.

"The convenience store at the corner of Main and Ellis was the latest target in a string of robberies. For the past month, police have been tracking a dangerous offender they call the Cobra because of the nature of his swift and violent attacks. Tonight's robbery marks an escalation in the level of violence seen so far. Dennis Smyth, the store's twenty-five-year-old clerk, was shot after activating the store's alarm system. Police remain silent on the condition of the store employee. Sources inside the police department say there may have been a witness to tonight's shooting. Police are refusing comment at this time. In other news . . ."

Noelle snapped off the television. The fine hairs on her arms rose in a ripple of goose bumps. Someone had told the press that there was a witness to the shooting. An icy ball crystalized in the pit of her stomach. She bit down on her lower lip. Okay, so what? The detective said she wasn't in danger. The news report said *maybe* there was a witness. It didn't say, "Noelle Ryan of Winslow Crescent can identify the shooter." Her stomach flopped at the memory of the gunman's eyes sweeping past the magazine rack. *Had* he seen her? What about her car? He had to have noticed her car. Could he find out who she was?

Stop it. You're letting your imagination run wild. The gunman wouldn't waste time writing down license plate numbers while making his getaway. He wasn't a cop. He couldn't run a plate and figure out who she was.

She was safe as long as she didn't discuss this with anyone. That's what the detective had said.

The room was eerily quiet without the background noise of the television. Abruptly Noelle stood and crossed to the window, pulling the drapes closer together. From there she moved to the front door, checking the lock, holding the deadbolt between her fingers as if strength of will would lock it tighter. She would have switched the porch light on but the bulb had burned out the week before. For once she wished there was a wall of nosy neighbors behind her house, instead of an empty field. Tomorrow she'd put blinds on the window over the kitchen sink.

Stop it. The doors are locked. You're safe.

She moved to the kitchen, checked the dead bolt on the back door and poured another glass of wine. Outside the exposed window darkness waited. She retreated to the living room. Jackson raised his head and whined.

"Sorry, buddy. I can't help it," Noelle muttered, stooping to pat his head. She was fine. She had a dog for protection. Yeah right. Jackson was as much protection as a feather duster. He would lick an attacker to death.

The phone rang. Noelle jumped. Her hand clipped the edge of the wine glass and a river of ruby merlot poured over the carpet. She flinched, remembering the clerk lying in a pool of red.

"Damn!" She jumped to her feet. "Get a grip, Noelle. It's the phone." She shot a glance at the clock and hurried towards the kitchen grabbing the phone mid-ring.

"Hello?" Her voice was edgy and breathless.

Silence.

"Hello," she repeated.

"Noelle Ryan?"

"Yes."

"This is Visa. We are calling about a purchase you made this evening."

Noelle's knuckles turned white. Stop it. It could be Visa. The police could have contacted them to . . . Her Visa. She had left it on the counter before going back to the drink counter. Her stomach turned. Her heart pounded. She dropped the phone and ran down the hall to her bedroom.

Her backpack was leaning against the wall. She grabbed it, pulled open the drawers of her dresser and started cramming clothes into the pack. She wasn't staying here. She ripped off her robe and dressed in jeans and a t-shirt, yanking on socks and runners before tossing the pack onto the bed. Hands shaking, she zipped the pack closed.

How did he get her phone number—the name on the Visa? He'd swept the money and everything from the counter into the plastic bag. He had the card. It would be easy enough to look her up in the phone book.

"Jackson, come," she called, grabbing his leash and snapping it onto his collar. She pulled her coat from its hanger and flipped the OFF switch on the gas fireplace.

She made it as far as the front door and stopped. She was afraid to stay in the house and terrified to leave. She held the leash so tightly it left an imprint of the braided cord on her fingers. The phone rang again and she bolted for her car.

8

Wet pavement gleamed under the light of the headlights. Rain or ice—Noelle couldn't tell. Was it cold enough to freeze the top layer of pavement? She didn't care. She accelerated around the corner onto the main road, the back end of the car fishtailing. Too fast, slow down. She lifted her foot off the gas and forced her hands to relax their death grip on the steering wheel. Better. She sucked in a deep breath and checked the rear-view mirror. Were those headlights following her? The car behind her slowed and turned right.

Noelle felt a thousand eyes watching from behind the blank windows of the silent houses she passed. Beside her Jackson panted, drooling on the upholstery, delighted at the unexpected outing. Some of her fears melted.

"Sorry, bud. I'm not staying home alone. We'll go to Mom and Dad's for the night."

Her eyes strayed to the rear-view mirror again. Was that van following her? Had she seen that truck before? Away from Landings' city limits, she could drive faster. She reached the outskirts of Victoria and slowed. Traffic on the highway was sparse. The usual twenty-minute trip into the city took ten. She turned off the highway and made her way through darkened residential streets. The wind picked up driving the rain before it, sending clouds of water billowing over the pavement.

At last she turned onto the tree-lined street where she had grown up. She was already feeling foolish, second-guessing her decision to run. She should have stayed home. So what if she didn't sleep. Nothing would have happened. She parked in front of her parent's house. She'd sleep there tonight, have an amazing breakfast and go home in the morning.

Strange how here the unlit windows didn't hold a sense of foreboding. Did returning to the nest lay down a protective charm or was it just that there was safety in numbers? It was a good thing that she had never changed back to her maiden name. The man from the store couldn't link this address to her Visa card.

She climbed out, grabbed her pack from the back seat and freed Jackson. He ran past her, racing in ever-widening circles around the yard. Noelle climbed the steps to the front door, unlocked it and disarmed the house alarm. She closed and bolted the door behind her before resetting the alarm. Jackson trotted past to announce their arrival. Startled voices followed him into the hallway as the house's occupants straggled out, belting housecoats and slipping on glasses.

"Noelle, what's wrong? What are you doing here?" Louise Hamilton demanded.

"What's going on?" Noelle's father Jim frowned and flipped on the hall light.

Noelle's fears evaporated.

"Sorry to get you guys out of bed." Noelle shrugged apologetically. "I was too chicken to spend the night alone."

"Uh huh." Louise's eyes narrowed as she took in Noelle's baggy t-shirt and wrinkled jeans. "Why do I have the feeling coffee and a shot of brandy are in order?"

In answer to her own question she headed for the kitchen to turn on the coffeemaker. Coffee brewing, Louise returned to lean against the doorway of the family room. Father and daughter sat side by side on the couch. Jim's brow furrowed as he listened to Noelle. Forty years of marriage had given him some sort of telepathic link to Louise's approach and he looked up.

"Lou, you better sit. Noelle's had quite a night," he said.

Noelle relaxed against the thick cushions of the sofa. Sharing the evening's events eased her fear.

"Okay shoot," Louise directed, settling onto the edge of the couch. Outwardly she was calm. Forty years of working in a trauma operating room had taught her to hide her anxiety.

"Right," Noelle said. She took in a deep breath and started over.

By the end of the recital Louise's frown matched the one on Jim's face.

Jim spoke first. "Call that detective, the one whose card you have. He'll want to know about this."

"I know, but it's late," Noelle countered.

"Hon, he's probably on the night shift."

"I left the card on the counter," Noelle said, curling her legs beneath her. "The morning will be soon enough. I'll call tomorrow." She yawned.

Jim looked as if he wanted to argue.

Louise quietly left the room and returned with the coffee. A comfortable silence fell over them. Jackson curled on the floor in front of her. Noelle stretched her hand to accept the steaming mug and took a sip and missed the look that passed between Jim and Louise.

"Feel better?" Louise asked.

Noelle nodded. "It's been a long day. Maria insisted I go to Zumba." She grimaced. "Won't be doing that again. Hmm." She sniffed the coffee appreciatively. "The brandy smells good. I'll sleep after this."

The brandy-laced coffee slid smoothly down her throat, melting the icy coating around her stomach. They chatted of everyday things until Noelle's cup was empty. Rising she gathered the cups onto the tray and carried them into the kitchen. Setting the tray down, she turned to her parents and hugged each in turn.

"Thanks for being here. I didn't know what else to do," she said.

"Honey, of course you should come here." Louise returned the hug tightly.

Stifling another yawn, Noelle headed down the hall to her old bedroom. She climbed into the queen-sized bed, closed her eyes, and slid into sleep.

9

Noelle woke slowly, sleep seeping away. She yawned and opened her eyes to unfamiliar surroundings. Her heart lurched in panic as she sat up. Immediately, muscles abused by an hour of high-impact Zumba launched a protest.

"Ow, ow, ow," she moaned, falling back against the pillows. Clear-headedness returned. She was safe. He couldn't find her here.

Last night she hadn't pulled the curtains when she stumbled into the room. Now dim light shone weakly through the glass, drawing patterns of moving branches on the surrounding walls. The wind had blown away the clouds and she could see glimpses of blue sky.

Noelle sighed and burrowed deeper into the pillows. Her brain and body were in complete agreement; only a fool would leave the cozy nest of blankets this early in the morning. Besides, a little extra sleep might help settle the jitters still creeping under her skin. She tugged at the quilt, but it was snagged on something at the bottom of the bed. Louise was using the room to unpack Christmas decorations. Too tired to move the boxes, Noelle had pushed them to one side before sliding under the covers. During the night, Jackson had made the leap from floor to bed. Now he grunted and lifted his head, mouth dropping open in a doggy grin.

"Get off the bed!" Noelle shooed him away, hardening her heart to the reproach in his brown eyes. "This is Irish linen, not dog hair and paw prints," she said brushing his hair from the lace quilt cover.

Jackson jumped down and treated her to a woebegone stare before slinking to the door. Noelle lay back and ignored him. Last night she had expected gruesome dreams, but instead her dream lover swirled from the mist rekindling the fire of the night before.

She smothered a jaw-cracking yawn. If she closed her eyes would he come back? She smiled wickedly. It was worth a try, but Jackson had other ideas. He scratched and whined at the base of the door. If he couldn't sleep on the bed, she couldn't sleep at all.

Giving in, she climbed out of bed, shivering as her bare feet touched cold hardwood. Jackson barked and wagged his tail, nosing the doorknob before turning to look hopefully at her.

"Okay, fine." She pulled the closet door open and grabbed a housecoat from a hanger. Fat penguins skied down the front of the midnight blue fleece. Nice. She surveyed the frolicking penguins with disgust. This artifact was from her high school era of pink Kool-Aid dyed hair and trucker hats. She shrugged into it and padded barefoot towards the murmur of voices and the aroma of freshly brewed coffee.

"Good morning," she said, helping herself to a steaming cup.

"Morning," Jim mumbled. He didn't meet her eyes.

Noelle raised her eyebrows and studied the matched guilty looks worn by her parents.

"What gives?" she said. "If I were a kid and looked like you guys, I would be grounded immediately." She added a splash of milk to her coffee.

Jim leaned back in his chair. His balding head gleamed softly under the overhead light. His blue eyes were minus their usual twinkle.

"That's because you could never tell a lie without looking guilty." He took a sip of coffee and continued. "We were talking about last night—about that phone call. What if he'd shown up at the house, instead of calling?"

"Yeah, I know, that's why I left." Noelle suppressed a shiver. She didn't want to talk about it. First, she needed time to process the events of the night in private. Judging from their long expressions, Jim and Louise weren't going to let that happen. With their worry radar awakened, they'd be joining forces to nudge her in the direction they thought safest. They hadn't used that tactic since the days of Jake. She scowled. Jake, now that was a problem she needed time to process.

"I think you're safe here. The guy can't figure out where you are—unless he followed you last night."

"No, I watched. There were hardly any cars on the road." Noelle took a sip of coffee, cradling the cup in her hands.

"The thing is . . . he knows where you live," Jim carried on.

"I know," Noelle repeated irritably. "That's why I'm going home to get that detective's number . . . right after breakfast." She put the cup down in favor of snooping through the well-stocked cabinets in search of something to eat. She already regretted running away the night before. In the cold light of day, it was clear that she had overreacted. She'd call the detective . . . right after she had something to eat. Her stomach growled in agreement. Last night's yogurt was a long time in the past.

"Noelle," Louise interrupted her search. "Sit down for a minute. We want to talk to you."

Noelle turned to find their guilty looks had spread. She tossed them a quizzical look, pulled a chair out and flopped down at the table.

"Okay, what?" she prodded, leaning back.

"Last night, I, umm," Louise hesitated and glanced over at Jim.

Jim shot his wife an amused glance and took over.

"Honey, what your Mom is trying to say is, we don't have experience with this type of thing. She called Jake."

"What!" Noelle's cup banged onto the tabletop, coffee sloshing over the rim.

Louise jumped up and grabbed the dishrag from the sink.

"Call him back. Tell him no!" Noelle paced the length of the kitchen. "How could you—don't you remember . . ?"

The doorbell rang.

"I'll get that," Jim said, bolting from the room.

"That would be Jake," Louise said calmly, mopping up the spilled coffee.

Noelle froze. Jim and Louise meant well. She knew that, but couldn't they see what this was doing to her? Seeing Jake, even after all this time, brought a sharp stab of grief, and the memory of waking up in a cold recovery room, a tear-soaked pillow beneath her head. No baby, no Jake. He hadn't been there. To ask for his help now . . . the thought burned. She couldn't . . . she wouldn't. She took a deep breath. She could hear Jim's whisper like the drone of an extra-large bumblebee at the front door.

If she were going to meet Jake, it would be on her terms, and when that meeting took place, she would not be wearing a rabbit suit, or a penguin-patterned housecoat. She stalked past Louise and fled to the safety of her room to prepare for battle.

***

An hour later, Noelle emerged from the bathroom freshly showered and dressed, her hair gathered in a long wavy ponytail secured below her right ear. She leaned into the mirror and stroked a palette of smoky eye shadows onto her lids, before rimming her lashes with charcoal-colored liner. She added a touch of red gloss to her lips, and stood back, studying the effect. Better.

Digging through the dresser drawer, she found a pair of gold hoop earrings—another remnant of the pink hair days—and slid them into place. A quick spray of a light floral perfume and she was ready. This time she was meeting Jake under different circumstances. She was taking charge and conducting things her way.

She turned away from the mirror. The thought of the man sitting in the kitchen sent butterflies fluttering in her stomach. It's okay, she told herself. Don't give him the power to affect you. Go out there and tell him you don't need his help.

Right, she scoffed. He has no effect on you. That's why you just spent more time getting dressed than you have in the past ten years. Be honest. You want him to see what he abandoned. She scowled.

The walk from the bedroom to the kitchen was too short. She lingered in the hallway waiting for her courage to catch up with her. She could see the kitchen's occupants, but they were still unaware of her presence. Jake was sprawled in a kitchen chair, the sleeves of his sweatshirt pushed up above his elbows, his broad shoulders filling the chair. He held his coffee mug poised to take a sip as he listened to something Louise was saying. Noelle took a tentative sniff. From the lingering scent of bacon, Louise had rolled out the fatted pig. There was no sign of leftovers, so Jake must have done justice to the home-cooked meal and deprived her of breakfast.

"Jerk," she muttered indignantly. Look at him worming his way back in. Jim and Lou appeared to have forgotten that ten years ago, he had dumped her and walked away without a backwards look. Even man's best friend was a turncoat. Jackson lay at Jake's feet, tongue lolling, his gaze fixed adoringly on his newfound friend. Jake had probably fed Noelle's ration of bacon to the dog. It was time to end this happy little scene.

***

Jake glanced up at Noelle's entrance. From the sparks in her green eyes, she was none too pleased to see him. He placed his cup on the table, regretting the end to the easy comradery of the moment before. He hadn't realized how much he missed seeing his folks until he sat down with Jim and Lou.

He rubbed his chin to cover a grin. It didn't look as if Noelle was planning to make nice. He patted Jackson's head, buying time as he covertly studied Noelle. She greeted her parents and poured a cup of coffee. The greeting she offered him was cool—downright frosty.

"Noelle you're looking well. I mean don't get me

wrong, the bunny suit was nice, but it's always good to have a few different looks," Jake said, sending her a wicked smile. Was that smoke pouring out of her ears?

Noelle pulled a chair out from the table and sank gracefully into it. She lined her cup up with the edge of the placemat before speaking.

"Jake," she began. "It was nice of you to come by but Mom and Dad shouldn't have bothered you. I don't need your help." She sent them a frosty glare. "I am dealing with this."

Jake leaned back. He hadn't expected to be greeted like a long-lost friend, but open hostility? Their last fight was a long time ago. If he recalled correctly, she had fired the first salvo and landed the last shot. If anyone should feel wronged, it was him. Noelle had gotten a restraining order from her lawyer and sued for divorce without even trying to make amends.

Hell, the marriage had been rocky anyway. You had to have more in common than good sex. He studied her over the rim of his coffee cup. Okay, great sex. All those fights meant lots of making up, but over time, something had to give. When he'd left for police training, he had been tattered and torn. The guys he'd trained with called him "Ice." Noelle had frozen him out, refusing to see or speak to him. He'd had to let her go. He studied her flushed face and his eyes narrowed as she dropped her gaze. His cop instincts stirred. What was she hiding?

"Noelle, we're only asking for Jake's advice," Louise said mildly, unspoken reproof in her voice.

"Don't bother. I'm handling this," Noelle said. "I don't need Jake's help." She shoved her chair back. The legs scraped loudly over the ceramic tiles. Standing, she carried her cup to the dishwasher.

"I'm going home to call that detective. I'll see you later. Jackson, come," she said, and stalked out of the room.

The front door slammed. Louise and Jim looked helplessly at Jake. He sighed and took a sip of his cooling coffee. Some things never changed.

10

Damn Jake. Noelle stalled her car at the light, dropped into first gear and bunny hopped through the intersection. She gritted her teeth and shifted into second, trying to concentrate on driving, not what she wanted to do to Jake. Okay he was back. Deal with it. Move on. Avoid him. His holiday would end and he would fly off into the sunset never to be seen again. She was bigger than this. She would survive. It was Christmas—peace on earth, good will to men, including ex-husbands.

The light turned red in front of her and she stomped on the brakes. Jackson lurched forward, woofed and stood. Noelle looked to the left. The occupants of the car next to her were staring openly. She frowned. The world was full of strange people. She looked up and glimpsed her face in the rear-view mirror. Great. She looked like the psychotic lead in a horror movie. She forced a smile to her frozen lips and accelerated away from the gawkers as the light changed. Damn Jake, he was making her crazy.

She flipped the radio on. Mick Jagger was wailing out his lack of satisfaction.

"I hear you, Mick," she muttered, flipping the channel. The song reminded her of Jake's reason for his early morning visit—CDs. She sniffed. That must be the lamest excuse of all time. No wait, she knew of something lamer—wearing a bunny suit to answer the door.

By the time she pulled into her driveway, her cheeks burned as if she had been standing too close to a blast furnace. Why was she letting Jake get to her? Ever since he'd appeared on her porch, she had been acting like a fool. The school secretary thought she was in the midst of a family crisis, Maria was honing her counseling skills, and Jim and Louise were behaving as if she were twelve, not twenty-nine. She turned off the ignition and yanked the key free.

"No more," she promised grabbing her purse. Jackson bounded past her and began his ritualistic tearing up of the yard. Too bad she couldn't work off her restless energy that easily. Instead, a headache throbbed in time with her tumbling thoughts. She leaned against the car and waited for Jackson to wear himself out. There were fewer disasters if he vented his energy before entering the house. His tail— a weapon of mass destruction—was lethal to anything not cemented down.

Finally, panting happily, Jackson joined her on the porch. Noelle stood in front of the door staring at the deep charcoal paint. Now that she was home, she wasn't so eager to turn the handle and step inside. She'd been so bent on escaping Jake's company that her only thought was about getting in the car and putting distance between them. Now in the full light of day she felt the weight of unseen eyes watching from the shadows.

Funny, right now she would welcome even Jake's company. Was he packing a gun? She shivered. Yeah, she would happily take Jake and his gun as back up. Not good, considering she was about to enter her own house. She turned and looked down the quiet row of houses lining the street. Maybe not so quiet, she thought with relief. Across the road, a neighbor scraped the ice from his windshield. Another was stringing Christmas lights along the eaves of his house—ordinary activities that, coupled with the faint December sun, made her feel foolish for her fears.

She shoved her key into the lock, turned it and twisted the doorknob to enter. Jackson growled. The hackles on his neck rose as he bared his teeth. Noelle froze as he turned towards her, leaning the weight of his body against her knees, pushing her back.

"Jackson down," she commanded, trying to see through the gap in the door. Last night she had closed the curtains. Now she wished they were wide open.

Jackson sat but his deep growl rumbled on. Noelle put her foot against the bottom of the door and pushed. The dog barreled past, ears slicked to his head, his tail flat. Noelle started to follow, but he turned back, the rumbling growl beginning anew.

Slowly, Noelle stretched her hand into the shadows and groped for the light switch. She half-expected something to grab her and drag her into the empty house. The keys in her right hand left sharp divots in her fingers. Her heart thumped as she ran her eyes over the living room.

"Jackson, what's wrong with you?"

Everything was the same as it was the night before.

"There's nothing here!" She snapped her fingers. Jackson's head swung towards her. The growling stopped.

"See, you're fine. Calm down." She patted his head. His ears stayed flat against his skull.

Sighing, Noelle dropped her purse and keys onto the chair. The detective's card was on the counter in the kitchen. Unfortunately, that meant moving from the handy escape route of the front door. She wasn't ready for that.

"Get a grip," she muttered and crossed to the window, yanking the curtains back and letting the light flood in.

Too bad she couldn't rip back the mocha-colored walls and see into the kitchen down the hall. Jackson sniffed at the overturned wine glass with its river of Merlot. His tongue darted out in a tentative lick. The deep red stain had pooled in the carpet. If she didn't clean it up soon, she would have a permanent reminder of the night of the shooting. First she'd call the police, then she would deal with the mess. She pictured the business card resting on the kitchen counter.

You're stalling, Noelle. Her gaze strayed back to the stain. It looked like blood. Was the clerk still alive? She shivered and looked over her shoulder. Don't be an idiot. If there were someone in the house, Jackson would be going ballistic. Instead he had taken the time to do some personal grooming. She kicked the door shut. Stain first, then the police. That way she would have time to get her thoughts together.

Jackson stood and shook. Dog tags jingling, he trotted towards the kitchen. His tail was still angled downward, but his ears were back in upright position. Noelle followed him, her confidence returning.

"Dog, you freaked me out," she scolded, shaking her head in disgust.

She had let her imagination turn the house into the set of a horror movie. It was an empty house—a cold, empty house. She shivered, hugging her jacket closer as an icy draft raised goose bumps on her arms. Last night she had checked every window and closed all the curtains. There was no way an arctic gale should be blowing down the hall. Feet dragging, she stepped into the kitchen. There was also no way that the back door should be wide open, but it was. Her gaze locked on the open door as a gust of wind caught its edge and swung it wide. It banged against an overturned chair. A handful of shattered glass tinkled to the floor.

Noelle flinched and stumbled back. Her elbow clipped the edge of the counter and pain lanced up her arm. Jackson lumbered to his bowl and buried his muzzle, slurping up yesterday's dog food. Noelle looked from the dog to the open door and crossed her arms tightly across her chest. Cold air wafted over her.

She heard the soft thud of the front door closing, and swung towards the sound. Her heart hammered in her chest. Panicked, she looked around the room for a place to hide.

Heavy footsteps drew nearer. Jackson trotted down the hall, tail wagging.

Noelle collapsed against the counter. Her legs were the consistency of warmed jelly. Whoever it was, Jackson recognized. A low voice greeted the dog's noisy welcome. Jake advanced into the kitchen waving a white t-shirt in a flag of truce.

His eyes rested on Noelle's face and moved rapidly over the room, taking in the broken glass and the open door.

"Noelle!"

Two strides closed the distance between them. His hands dropped onto her shoulders. "Noelle," he repeated, giving her a little shake.

His sharp tone cleared the roaring in her ears.

"I'm going to check the rest of the house," he said, turning away from her. "Jackson, stay."

Jackson dropped to his haunches and whined.

Vaguely Noelle noted Jackson's obedience. He seemed to have chosen Jake as a doggy rock star.

The doorbell rang. Noelle automatically stepped towards the front of the house. Jake was ahead of her, moving swiftly down the hallway, pulling the door open to confront the man on the step.

11

Detective Dan Ryerson's finger hovered over the doorbell poised to ring again. The abrupt opening of the door sent him back a step.

"I'm looking for Noelle Ryan," Ryerson said meeting the hostile glare of the man in front of him.

"You the detective from the Landings detachment?" Jake asked.

"And you are . . ?" Ryerson said in answer.

Noelle tried to nudge Jake out of the way. Unable to move him, she planted both hands on his chest and heaved. Jake gave way grudgingly.

"Detective Ryerson, come in." She frowned at Jake, reaching past him to pull the detective through the doorway.

Jake glowered back and shoved his hands into his pockets. He leaned one broad shoulder against the doorframe and waited.

"I thought I would do a follow up with you, see if you remembered any other details," Ryerson said.

Jake snorted rudely, rolling his eyes. The detective's cheeks reddened.

"Someone broke into my house last night," Noelle cut in.

Noelle saw Ryerson glance at Jake. The detective would have to be thick-skinned not to feel Jake's animosity. Ryerson's eyebrows rose slowly. He returned Jake's challenging look with an assessing one of his own.

"And this is?" Ryerson gestured towards Jake.

"This is just leaving," Noelle stated, shooting Jake another annoyed glance.

"Actually, Noelle, I think I'll hang around. The detective could probably use some help. Professional courtesy and all, you know." Jake straightened from his casual lounge. "I'm Jake Ryan." He reached into his back pocket and pulled out his wallet, flipping it open. He offered his identification badge.

Detective Ryerson took the ID. "I figured you were a cop," he said dispassionately.

Jake nodded.

"Now that that's done, tell me what happened," Ryerson said.

Noelle closed the door, taking the time to shoot another evil glare at Jake. What was he up to? Why wouldn't he take the hint he wasn't wanted and leave?

"Hey Noelle, the detective would probably appreciate a coffee. It's cold out. Maybe you should put a pot on before you tell him what happened," Jake said blandly.

Noelle nodded. Good idea. She should have thought of that. Making coffee would help her organize her thoughts. It was only as she was dumping the coffee into the filter that she realized Jake had maneuvered her out of the conversation.

What was he up to? When he'd suggested coffee, the detective had looked so grateful that Noelle found herself acting like Suzy Homemaker before she thought it through. She banged the pot down with more force than necessary. Jake had better realize she was on to him. As soon as the detective left, she was getting rid of him for the last time.

***

Ryerson looked at Jake. "I don't think she's very happy with you," he observed.

Jake shrugged. "She never is, but she'll get over it. I need to show you something. Noelle hasn't seen it yet." He led the way down the hallway to the bedroom, insinuating a familiarity with the layout of the house that the other man was free to interpret any way he wished.

The closed blinds in the bedroom made the room as dark as a cave. Jake used the sleeve of his jacket to flip on the lights and stepped back, letting the detective see what he had discovered a few minutes earlier.

"What's going on?" Noelle demanded, pushing Jake aside. He made a half-hearted attempt to block her view, then sighed and stepped aside. She would see it eventually.

He felt the tension grip her as soon as she moved past him. Her shoulders stiffened at the sight of the kitchen knife driven through her pillow. He wished he could protect her, but he couldn't. He didn't have the right. Besides the move would probably earn him a black eye.

He met Ryerson's gaze and looked back at Noelle. Had she seen the writing yet, or was she still taking in the shattered picture frames and torn bedding? The writer had used a black felt marker to express his frustration at missing his victim. The heavy block writing had shredded the tip of the uncapped marker lying on the floor beside the wall.

You're dead bitch! The message was short and to the point. The writer apparently didn't like to mince words. He cared about punctuation too, judging by the exclamation mark he'd used to express his feelings.

Noelle sagged against the doorframe. Her shoulders heaved once. She bolted from the room. Jake watched her go, wishing there was something he could do to shield her from the ugliness. He frowned and shook his head. The reality was, he'd seen worse.

***

Moments later Noelle rested her forehead against the bathroom wall, grateful for its support. Her stomach was empty and her head spinning. Straightening slowly, she leaned over the sink and splashed cold water on her face. The sight of her corpse-white cheeks made her grimace. She looked like the undead. She pinched color back into them, grabbed her toothbrush, and scoured her mouth free of the acid taste of bile. Her curls were damp with sweat. They had broken free of the ponytail and now straggled over her eyes. She shoved them back and laced her fingers together to stop their shaking.

Until now she had convinced herself that the break in was random. The shredded pillow and trashed room dispelled that myth. This was personal. The guy from the store not only knew where she lived, he wanted her dead.

She slumped against the wall. She couldn't face Jake like this. His reappearance had knocked her carefully ordered world apart. How could she think straight when the sight of his rock-hard body and lazy smile melted her brain into a puddle of irrational thought. She closed her eyes. She wasn't up to dealing with Jake and evading a crazed psycho killer at the same time.

Stepping into the hall, she followed the sound of voices to the living room. The detective, his back to her, was speaking on his cell phone. Jake stood beside the antique wall hutch, his hands tucked into his pockets as he studied the bank of family photographs lining the shining wood grain.

He turned at the sound of her footsteps, pulled his hands from his pockets and crossed the room towards her, reaching out hesitantly. She couldn't help it. She slid into the shelter of his arms. Just this once, she promised herself.

The detective pocketed his phone.

"The department is sending a couple of techs to do some finger printing. Tell me exactly what happened last night and this morning. Don't leave anything out. We'll need every piece of information we can get to find this guy." Ryerson looked worried.

"I'll get the coffee," Jake said and left them.

Noelle sank onto the couch, grateful for the support of the cushions beneath her legs. The detective sat on the chair across from her waiting for her to recount the events of the night before.

Silence closed in. In the distance, she heard the homey sounds of Jake moving about the kitchen. Her brain shuddered to a stop and rewound. Jake and homey? Since when did those words belong in the same sentence? Frivolous, carefree, opportunistic, sexy, she gave herself a mental shake. What was the matter with her? Thoughts of Jake were turning her brain to marshmallow.

"Here."

She looked up to find him next to her, handing her a cup of coffee. He moved like a hunting cat—sleek grace and hushed deadliness. Her eyes widened at the thought.

"I put sugar in it. You need the energy hit it will give you," he said.

"Thanks." She took the cup, wrapping her fingers around it, savoring the warmth.

Jake handed Ryerson the other cup and settled onto the couch beside her.

"Take your time, Noelle. Tell me what you remember about the caller," Ryerson said.

Noelle took a sip of coffee, taking a moment to gather her thoughts. Beside her, Jake's big body offered steady warmth and altogether too much distraction. She caught herself staring down at his thighs, admiring the way his faded jeans hugged his legs. Hastily she pulled her eyes away, looking up to find two sets of male eyes trained on her reddening face.

"It's okay, Noelle, it's natural to be flustered by everything that's happened," Jake said soothingly.

Noelle's cheeks flamed. Flustered? It was a good thing he didn't realize what was actually flustering her.

"Okay, so last night when you got home…" the detective prodded.

After that, it was easy. Noelle recounted the events of the night, finishing with her arrival at the house and Jackson's behavior. "When I opened the door, Jackson went nuts." As if called, the dog strolled into the room and settled at Jake's feet. His tail softly thumped the ground.

Quiet settled over them. Both men appeared lost in thought. Jake's eyes had taken on a hard look that Noelle had never seen before. Fascinated she watched him from beneath her lashes.

The detective shook his head. "This guy is ramping things up, but we're no closer to catching him then we were a year ago." He sounded frustrated.

"Security tapes?" Jake asked.

Ryerson shook his head. "He keeps his face away from the cameras. The guys have taken to calling him the Cobra. He's in and out without leaving a fingerprint. If someone gets in his way, he strikes. No one recalls much about him. This is our first break."

"You think he scouts out the stores ahead of time, marks where the cameras are, and goes from there?" Jake said.

"Could do. We'll take a look back through earlier loops, see if we can pull something from them. Good thought." Ryerson frowned, tapping his pen against his note pad.

Jake's silence made Noelle antsy. What was he thinking? He was staring at the deep red stain on the carpet.

Ryerson apparently saw Jake's silence as ominous as well. "Look, I know this is tough for you. You're used to running the investigation, but we know how to do our job."

Jake's face grew expressionless.

Ryerson sighed. Noelle looked at him, but Ryerson seemed to have forgotten her presence.

"Listen. You need to step back. Don't make this personal and get in our way."

Jake nodded tightly. "Don't worry. I know my limits. I won't do anything unless Noelle is threatened. Her parents asked for my help."

"Jake, I don't need your help. The police are capable of doing their job." Noelle's gaze rested on the two men. Their words didn't match their behavior. It was as if they were conducting a secret conversation. Worse, they were ignoring her completely.

Jake shrugged and sipped his coffee. He looked like he was drinking varnish, instead of freshly ground Kona blend.

Apparently satisfied he had delivered his message, Ryerson flipped his notebook shut. "The evidence team will be here shortly. If we're lucky, they'll get a print. From there, we might be able to get an ID. Criminals aren't very bright. That's why the jails are full." He shoved the book into his jacket pocket.

"You aren't planning to stay here, are you?" he asked Noelle.

"No . . .I'll be at my parents' house."

"Give me their name and address so I'll know where to reach you if anything turns up. Stick around until our people finish collecting evidence, and then you can do something about your back door. I'll call you later to see how you're doing."

"Don't worry. Noelle won't be alone. I'll keep an eye on her," Jake said.

The detective slanted him a mocking smile and stood. "I'll bet," he muttered.

12

Noelle walked Ryerson to the door. Her stomach was a hard knot and anxiety buzzed beneath her skin like a swarm of angry bees. What if she'd been here last night? What if he had been waiting here this morning?

"Hey." Ryerson nudged her arm. "We'll get this guy. In the meantime, we'll keep you safe."

Noelle smiled wanly. "I know, it's just . . . I don't see this stuff all the time. I mean . . . my take on violence is watching a cop show on TV, or seeing it on the news. That doesn't make it real."

Ryerson sighed. "Oh, it's real all right . . . Listen, this guy is a badass. He's not afraid to use violence and intimidation to make his point. You have to be on the ball. Keep your eyes open."

"I am. I will be." Noelle looked out at the quiet street. Until this morning, home was a refuge.

"That means, don't put yourself at risk. Don't go places by yourself. Just for a while," he added. "But it looks like I'm leaving you in good hands." He gave her a quizzical look.

Noelle sighed and rolled her eyes. "Yeah. I'm sorry about that."

Jake's attitude towards the detective had been condescending and rude to say the least, a pit bull growling over a T-bone steak. Noelle found herself chattering inanely, compensating for his behavior.

"It's so cold. I wouldn't be surprised if we have snow for Christmas," she said brightly.

"Maybe we will," Ryerson answered. "It would be good for the ski hills, give them a kick start on the season. Do you ski?"

"A bit. I try and get out a couple of times a year," she said. She heard a muffled snort from the living room and then the heavy tread of footsteps retreating towards the kitchen. "My class is bouncing off the walls at the thought of snow."

They reached the door and Ryerson gave her a friendly smile.

"I'll be in touch if we hear anything," he said.

"Thanks." Noelle stepped onto the porch holding her hand out for a quick shake. She watched the detective cross the road to his unmarked car and shook her head in disgust. Why did she feel the need to make up for Jake's rudeness? The answer was simple. His heavy silence, crossed arms and pointed glares made her feel she had to step in and carry the conversation. Ryerson was just as bad. He had gone out of his way to put Jake on the defensive, asking mocking questions and casting doubts on Jake's background. What was it with men? Why did they have to make it a pissing match? She rolled her eyes.

The detective climbed into his car. Another car, Jake's rental she supposed, sat in front of the house—a reminder—if she needed one, of what waited inside.

For her own preservation she had to get rid of her unwanted bodyguard, and she had to do it before she fell under the Jake spell. Been there, done that. It was so not going to happen again, she vowed.

Last night's storm had left the tree branches coated in a rime of ice. She tucked her hands into the pockets of her jeans, shivering as a gust of wind struck her. Inside the house, it was warm and dry. Inside she was face to face with violence. This time her shiver had nothing to do with the temperature.

What was she going to do about Jake? Five minutes in his company and she was rising to his bait like a hungry fish. That wasn't good. She knew what happened to any poor unsuspecting fish he reeled in. She forced a smile to her lips and waved a last good-bye to the detective before stepping inside and closing the door. Standing in the hallway she contemplated how to tell Jake where he could go. No, she corrected herself. She would be nice. She would politely point out that she didn't need his help.

Jake had settled into a chair at the kitchen table and was scowling at the back door. He looked up as she entered the room. His expression changed to one of mocking affability.

"So did you send the good detective on his way?" he asked.

Count to ten, Noelle reminded herself. Don't answer until you count to ten.

"Unlike you, Detective Ryerson is very nice. Maybe you could ask him for some lessons on public relations. I hate to think how you deal with your clients."

Jake smiled. "I don't have to worry about it. My clients are dead. They tend not to say too much."

"You must have to work with the living sometimes."

"I have a partner for that. She does all the nice-nice stuff. You'd like her. I annoy her too," he answered.

"Jake, you have to go. I don't want you here." She didn't, she told herself. She just needed to convince the little voice in her head that kept whispering how hot he was. Jake was poison. He had proven that in the past—distracting her from school, tempting her from her chosen path and breaking her heart. The list went on and on. She couldn't afford to let him get close enough to do it all again.

Jake stood. The last ten years had filled his six-foot-two-inch frame with muscle. He towered over her, but she didn't feel threatened. She licked her lips. She couldn't think when he stared at her like that.

"I'll get your jacket," she murmured, turning to go.

"No wait," Jake said. He touched her arm and turned her back to face him.

"What?" she said.

Her heart stuttered, restarted and beat faster. Jackson was barking at the back door.

"Leave him. He's fine. He's chasing seagulls." Jake's voice was low and husky.

A thrill rushed through her. The ice she had cultivated so carefully melted in a quick thaw as her blood ran hotter.

Ten years ago, he could make her palms sweat with one look.

"You're standing too close," she whispered.

"I don't think so." Jake stared down at her.

She lost herself in the blue of his eyes. The heat from his body drew her like a moth to a flame. A tiny voice in her head shouted warnings, but she couldn't move. Once again, she had taken the bait.

His head dipped and his lips captured hers in a soft kiss. Noelle tensed and tried to pull back from the edge. He trailed tiny kisses over her face. Butterfly kisses. She wanted more. Resistance vanished in the white-hot fire racing through her veins.

She cupped his face pulling him closer. Her lips parted. His tongue met hers. The kiss deepened. She leaned in. Closer, she had to get closer. His fingers tangled in her hair, pulling her in tighter. Jake groaned. His hands dropped to her hips, molding her to him. His need strained the fit of the jeans she had admired earlier. He rocked against her.

The doorbell rang. Reeling, Noelle panted, pulling away. Jake's arms dropped to his sides. Their eyes locked. Breathless, Noelle backed up. A shuttered look closed off her face as she fled to answer the door.

13

What the hell just happened? Jake leaned against the kitchen counter, the edge of the granite smooth and cold beneath his fingers. He hadn't meant to kiss her. It was a mistake. No, not a mistake, a calculated risk. He had wanted to break through her reserve, get past the walls she had built. Instead the kiss left him squirming like a schoolboy on his first date. Whoa there, Jake—think before you leap. Kissing Noelle was like hurtling off the highest cliff and freefalling through heaven. He raked his fingers through his hair and took a deep breath. What was he thinking? He'd walked this minefield before and look how well that had turned out. Noelle was his past, any attraction to her over a long time ago.

The sound of voices made him straighten. He forced his face into a blank mask as two plain-clothed officers followed Noelle into the room. Her cheeks were flushed, her hair rumpled. She looked like she'd crawled out from between the sheets after a session of hot, steamy sex. Jake smiled. Noelle blushed and turned away, answering the officers' questions as if her life depended on it. Maybe it did.

Jake scowled as once more reality raised its lousy head. The technicians were already unsnapping their equipment cases, getting down to business. Jake looked away. He had been part of this scene hundreds of times, but never from this side. Did Noelle realize the finger printing powder clung to every surface, defying all efforts to remove it? A pang of guilt reminded him of all the times he had left a crime scene with the words, "We'll be in touch." He never had to worry about the cleanup. He had a feeling he was about to learn exactly how tough of a job it was.

Noelle watched the men, wanting to toss everyone out and lock the door. Jake's kiss burned on her lips. The heat of his touch tingled on her skin. She gritted her teeth, angry at her body's betrayal. It was a kiss! That's all. Why was she working herself into such a lather? She'd been kissed since Jake. It meant nothing.

"Liar," the annoying little voice chirped. "If that were true, why are you acting like this?"

"Hormones," argued another little voice. "You've been single so long that you turn into a ball of churning hormones at the careless brush of a lip. It's a case of wrong man, right time."

She smiled vaguely at the two technicians, trying to portray an air of casual detachment as she walked past Jake. With luck, he wouldn't see her move as the slinking retreat it really was. Coffee. She'd make coffee. That appeared to be all she was good for this morning. She could start a business—*Burgled or attacked? Call Noelle. She has the grounds to make it better.* The simple act of washing the carafe and reassembling the ingredients was a distraction. It helped push away the memory of her toe-tingling, body-melting response to Jake's kiss. Her reaction was a symptom of fatigue—nothing more, nothing less.

"Noelle, the techs want to know if he took anything."

Jake was so near that his breath tickled her ear.

"Stop doing that," she hissed.

Jake smiled.

She flung the dishrag into the sink.

"Jake, I can . . ." The words died under the heat from his blue eyes.

"The techs? Is anything missing?" he prodded.

She looked away. Great, he probably knew exactly what she was thinking. Jake had always read her like an open book. Look at her. She was a hot mess, all because of one measly, little kiss. She pursed her traitorous lips and stepped back. From now on, he could keep his kisses to himself.

"I'll, um, go check."

She escaped, prowling the house, checking the rooms, looking for anything out of place. As she stood in the open doorway to her bedroom a shiver tracked down her spine. Had the gunman stood here? Cobra—she ran the word through her mind. Swift and deadly like the snake he was named for. Had he imagined her sleeping? Was a quick stab of the knife what he had planned, or was there more? They'd find him. They'd find fingerprints, DNA, tissue, something. That's how it worked on TV. She backed away, called Jackson and took him out to the backyard to play fetch.

When she came back in, the techs had finished collecting fingerprints. A powdery gray residue stained the white wood. Its oily haze extended over the door and around the broken window. One of the techs looked up as she entered. Jake eyed her expressionlessly. He had straddled a chair and was watching the men work.

"From what I can see, nothing's missing," Noelle said. "Did you find anything?"

"Sorry." The nearest tech glanced up with an apologetic smile. "There's not much we can tell you right now, but we're pretty much finished." He wiped his fingers on a rag.

The other tech closed the lid of a case resting on the floor. "We'll need a set of yours and Detective Ryan's prints to compare against whatever we've found." He paused, carefully snapping the lock shut, before continuing. "To be honest, I don't think we'll turn anything up." It was cop to cop now. "This is a careful guy. We have yet to find a single print to link him to a crime scene."

Once again, Noelle was the invisible woman.

"When will you know?" she asked, steering the conversation back her way.

"Maybe later today. Detective Ryerson will get back to you."

The men fingerprinted them and packed up the rest of their gear. Noelle watched them leave, standing in the doorway, rubbing the grainy powder from her fingers. Again, she had the uncomfortable sensation of eyes watching. You're paranoid, she told herself as goose bumps lifted the hairs on her arms. She pulled her sweater tighter.

Yeah right, paranoid, but was it paranoia if someone really was out to get you?

Closing the door, she made her way back to the kitchen.

"Okay, appreciate it. Bye." Jake ended his call and looked up at her. "I called Paul Jeffries. He's a glass fitter and locksmith now. He'll be here as soon as he can. You remember him? I played hockey with him. I figure he owes me a favor for all the times I saved his butt back in the day."

Noelle gritted her teeth. He was doing it again; taking charge, telling her what he had done after he had done it. The man would drive a reasonably sane woman to…. Breathe, Noelle. She stopped herself, breaking the direction her thoughts were taking her. Do not let him get to you.

"Something wrong?" Jake asked.

"No . . . yes. I can do it myself," she said.

Jake shrugged. "Just getting the ball rolling."

Noelle grabbed the spray cleaner from under the sink and started scrubbing the oily residue on the window frame. Jake had already swept up the broken glass. The cleaning must have worn him out because he collapsed into a chair at the table to watch her work.

"Hey, happy birthday," he said.

She looked up.

"Tomorrow, Jake." He'd never gotten it right. Although to be fair, he'd only been around for one of them. Funny, in the turmoil of the past twenty-four hours, she had forgotten about her birthday.

"You know the police have this under control. Detective Ryerson said the guy is as good as caught," she lied. "Don't feel you have to hang around."

Jake stretched and settled deeper into the chair. The heat in his blue eyes left her breathless. She looked away. This shouldn't be happening—not now—not ever.

"No," he said. "No worries. I don't have anywhere I have to be. Besides I said I would keep an eye on you."

The doorbell rang silencing further argument.

"I'll get it. In case you aren't clear, this is my house," she said.

"Suit yourself," Jake answered, subsiding into the chair.

Noelle stalked out of the room missing the speculative look that followed her.

Paul Jeffries was on the other side of the door, fifty pounds heavier and with a bigger mouth than ever. He grabbed her in a hug that lifted her off the ground and left her wanting a shower. How could Jake stand him?

"So Noelle, you and Jake are back together. That's great. I always knew it was a mistake for you two to split up, but hey, sometimes those old hormones just can't be helped." His eyes slid over her breasts.

"Jake is in the kitchen. He'll show you what I need done. I need a shower," she muttered and pointed towards the kitchen before escaping to her room. Hormones! Huh! That slob wouldn't recognize a hormone if it bit him in the ass!

She spent the next hour gathering feathers and picking up glass. In the distance, she heard the rise and fall of voices punctuated by Paul's hearty guffaws. She wrinkled her nose in disgust and focused on the job in front of her. She had hoped that cleaning the oily fingerprinting chemical from the walls would take her mind off Jake and his honey kisses, but instead, she couldn't stop thinking about the feel of his lips on hers. What was wrong with her? One kiss and she was careening over the rails on a thrill ride only Jake could give her. The bedroom door squeaked. Noelle swung around to face the root cause of all her problems. Jake's broad shoulders filled the doorway. He looked out of place against the feminine surroundings, his height making the room impossibly small and intimate. The hormones Paul had blamed roared back to life.

"He's gone," Jake said in greeting. "Was he always such a wind bag?"

He strolled into the room and flopped onto the bed. Jackson followed. The dog shot a quick glance at Noelle and gathered himself for the jump to the mattress.

"No," Noelle said firmly. Jackson whined and dropped to the ground.

Jake sat up, leaned over, and patted his head. "Sorry old guy, beds are for people."

The look he sent Noelle generated a wave of heat to her cheeks and a raging flame to parts more southern. Judging by Jake's smirk, he knew exactly where her mind had gone.

She dropped the pillow she was clutching over her breasts and glared at him. "You know, Jake, some things never change. Where's the new key?"

Jake dangled it in front of her. "What will you give me for it?"

Noelle snatched it from his hand and pocketed it.

"Nothing."

She rubbed her fingers against her thigh. The brief contact had generated a spark. Flustered, Noelle grabbed a suitcase from the closet and began stuffing clothing into it. Jake propped a couple of pillows behind his back and leaned against the headboard, watching her move about the room.

Was it hot in here? Noelle snuck a peek at the mirror. Her cheeks were flushed and her eyes glittered. She ducked her head and pulled open the drawer holding her underwear. She plunged a hand in and scooped up the only panties left, a pile of lacy thongs. They would have to do. She wasn't dragging her dirty laundry with her. She would get to that when this was over. For now, she needed to be as far from Jake as she could.

"Okay, I'm ready," she said, zipping the case shut. "Thanks for your help, Jake. I'll see you around."

She stuck her hand out in a formal gesture of farewell. Jake's hand, stronger, warmer, engulfed hers, hanging on a moment longer than necessary. Okay, the handshake was a mistake. She jerked her hand free and fumbled with the case dragging it off the bed and onto the floor.

"Hey, Noelle," Jake called.

She turned around.

"You dropped one." Jake held up a hand, twirling a lacy black thong around the tip of one finger. A tiny red plastic apple dangled from the elastic waist. "Forbidden fruit?" he asked, flashing her a devilish grin.

Noelle's cheeks boiled. She snatched the offending morsel of clothing out of his hand and shoved it into the side of the suitcase.

"Do you want me to carry that to your car?"

"No. I can do it." She dragged the case down the hall to the front door and grabbed her jacket from the chair where she had tossed it. Jake followed.

"The back door is locked. I did a quick sweep of the yard. Everything looks secure. The gate was open. That's probably how he came and went."

"Thanks, Jake."

"No problem. Make sure you have someone with you if you go out, okay?" Jake was serious now. "This guy is psychotic. It's a game to him."

"Yeah, I know. Detective Ryerson said the same thing."

"Be aware of your surroundings. Be careful."

Noelle held the front door open for Jake to pass through. He stepped onto the porch and Noelle slammed the door shut twisting the deadbolt. Leaning against the door, she listened until she heard the sound of his steps leaving the porch. Heaving a breath of relief, she hurried down the hall to grab some toiletries. She wanted out of this house, out from under the malevolent silence. As for the Jake problem, she'd avoid him. It would be easy. After all, Christmas was coming and there was never a shortage of things to do.

***

Jake leaned back in the driver's seat of the black Mustang he had rented. This was the second time in twenty-four hours she'd pushed him through the door. The first time he had left with a smile on his lips; now a frown that would frighten his toughest snitch, twisted his mouth. He shook his head, mulling over the information he had learned from the techs. The situation was growing more dangerous by the hour and they still had no solid leads. There were too many unknowns marring the investigation, and Jake didn't like that factor in any case he worked. The police had nothing to go on, and if he guessed right, the evidence guys wouldn't turn up any usable fingerprints. The guy stalking Noelle was a sick puppy. The message he left confirmed that.

Noelle might not like it, but until they caught a break, he was going to follow her closer than any shadow. Jake eyed the surrounding neighborhood, studying the cars parked nearby. Someone must have heard something last night. He'd follow it up with that detective. What was his name? Ryeson, Ryers? Whatever. He'd get hold of him and find out what he had on the case, professional courtesy and all that stuff. At the same time, he'd let him know that Noelle didn't need any of the protective services he was offering. The detective was a little too aware of Noelle's charms. Jake could look out for her just fine.

The slamming of the front door brought his eyes back to the problem at hand. Noelle flung her purse over her shoulder and scurried to her car. Without pausing to look around, she ducked her head and threw her suitcase onto the passenger seat. Letting Jackson into the car she climbed into the driver's seat and started the engine. She reversed out of the driveway, spinning the tires as she accelerated.

Jake frowned and started the Mustang's engine. The girl had a lot to learn about personal awareness. He pulled out and followed her down the road.

***

The late model Buick accelerated from behind a parked van and followed the black mustang. It amused the man behind the wheel that the police had failed to notice him. Anonymity. That was the way to do it. Blend with your surroundings, be a chameleon, and no one would spot you. He smiled. Cobra. It was a name that fit his brilliance. Twenty-seven convenience stores, and the cops still had no good ID. He frowned, except for last night. Stupid cow. What was she doing out at that time of night anyway?

He reached up and rubbed his nose with the palm of one big hand. He didn't like the look of the guy who had waited for the girl to leave. He might be a complication but he had dealt with complications in the past. The big guys went down as easily as the little ones. He spat out the open window and his mouth twisted into a sneer. He'd find out what hole the girl was hiding in and that would be the end of this mess. Next time he'd be more careful.

14

Noelle leaned into the wall and poked her head around the corner. Good, she was alone. No one would hear her resort to begging.

"So you'll come to dinner?" she repeated, trying to ignore the hint of urgency in her voice. Silently she waited for Maria's reply, willing her to say "yes." You had to tread carefully with Maria. She was prickly about what she called "butting into family events." It didn't matter that in the Hamilton house there was always a family event going on. Judging from the pause on the other end of the line, a "no" was in the making.

"Please," Noelle begged. "These guys are driving me crazy. The shooting and the break in has everyone wired up." It had her wired up too. The thought that someone wanted her dead was more than a little unsettling.

"Did Nick really say women can't protect themselves?" Marie demanded, her attention caught by Noelle's earlier words. "Even your brother couldn't say something so stupid."

Noelle smiled. She'd known Maria would zero in on whatever Nick said. She had the sneaking suspicion that the animosity between Nick and Maria was a front for a dose of sizzling attraction. "You know Nick. The girls he dates need help to get a fake spider out of the bath tub."

Maria snorted. "That's because the girls Nick dates can't bend over to pick the spider up. They'd fall off their heels." Silence, and then, "He's worried about you. Maybe you should take a kickboxing class. If you went to the gym more often, you'd get better. The other night you did great. Add some martial arts and you might be able to take down one of Santa's elves, maybe even Justin Hall."

Noelle's smile slipped a notch. "Justin blindsided me. Besides the school board frowns on taking down little boys."

"Yeah." Maria's disgust was clear. "Like a five-foot-two, one-hundred and forty-pound anger management problem needs protection."

"He's ten, Maria. He said it was an accident." This wasn't the direction Noelle wanted the conversation to go.

She had to get it back on course before Maria launched into a description of sociopathic behavior. Noelle had solved the Justin problem. The next time he had the dodge ball, she wouldn't turn her back on him. "Come on, Maria. Come to dinner. I'll let you advise me on take down methods."

More silence and then Maria said, "Okay. Since you're asking so nicely, I'll come. Six o'clock, right?"

"See you then," Noelle said, ending the call. A twinge of guilt nibbled her, but she pushed it away. It would do Maria good to hang out with a big family group. She was too much of a loner. Besides, desperate times called for desperate measures. Since the break-in, Jim and Louise were intent on wrapping their Christmas baby, Noelle, in swaddling bands. Noelle sighed. She needed to get back under her own roof. Too much time in the family nest was making her loony.

Her parents had taken to spelling each other off in a tag-team system of baby-sitting. It was a wonder they let her go to the bathroom alone. If she had to endure one more hug or gusty sigh, she'd head home and post a welcome sign on the front door.

When Jim and Louise first heard about the break-in, they had wanted to cancel the open house. Noelle had threatened to install a security system and move home.

Detective Ryerson vetoed that with the threat of taking her into protective custody. She had thought he was joking, but the steely determination in his eyes convinced her otherwise. Jim and Lou had only agreed to hold the annual Christmas party after Noelle gave in and promised to listen to Jake's advice.

She shook her head in disgust. The Cobra had no idea where she was. Did they think he was going to dress up like Great Aunt Mabel and waltz through the front door? And how had Saint Jake, the great detective, weaseled his way into becoming so indispensable? Did the "ex" part of husband mean nothing?

The incredibly, awesome Detective Jake Ryan's presence threatened to hijack Noelle's favorite evening. Everyone would think he and Noelle were a couple again. Heads would be snapping so hard in their direction that she would have to hand out neck braces with the candy canes.

Maria had turned out to be the solution. She and Nick couldn't be in the same room without sparks flying. The heat between them would leave Louise so busy putting out fires, Noelle could kick back, relax and enjoy the night.

As for Jake, she'd hook him up with Aunt Mabel or Cousin Gina. Which would it be—bunions or hemorrhoids? Cousin Gina, she decided. An evening spent listening to

Gina's lurid tales of childbirth would curdle Jake's eggnog. By the time Gina finished describing Darren's role in cutting the cord, Jake would be halfway to the airport. That would teach him to play fast and loose with a woman's heart. She smiled a Grinchy grin. What better way to deal with the return of the prodigal son?

There had to be a way to spend Christmas near Jake and protect her sanity at the same time. Their kiss was haunting her sleep. Her dream lover had returned, and now there was no doubt that he wore Jake's face. Last night's stormy imaginings had left her body flaming like a roman candle. She had reached out to find the place beside her empty and her body on fire. The things the dream Jake did . . . Her face burned. If the real Jake did that, he wouldn't have shown up in Landings alone.

Soft footsteps announced Lou's arrival. Her arms were laden with tablecloths and napkins. Noelle ducked her head. If her mother saw her flaming cheeks, she would start looking for a thermometer.

"Plaid or poinsettia?" Louise asked, holding out a length of tablecloth. "I don't remember which one I used last year."

"Plaid." Noelle stood and stretched.

"Is Maria coming?" Louise asked. A worried frown puckered her mouth.

"She wouldn't miss it," Noelle said, masking a smile. She knew exactly what Louise was thinking.

"That's great." Louise was putting on a brave face.

Noelle felt another pang of guilt. No. She hardened her heart. They had brought it on themselves by inviting Jake. If she had to put up with Jake, they could deal with the fireworks between Nick and Maria.

Louise laid the pile of red and gold table clothes on the table and brushed away an imaginary speck of dust. "Everything done?" she asked.

"And then some," Noelle replied, snapping a salute. "Request leave to stand down, Drill Sergeant."

Louise glanced up at the vaulted ceiling.

"No, there are no spider webs. No self-respecting spider would risk spinning a web up there. What else do you need?"

"Nothing. You go and get some things done. This is your birthday. You deserve a chance to spoil yourself. Jake should be here in a few minutes. Oh, did you phone that detective? Maybe they've heard something. No," she interrupted herself. "Jake would have told us if they had."

Jake, Jake, Jake. Noelle frowned. She had to get out of here before he showed up. Tonight, she would have her fill of bodyguards–three older brothers and Jake—a full protective detail.

Louise held up a tablecloth, already lost in thought, planning her dinner setting. She had forgotten Noelle was in the room.

Noelle left the dining room and followed the sound of the vacuum to the living room. Jim was hoovering beneath the couch. Noelle leaned against the doorframe and fondly studied the backward-facing baseball cap he'd perched on his balding head. Jim was deep into the battle of sucking up dust bunnies and cat hair. Where *was* the cat? The last time Jackson and the cat had gotten together, Jackson had gotten his nose scratched for inappropriate sniffing, and stress had caused Mr. Meow to lose half his fur. She eyed a floating clump of fur. Maybe it was already too late.

Wait a minute. Why was she standing here doing nothing? Her keepers were distracted. Now was the perfect time for an escape. She could be gone before they realized their chick had flown the coop. Thoughts of shopping danced like sugarplums in her head.

Stealthily she lifted her coat from the rack by the door and grabbed her purse. Quietly opening and closing the front door, she ducked out of the house and escaped to her car. Her brother Ray arrived as she started the engine. He parked in front of the house and beckoned her over. One look told her big brother Ray was gearing up for a lecture on personal safety. She rolled her eyes. Why couldn't she have been one more girl in a long line of sisters?

Luckily she'd parked for a quick escape. She pulled onto the road ignoring Ray's frantic waves. She'd hear about that tonight, but it wouldn't hurt him to stew for a while. Besides, she was feeling too good to stop and argue.

She settled into the seat. Freedom. Escape made her feel almost normal. She hated everyone fussing over her. She needed to be out and doing, especially with Jake on the scene. Inactivity had left her feeling as nutty as leftover fruitcake.

At least she had caught up on her sleep. She had gone to bed early enough to wake up with the birds and slept like a log. She wrinkled her nose. Okay, maybe not a log, maybe more like a chicken in a coop full of roosters, a tired chicken. Her cheeks burned. Focus, girl, she muttered squirming, her thoughts sliding back to last night's dream. Why did her dream lover have to look like Jake?

Behind her, Ray waved frantically, demanding she turn around. She waved back cheerfully and shifted into third gear. If she stopped, they'd make her wait for a bodyguard. You didn't have to be a rocket scientist to guess whom that would be. She was not spending the day with Jake. Nights were bad enough. Besides she was perfectly safe. Detective Ryerson had said it was unlikely the guy would figure out where she was. The whole bodyguard thing was just about taking precautions. She'd keep her eyes open and everything would be just fine.

***

As Noelle's Honda rounded the bend in the road, a battered Buick pulled away from the curb. The driver flung a cigarette butt out the window and let the distance between the two cars double. This was simpler than he'd expected. The girl had been laughably easy to track, and today, the big guy was nowhere in sight. He could rid himself of his problem without distraction. A smirk crossed his lips. He was still the master, the Cobra.

15

Escape was almost too easy. Ray would never forgive her. She'd buy him something extra special to make up for ditching him, but it was worth it. Sneaking out before Jake arrived was brilliant. Her smile dwindled. The Jake issue was a serious problem. His arrival on the scene had started this catastrophe. He was sucking the merry out of Christmas. She shook her head. No. She wasn't going to waste time brooding over Jake. She was going to find her missing Christmas spirit and she was going to do it now. She poked the scan button on the radio, found a channel playing holiday music, and passed the time singing along to the carols. Traffic slowed to a crawl as she neared Victoria. She had timed her great escape to coincide with the arrival of a ferry from the mainland.

Impatiently Noelle drummed her fingers on the steering wheel. A trip that should take twenty minutes driving time warped into forty minutes of stopping and starting. By the time she reached the cobbled streets of the capital city's downtown, her *fa la la's* had morphed into "what the hells?" Only the sight of the city core returned the smile to her face.

In honor of the season, the merchants of downtown Victoria had rolled out a blanket of tinsel and lights. Glittering stars replaced the hanging baskets on the globed street lamps and twinkling fairy lights wrapped the trees. The capital city was open for business. The sun was shining and people were smiling. Even the most jaded of Scrooges would have a hard time finding fault with the holly-trimmed storefronts and colored lights. Noelle rolled down her window and breathed in the cold sea air. The weatherman was wrong. All the doom and gloom warnings of a heavy front moving in were a bad case of humbug. The sun was proof things were looking up in the weather department.

She slowed to let a huddle of shoppers cross the cobblestoned road in front of her. Judging by the crowds she wasn't the only one braving the nippy air for a shop. On the sidewalk beside her a family clustered in front of the display window of a chocolate shop. The littlest member of the group tugged the adults towards the door. His smile was warm enough to melt the giant chocolate Santa in the window.

Parking was at a premium. She squeezed into a space near the elevator on the bottom level of the downtown mall, locked her car, and jogged to the entrance. Her booted heels tapped sharply on the concrete, the sound echoing across the open space. Uneasily Noelle ran her eyes over the tightly parked cars, regretting the decision to park underground. No. Parking here made sense. If she parked on the street, she would have to walk six blocks to the mall. She shot another quick look at the empty cars. The sense of hidden eyes was back—this time so strong she considered telling Detective Ryerson about it. She shook her head. Relax. It was normal to feel nervous, especially when she was already suffering from a guilty conscience at sneaking off. Death threats and break-ins had a way of making the calmest person jump at shadows. If she told Ryerson, he would think she was nuts. Not to mention, he'd be ticked that she was out alone.

She pushed through the heavy glass door of the elevator lobby and pressed the call button. Rocking nervously on her toes, she waited for the elevator. Overhead the boom of the exhaust fans drowned out everything but the heavy thump of her heart. That organ was working overtime, sending blood swooshing through her ears.

Jingling her keys in her pocket, she peered out at the empty space on the other side of the glass wall. No, it was best to keep her feelings to herself. Protective custody was an experience she preferred to skip. The elevator bell chimed. She jumped, laughing shakily.

"You're letting your imagination drive you nuts," she muttered, ducking into the elevator and poking the third-floor button. Only when the compartment lifted did she relax.

The doors to the upper level of the mall opened and she stepped out. She had never been claustrophobic, but the caged confines of the elevator car had set her heart racing. Still rattled, she crossed to the edge of the foyer, leaned against the railing, and looked down on the open courtyard below. Scents of cinnamon and cranberry teased her nose.

She inhaled the tangy aroma and admired the Christmas decorating. The mall's design group had created a holiday wonderland, wrapping the massive ceiling beams in swags of cedar and holly studded with glittering lights and red iridescent stars. Flocked Christmas trees formed snow-covered forests watched over by gilded reindeer. On a raised dais at the center of the atrium a high school band played *Rudolph, the Red Nosed Reindeer*, their Santa hats and bells moving with military precision as they worked through the melody. The trumpet player sported green antlers and a red nose that glowed when he blew a note.

Christmas, traditional or new age, had something for everyone. Like trees—she preferred the traditional, but so what if someone else wanted the tacky, glow-in-the-dark trees across the courtyard. Or people—she watched a grandpa, wearing a Santa hat, swerve his red-nosed scooter around a group of elf-hatted teens.

Enough window shopping, it was time to get to work. She had a healthy balance in her bank account and the afternoon in front of her. No schedules, no deadlines, no report cards to write, and best of all, no pain in the butt ex-husband dogging her every step.

Humming along to the band's rendition of *Silver Bells*, she wove her way through the crowds. Not even the long line-ups at the cashiers dampened her enthusiasm. Toy shopping took the most time. Anything that forced her brother Ray down to ground level was worth considering. Ray's linebacker-sized posterior parked beside his four-year-old, was a sight screaming for capture on *Instagram*. She stopped to take a closer look at a set of miniature drums. Her two-year-old nephew would love playing rock star. She moved on. The drums would drive her pregnant sister-in-law crazy.

Reality returned with the sight of the huge hanging clock. She had set her phone to vibrate when she'd entered the mall. Now, she dug it out of her purse. Fifteen missed calls in the last four hours. She shoved the phone into her jacket pocket.

Time to go. She'd put a hefty dent in her bank account and reached her carrying capacity. She juggled her parcels and took a sip of the peppermint mocha she'd splurged on. If she left now, she would get to her parents' house in time to dress for dinner and help with a few final touches.

Jim and Lou Hamilton were huge Christmas fans. When their only daughter arrived a week before the big day, it was natural she be christened Noelle. To Noelle, the real Christmas blessing was she hadn't been born a boy. She might have ended up as Rudolph or Ebenezer.

Every year the Hamiltons hosted an annual birthday/tree trimming party. It started with a supper to celebrate Noelle's birthday and expanded to an open house where friends and neighbors filled the house with Christmas spirit and noise, a lot of noise. With so many people around Noelle should have no trouble avoiding

Jake. She might even manage to declare a Christmas truce. It was only one night. She was big enough for that.

She waited in the elevator queue, taking an occasional sip of the mint chocolate coffee, enjoying the blend of flavors on her tongue. It would be good to dump the shopping bags in the trunk of the car. Their weight threatened to leave her with one shoulder permanently lower than the other.

The elevator arrived and the doors opened. Everyone jostled in. She smiled at a little boy standing nearby and received a toothy grin in response. Her stomach dropped as the car descended. There would be others getting off on the bottom, she consoled herself, but the last of her fellow riders filed out on the floor above. The doors closed. The elevator dropped the final feet and opened onto the empty lobby.

16

Noelle hesitated, her shoulder butted up against the edge of the elevator door keeping her escape route clear behind her. Overhead the banks of fluorescent lighting chased away the shadows and bathed the alcove in cold white light. In front of her a wall of windows offered a view of what waited on the other side of the glass. Nothing. She ran her eyes over the empty space. There was nothing out there but cars awaiting their owners' returns. The door closed and bounced off her shoulder.

If there was no one out there, why were goose bumps trampling up her arms? Crazy, that's why. She was going crazy imagining hidden eyes and danger in every doorway, or in this case, behind every concrete pillar. She edged away from the elevator, shrugging the shopping bags higher up her arm. Leaning against the window, she peered through the glass.

Four hours ago, the lot had been full. Now a handful of cars were parked in the concrete cavern. Her car seemed a million miles away.

She bit down on her lower lip and considered the distance to her dependable old Honda. Time to go her brain told her, but her feet remained rooted in the concrete floor. She frowned and stared harder at her car. If only she could see through its darkened windows . . . Had the lights above it been out when she parked? She should have paid more attention. What had Jake said? *Be alert, be careful.* She shifted restlessly, juggling bags and coffee cup into a more comfortable position. The alert part she had under control. The careful part . . . well, it was too late to fix that.

Maybe she should go back in and have security walk her to her car. No, that meant going all the way to the third floor and hunting for the security office. It would take too much time and she had been gone long enough. *Grow up. You've walked through a million parking lots. Don't be such a chicken.* Her feet stayed fixed. She sighed. So much for the pep talk—it clearly wasn't working. More than ever she wanted to turn around, punch the elevator call button and flee the empty lot.

She gazed out the window. It was natural to be nervous. The past few days hadn't been exactly routine, but she needed to get a handle on her fear or it would take over her life. It's a parking garage. It's daylight. Nothing is going to happen.

She opened the door and stepped onto the lot. Overhead the giant exhaust fans wheezed and clattered, blanketing the space with mechanical groans. A gust of forced air stinking of oil and dirt oozed over her. Noelle's blood cooled, gelling under her skin. Her heart thudded in time with the boom of the fans. Her imagination kicked into overdrive, altering the familiar lot, growing the shadows and stretching the distance to her car. The dimly lit parking lot was the perfect setting for a horror movie. She imagined the victim crossing the deserted lot. "*Go back, go back.*" Jake's words returned in a flood of ice. *It's a game to him. He's psychotic.*

What kind of game—hide and seek? Only maybe he was doing a better job of hiding than she was. She shot a quick look at the parked cars and moved faster. She should have gone back up. She stopped, turned around and looked towards the brightly lit elevator alcove. It was as far back as it was to go on. She was committed. Don't be a victim. March up to your car and get the hell out of here. She trotted forward, shopping bags swinging, striking her knee with every step. *Run, bang, run bang.* Ow. She was going to have a bruise from the sharp edge of the toy drum set.

The nearest car to hers was a battered Buick parked crookedly, facing outward. Positioned for a quick escape or abandoned? It looked abandoned. No, it looked like it belonged on the set of a horror movie. She shivered. Her heart thumped harder, threatening to crawl into her throat.

Enough drama. The car is close, just a short dash. She fumbled with the bags, juggling her mocha, trying to reach the keys in her pocket. She should get a new car, one with a security system and a key fob, a key fob with a great big panic button.

"Stop it, Noelle," she muttered.

Her voice echoed. How long was she going to be this way—jumping at shadows, seeing muggers behind every cement post? The parking lot was well lit. It was empty... The night of the shooting the store had been well lit. Her house had been well lit. Had he watched her house, seen her shadow moving behind the curtains? Her heart rate ratcheted higher.

She ran the last few steps to her car, abandoning any thought of putting on a brave face. Glass crunched under her feet. She looked up. The bank of lights above the parking space was smashed. Wires leaked from the broken fixture. Why hadn't she noticed the glass when she parked? Did vandals have no Christmas spirit?

A car door slammed. A spurt of relief melted her frozen muscles. She wasn't the only life down here. She reached the back of her car. A yellow panic button sprouted from the side of a nearby pillar; big letters spelled out the word HELP. Did muggers give you time to push the button?

She tripped on an uneven piece of concrete and hot mocha splashed her fingers.

"Damn," she muttered, banging her knee on the car bumper. Her relief at reaching the car escaped in a quiet breath. She had let her imagination take hold and panic set in. She rested her drink on the trunk and, balancing the parcels on one knee, dug deeper into her coat pocket in search of the keys.

Something moved in the shadow of the HELP pillar. She looked up. A man straightened from beside the concrete slab. His eyes met hers as his lips twisted into a cold smile. Noelle dropped the bags and raised her hands in self-defense. He tossed his cigarette aside and took two steps towards her. Noelle retreated. The back end of her car butted up against her legs. He rushed at her, coming in hard and low. The weight of his body slammed against her, pushing her into the car. She hit the bumper, riding up and over the trunk. Metal groaned under her weight. Pain lanced through her hip.

He wrapped his fingers in the front of her jacket hoisting her high leaving her feet dangling. Noelle tried to scream, but only a muffled croak emerged. She kicked and clawed, trying to break the chokehold. Starved for air, she raked her nails over his cheek. Cursing he let go. She fell and her head thumped the ground. Stars spun in front of her eyes. Gasping and gagging, she scrambled away. He grabbed her ankle, hauling her back. Knotting a fist in the front of her coat, he yanked her to her feet. Noelle's head wobbled on her neck. His hands were iron claws at her throat. His breath bathed her face. She struck blindly. He dodged, laughed and pulled her in.

"You shoulda minded your own business!" he growled and threw her back against the car.

She bounced off the driver's door, her breath escaping in a solid whoosh. Retching, she pushed herself up. Her fingers slid over the cold smooth glass of the car window.

"Bitch!" he swore and punched her.

The blow caught her below the left eye and snapped her teeth shut. She tasted blood. Falling, she twisted onto her side and curled into fetal position.

"Stop," she whimpered.

He kicked her in the ribs and stooped, bending over her. He leaned in, slowly sliding a knife from a sheath on his belt. His eyes were cold dark pits. She was going to die. He smiled and her blood congealed. Flicking the knife open, he pressed the point to her throat. It dug into her skin.

"You remember me?"

Noelle swallowed. The knifepoint pricked deeper.

"I can cut your throat before you say another word," he said. "You should have been home tucked up in that snug little bed of yours, not out running around. Your loss, babe."

"I won't say anything," Noelle croaked. "I didn't see your face."

"But you have now. You have nothing to offer me, unless . . ." He lessened the pressure on the knife.

Noelle flung herself to the left and kicked his knee with the heel of her boot. Caught off guard, he tripped and almost went down. Catching his balance, he lunged, slashing out wildly. The tip of the knife caught the woolen sleeve of her coat. He drew back for another stab.

"We should have waited and got it on sale. You always want everything right away," a man's voice complained.

"I don't. You just can't make a decision," a woman answered, laughing.

The voices came closer.

"You're lucky, bitch!" Noelle's attacker leaned closer. The stench of cigarettes and body odor stirred the hairs around her ear. "Next time you won't be!"

He straightened and ran towards the old Buick. The door slammed and the Buick flashed past catching the front corner of her car. Gasping against a sharp stab of pain, Noelle rolled over colliding with the tire behind her.

17

"**H**ey! What's going on? Jean, call 911." Voices cut through the fog surrounding her, driving it back.

Noelle gagged. Agony clawed her lungs. Gentle hands clasped her shoulders and rolled her over.

"Hey, you okay? Jean, call the police." The man passed his cell phone to his wife and anxiously patted Noelle's arm.

"No." Noelle exhaled painfully and struggled to sit. "Wait." She grimaced. Her thoughts tumbled in disconnected strands. She didn't want the police. She'd call them later, from safety. Not from here.

"You need a doctor. Paul, tell her . . . Your poor face. . ." Jean bent over her and gently touched her cheek. "That car did a number on you. Thank God we were late leaving the mall," she murmured.

Noelle grimaced. She was sure the sister to that bruise was growing on the back of her head. She lifted a hand to her face. Her cheek burned, but her fingers came away bloodless.

"Can you help me up?" She extended her hand to the man, Paul. Reluctantly, he took it, hauling her to her feet.

She swayed and the parking lot swam before her eyes. Paul grabbed her arm, steadying her. Slowly the world righted itself, leaving her standing.

"Did the car hit you?" Jean asked.

She shook her head. Pain stabbed her temples. They thought that she was a victim of a hit and run? Hadn't they seen him?

"If you won't let us call the police, let us call an ambulance. You're pretty beaten up. You took quite a fall. People drive like idiots. They don't watch for pedestrians. It was probably a new driver," Jean said.

"Did you see him?" Noelle asked.

"We heard a thud." Jean wagged her head solemnly. "Some lunatic drove away fast."

Noelle unhooked her keys from the lining of her pocket. Carefully she unlocked the trunk and bent to pick up her bags. The ground heaved as the world tilted.

Hands pressed her to sit. They picked up her bags and stowed them neatly in the trunk.

"Are you sure you can drive." Paul asked doubtfully, eyeing her ashen face.

Noelle nodded, cleared her throat and spoke more firmly. "Yes, I'm fine. I just want to go home."

Paul helped her into the car and closed the door. Waving her thanks, she started the engine and backed out of the parking stall. In the mirror her face was pasty pale, the purple on her cheek spreading. She stopped at the pay booth, dug a bill out of her wallet and dropped it into the attendant's hand. The barrier rose and she drove off, oblivious to his calls to come back for the change he was waving.

Nausea churned in her throat. She pulled into an empty lot, scrambled to open the door and vomited her lunch. Sagging in her seat, she closed her eyes and prayed for the world to stop spinning. When she opened them again, everything stayed where it belonged. She dragged a shaky hand across her face. Thinking was an effort, but she needed a plan. Once she called the police, they'd put her in protective custody. Worse, if she showed up looking like this, she'd scare everyone half to death.

A tear broke past the barrier of her lashes and she scrubbed it away. The shaking started in her fingers and spread through her body like a fast burning wildfire. She hugged herself and cried as her sense of safety popped like an over-inflated balloon. While she had been congratulating herself on how clever she was, he was watching, waiting for the moment to strike.

Anger took over from self-pity. Once she called the police, someone else would assume control of her life. Say good-bye to freedom, Noelle. You thought it was bad before; it's about to get a thousand times worse.

She glared at the steering wheel through a blur of tears. Did she have to tell the police right now? What if she kept quiet—just for tonight—and pretended that everything was normal? No, that would be stupid. The police needed to catch this guy. But what difference would one night make? She could have tonight and call the police tomorrow. Then they could smother her in all the protective custody they wanted. They weren't going to find him tonight.

She angled the mirror down and examined her battered face. She'd buy cover up and hide the marks. The black eye wouldn't come until tomorrow. She pressed her fingers to her cheek. It hurt, but nothing felt broken.

She shoved the mirror back into place. It wouldn't be the first black eye she had hidden. She'd once taken a soccer ball to the face on the eve of a friend's wedding. She'd concealed that bruise so well that no one knew it was there. Nobody would see the bump on the back of her head, and if anyone got close enough to witness the boot mark on her ribs… well, she was at the wrong party.

Okay, she would keep quiet, get through tonight, and call Detective Ryerson tomorrow. Her parents had been planning the big birthday/Christmas bash for months. If they knew about the attack in the parking lot, the night would be ruined. No—tonight she would be safe enough surrounded by her army of bodyguards—tomorrow she would fess up. She forced a smile in the mirror and watched the puffy purple mark on her cheek stretch. She flipped the mirror back up. She'd make sure the cover up was industrial-strength.

18

Noelle propped her elbow on the counter and studied her image in the mirror. The *Cover Me Extreme* concealer had lived up to its promise, leaving her face smooth, her complexion flawless. Even under the unforgiving glare of the fluorescent lights, the beige-toned cover up hid the purple bruise surrounding her eye.

She turned her head side to side, critically studying the effect. Not bad. She nodded in satisfaction. Her face had a polished look—very glamorous and intriguing. Of course, all that concealer demanded a heavier hand with the rest of her makeup. She had selected a pallet of colors she would normally skip, figuring that the roses, violets, and purples would help hide the bruising if the *Cover Me* faded. Yes, she decided, very nice. Except, way too exotic for what she'd planned on wearing tonight. She tossed the concealer into her purse. If she arrived looking like an understudy on opening night, she would draw everyone's attention. She may as well strap on a neon sign and announce something was wrong. She sagged against the counter and rested her chin on her palms. There had to be a way out of this mess.

It was another thing she could blame Jake for. If she weren't so desperate to avoid him, she would never have gone off on her own. Okay, maybe she would have, but Jake made her so crazy that all she could think about was getting out of the house before he arrived.

She straightened and cast another look in the mirror. If she had any hope of pulling this off, she needed a dress to match the fashion model makeup. At least she could cross runway model off a list of dream careers. The makeup itched. She wanted to scrub her hands over her face and free up her pores. She made a mental note to avoid open flames. The heat would probably melt her face.

She scooped the rest of the makeup into her purse, left the ladies room, and waded through a herd of teenage girls surrounding the cosmetics counter. The scent of cheap florals and expensive musk perfumes drifted over her and made her stomach heave. The girls' shrill chatter made her head pound.

Standing on the sidewalk outside of the drugstore, she breathed in the frosty air. The store's heat was suffocating, the heavy perfume cloying. She liked perfume, but ten different scents on five people made her nose itch. Worse, she couldn't risk scratching it and marring the finish on her carefully prepped face. Tentacles of cold snaked through her open jacket. Shivering, she pulled it tighter. Maybe the weatherman wasn't so far off in his predictions for a white Christmas. Fine with her, she wasn't going anywhere.

Her fingers tangled in the cut sleeve. She was lucky the knife hadn't ripped more than the thick wool. She could be sitting in a hospital bed explaining why she was alone at the mall in the first place. That is, she swallowed, if she had managed to fight him off. If that couple hadn't come along when they did . . . She pushed the thought aside. They had, and she was fine. She needed to get a dress and carry on with this farce.

Somewhere in all these stores was the answer to her dilemma. A bank, a drycleaner . . . forget the hardware shop, unless she needed a power washer to get the makeup off later . . . a deli, and the dollar store. She smiled . . . there it was.

Helena's Fine Gowns and Dazzling Apparel— Landings' answer to designer dresses. Helena and Frieda

Chong worshipped their fellow twins, the Gabor sisters. Helena and Frieda, with their bleached blonde hair and four-inch heels had tottered around their store for as long as Noelle could remember. If anyone had a dress to match the makeup, they would. If not, she may as well go home and fess up to the day's adventure.

Squaring her shoulders, she opened the door and stepped into the store.

"Good afternoon." A salesclerk sent Noelle a beaming, patently phony smile of welcome. "Welcome to Helena's. Is there anything I can help you find?"

"Er, no, just looking," Noelle muttered, edging past her, feeling the plush pile of carpet give way beneath her feet. Keep moving. If you don't make eye contact, they won't attack. The trick worked with dogs; maybe it offered the same protection from circling salesclerks.

She found the eveningwear section at the back of the store. It was marked by rows of dramatic black gowns, fiery sequined red sheathes, and shiny pink taffeta dresses pinned to the wall. The gowns were more suited to fading starlets than the store's clientele of graduating high school students.

Gold signs proclaimed huge sales discounts.

"May I help you find something?" An elaborately made up clerk straightened from the rack she was sorting and ran a critical eye over Noelle.

Noelle forced a smile. "I'm just looking, thanks."

"We have some lovely evening dresses perfect for the holidays," the clerk continued ruthlessly, pulling a shimmering strapless gold mini dress from the rack. She held it up.

"That's very nice, but I think I'm looking for something a little more understated."

The clerk pursed her lips and returned to the rack.

Noelle concentrated on the dresses, trying to ignore the jangle of hangers behind her.

"*This* is a copy of a dress Angelina Jolie wore in Cannes." The clerk reverently lifted a long flame-colored sheath from the rack. "She was the envy of all the stars, and made the top-ten-best-dressed list."

Noelle faked a smile. If Angelina wore that, it wasn't the top ten best-list she made. The dress would bare all to the cameras; more porn star than movie star. No wonder the sales tag proclaimed seventy-five percent off.

"It's lovely," Noelle murmured dutifully.

The clerk nodded regally and returned the dress to the rack.

"It's a bit more formal than I need," she added and flitted to another rack hoping the clerk wouldn't follow.

"This one is fun. It's all the rage in Hollywood. We also have some lovely bustiers," the salesclerk continued, her eyes dropping to eye Noelle's chest. "They give you lift and enhance your cleavage."

"Thanks, but I think that this might be more what I'm looking for." In desperation, Noelle yanked a short black cocktail dress from the rack. She held the dress up and looked at it more closely.

"That's a wonderful option," the clerk gushed. "Obviously, you aren't a stranger to the dramatic make up needed for that dress. After all, we want the men to see more than the dress."

Wait a minute. Did the clerk think she was a hooker? Noelle snuck a peek at a nearby mirror. The makeup wasn't that garish.

"Yes," the clerk continued. "Your body type will let you wear that dress easily. What size are you looking for?"

"A six," Noelle answered.

The clerk plucked the correct dress size from the rack and led Noelle to the fitting room. Noelle pushed the door closed and leaned her head against it, grateful for the coolness beneath her brow. She should have grabbed a bottle of painkillers at the drugstore. Her headache fueled a growing nausea. She closed her eyes and wished for the dizziness to go away.

Turning back to the dress, she held the spandex edge between her thumb and forefinger. This was a first. She had never tried on anything this seductive. Could she pull it off? The slinky dress would hug every curve, while the plunging neckline would show more skin than she was used to revealing. Intriguing. It was the perfect dress to entice a man's interest, perfect for an evening with someone special . . . or showing an ex-husband what he was missing.

She turned her back on the dress, pulled her shirt over her head, and dropped it onto the bench behind her. Sloughing off her jeans, she spotted the bruise encircling the base of her ribs. Gently she ran her fingers over it, wincing at the slight pressure. She was lucky the kick hadn't broken a rib. She shivered. Thank God she'd rolled when she saw it coming. If his boot had really connected . . She frowned and goose bumps rippled up her arms. If the elderly couple hadn't arrived . . .

At least now she could give Detective Ryerson a description—dark eyes, a sharp beak of aquiline nose, and thin lips pulled back over even white teeth . . . He'd been waiting for her. How long had he sat in the underground lot? Had he tracked her from the start? That was a stupid question. He hadn't magically picked the exact spot to wait for her. She sank onto the bench, the dress forgotten between her fingers.

"Hello, do you need any help."

Noelle jumped at the sharp knock, barking her shin on the low bench. Cursing softly, she rubbed her leg. Another bruise to add to her collection.

"No, I'm fine," she called out.

Hastily she stepped into the short, clinging dress, reaching behind in a series of contortions to pull the zipper up. The exertion left an oily film of sweat clinging to her forehead. She took a deep breath and gasped as pain clawed her ribs. Dots danced in front of her eyes. Abruptly she sat down. When the dizziness cleared, she stood and faced her image in the mirror.

The dress clung like a second skin. The silky black fabric cupped her breasts, pushing them up. The skirt flowed over her hips, stopping mid-thigh to leave a flattering view of Noelle's long shapely legs. Noelle blinked. The simple sexy dress coupled with the sophisticated makeup, completely altered her appearance.

"If you'd like, there's a better mirror out here," the clerk called from where she lay in wait outside the fitting room.

Noelle unlocked the door and stepped out.

"It's perfect," the clerk said clapping her hands together. "Sooo glamorous. That dress calls for just the blend of sexy eyes and dramatic make up that you're wearing. Is it a special occasion?"

Noelle nodded. "My birthday," she said, pivoting to check the fit of the dress.

"Well, that's certainly a reason to buy this dress. Who doesn't want to get dolled up on their birthday? And at Christmas to boot!" The clerk looked ecstatic.

Noelle smiled. "You're right," she said. Who wouldn't want to look her best, especially when an extra-annoying ex-husband showed up uninvited? A classic case of too bad, look what you walked out on. No one would think twice about the reason behind her sudden glamour.

She checked her watch.

"I'm late, so I am going to leave it on," she said. By now her wardens had worked themselves to full-fledged panic. She had sent a text saying she was running late, but even that was pushing her luck. She was in for an earful when she got home.

"I'll get you some nylons," the clerk said, casting a disapproving look at Noelle's red and green ho, ho, ho socks. She hurried off.

A moment later, she returned, and Noelle retreated to the change room to pull on the sheer black hose.

She paid for her purchases, waiting patiently as the clerk clipped off the sales tags, gushing over the dress as she snipped.

"There's a shoe store a few doors down. Check there. They'll have the perfect shoe for this dress, something strappy and high that will enhance your rear. High heels make men crazy." She frowned. "I wish they had to wear them for an evening." She handed Noelle the receipt.

Noelle thanked her, and headed to the shoe store where she bought a pair of strappy black high-heeled pumps. She wobbled to the safety of her car, ignoring the appreciative cat calls of some passing construction workers.

19

Noelle slid into the driver's seat and winced as cold leather met the back of her exposed thighs. She hammered down the lock button feeling a wave of relief at the sound of the lock engaging. There, safe—all tucked in and free from harm. Right. She would believe that when she was back behind four walls. But for now . . . she leaned forward, stuck the key in the ignition and turned it with a shaking hand.

The drive across town was uneventful. Noelle's eyes constantly strayed to the rear-view mirror, straining for a glimpse of the battered Buick with its crumpled fender. At each red light, she searched the face of the driver beside her.

Somehow her attacker knew where to find her. The thought made her heart stutter in her chest. He could be anywhere waiting for her. He had watched her leave this morning and followed her downtown, biding his time until he caught her alone.

She turned the corner onto her parent's street, oblivious to the bright display of Christmas lights flanking the road. She had the jittery feeling of having sipped too many espressos. In the words of her brother Nick, she was wound up tighter than the Tasmanian devil on a caffeine jag. Her gaze lingered on the parked cars lining the curb. No Buicks. Naturally, she chided herself. Give the guy some credit. He had brains. That's why the police hadn't caught him. She wouldn't be in this mess if she had credited him with the smarts to plan an ambush.

Slowly her heart rate stabilized. From what she could see, the cars parked here belonged. She looked for the rental car Jake had driven earlier. Bonus. It was nowhere in sight. With luck, it would stay that way. She pushed open the door and leaned over to gather the bags from the passenger seat. The things in the trunk could wait; she wasn't up to lugging them into the house right now.

Across the road, a horn honked. Noelle looked up to see Maria climbing out of her car. Noelle waited so that they could walk in together.

Maria straightened from the low seat of her BMW convertible and twitched her sleek red dress into place. The dress, ending mid-thigh, showed off her long dancer's legs. Casually Maria raked a hand through her thick black hair, sending it cascading over one shoulder. She placed a braceleted hand on each hip and whistled appreciatively.

"Well, well, well, what have we got here? You look gorgeous. What's the occasion? Other than your birthday?"

"Nothing." Noelle linked arms with her, ignoring the sharp twinge of pain the movement brought. "I thought that tonight, I'd give you a run for the money."

Laughing, they sauntered up the sidewalk. Before Noelle could put her key in the lock the door opened.

"Noelle, where the hell have you..." Nick's voice trailed off as he caught sight of Maria. "Maria. Welcome, come in."

Maria smiled brightly and let Nick tug her into the house. Noelle hid a smile. Judging from the look on Nick's face he had forgotten all about Noelle and her adventures.

"Noelle!"

Okay, maybe she should have waited before congratulating herself on her escape. Ray wouldn't be as easy to distract as Nick.

"You saw me this morning! Why didn't you stop when I called you?" Ray took up most of the doorway. He crossed his beefy arms across his chest and scowled. "Did you stop and think that maybe you shouldn't be out running around by yourself? No, wait. You wouldn't do that, would you?" Ray's chin jutted belligerently. A vein throbbed in his forehead.

"Relax, Ray, I'm fine," Noelle interrupted. "I had some last-minute shopping. Nothing happened." Noelle crossed her fingers behind her back at the lie. "See." She held the bags up.

Grudgingly, Ray stepped aside to let her pass.

"We're not done yet," he warned, closing the door behind her. "I have lots more to say on the subject."

Noelle hunched an irritated shoulder at him. "Enough, Ray. You aren't my mother."

"But I am."

Lou and Jim were waiting in the foyer. Noelle winced as the combined weight of their disapproving gazes fell on her.

"I'm sorry." She held up her free hand and flashed them the look of contrition she had perfected during her teen years. "Time got away on me." She told the little white lie and wondered if her nose was growing. "Look who I found outside." She pushed Maria into the limelight and excused herself to put the parcels in her room.

In the quiet of the bedroom, she ransacked the medicine chest for pills to quell her head's persistent pounding. How was she going to pull off the mammoth task of pretending nothing had happened? She checked her make up. It hadn't melted off. She could do this. If she didn't stay in one place long, no one would see though the makeup. Easy. Hah. She shook her head. Whom was she trying to kid?

In her absence, her third brother and his family had arrived. In typical Hamilton house fashion, the noise level spiked as everyone spoke at once. Noelle's three nephews bounced around the room, touching decorations and sneaking appetizers from platters. Noelle entered the crowded living room and waved to an aunt and uncle.

"Welcome to the annual Hamilton family mad house," she greeted her aunt.

"Look at you," Aunt Beth said, leaning in for a hug. "Way to go, girl. Show him what he's missing." Beth winked.

Noelle stepped back and offered a greeting to her Uncle Bob. His bear hug almost brought her to her knees. A blast of rum and eggnog wafted over her. It looked like Lou had broken out her patented homemade potion.

Noelle smiled and moved away. She pretended to fuss with the branches of the twelve-foot-tall blue spruce in the corner and carefully took a breath. Had Uncle Bob's hug finished what the kick had started?

Scents of cinnamon and spruce flavored the air. Twinkling lights nestled in the branches of the tree illuminated the crystal stars hanging from its limbs. The elves had been busy while she was away. They had placed the glittering gold star at the tree's peak and filled wicker baskets with ornaments. There was one rule to hanging a decoration. Once placed, it stayed there. It never ceased to amaze Noelle that with so many people hanging ornaments, the tree looked fresh from the pages of a decorating magazine. Maybe it was the vaulted ceiling of the West Coast-style house, or maybe the act of hanging a decoration was usually a group decision.

In the corner, Nick was managing a make shift bar, struggling to mix drinks and impress Maria at the same time. Noelle smiled. She had known there was a spark there. From the besotted look on Nick's face, he would be distracted for the rest of the night.

No sign of Jake. Maybe he had taken the hint and wasn't coming. The doorbell chimed. Her hopes evaporated like a snowflake in the Sahara. Jake, she identified the arrival's voice. She hunted for an escape.

"Kyle, don't. I'm telling! Mom!"

Noelle seized on the growing hostilities between Andrew and his little brother Kyle and waved her sister-in-law off. Two little boys on a candy cane high were the perfect distraction. She called her nephews over. They barreled up to her, voices shrill with excitement, each trying to out-shout the other. Every yell sent a stab through her head. She found crayons and Christmas coloring books and set them up in a corner. Heads bent in concentration, the boys settled down to creating a masterpiece for Santa.

From there she drifted from group to group, accepting birthday hugs and kisses, catching up on family news. Nobody mentioned the robbery. Perhaps her parents had decided to keep the news to themselves until the police finished their investigation.

Finally, she worked her way to the kitchen and poured a glass of water. Peace. A few minutes of quiet before the dinner circus began. So far, the instant relief cure promised by the headache tablets hadn't materialized.

A soft woof recalled her to her surroundings. Jackson whined and stretched. His collar jingled softly as he rose from his place on the mat by the back door. Jackson and

Lou had an understanding. If Jackson stayed on the kitchen rug, he got turkey. If he moved off it, he went outside.

Noelle bent and scratched behind his ears. His tongue rasped over her wrist and his tail beat the floor.

"No wonder they call it a dog's life. I wish all I had to worry about was turkey scraps," she told him.

Her mind returned to the afternoon. Second thoughts were setting in. Should she have called the detective right away? She stared out the window at the lights of the house behind. When she had decided to keep quiet, it had seemed like a good idea, but now ... she shook her head. The shooter knew she was here. Right now, he could be outside waiting, like a spider. Come into my parlor, little girl. She shivered and paced the kitchen. Was she putting her family at risk? Was she keeping the police from catching him because she had chosen to keep silent?

She stared down at Jackson. This whole mess was making her nuts. Once everyone was gone, she'd call the police. Maybe she could stay in a hotel until things cooled down.

The sound of footsteps made her force a smile and turn to face the door. Jake. The smile faded.

He strolled in and snagged a glass from the cupboard. Filling it with water, he looked back at her. For once his blue eyes were minus their amused glint. Her guilty feelings multiplied. Her chin rose in challenge.

"What?" she demanded.

"Nothing." He straightened and took a step towards her. "Feeling guilty?" he asked softly.

Noelle forced a brittle smile to her lips. If she couldn't fool Jake, she had better give up right now.

Jake took a sip and studied Noelle's perfect makeup. He had seen camouflage like it on battered women back in his uniform days. In fact, he would almost swear Noelle was trying to cover up one hell of a shiner. Her cheek looked swollen and there was a faint discoloration around her eye. The Noelle he remembered would have been the first to make a joke out of an accidental injury. She had gotten a black eye before a friend's wedding and disguised it so well that he was the only one who knew. If she wasn't talking, she was hiding something.

He looked away as Lou entered the kitchen. Noelle seized the moment to escape.

"Chicken," he muttered as she grabbed a basket of buns and fled.

Whatever she was hiding, he was going to enjoy the challenge of getting to the bottom of before the night was through.

"If you're going to stand there, you're going to be put to work. Take this to the table." Lou handed him a steaming casserole and shooed him from the kitchen.

Dinner gave Jake the opportunity to watch Noelle more closely. As the guest of honor, she had bumped her father from his customary chair at the head of the table. Jake slid into a seat between Nick and one of Noelle's uncles. When he had arrived back in Landings, he had expected things to be awkward with Lou and Jim. He would not have contacted them if he hadn't seen Noelle in her bunny suit that first day. His plan was to use them so he could see Noelle again. He hadn't counted on enjoying their company.

"That was a tough time Jake. Words were said and things done . . ." Lou had said, and then suddenly tightlipped, changed the subject, asking Jake about his career and life in Toronto. What things? That conversation was another mystery that Jake meant to solve.

As dinner progressed, Noelle dropped her guard. Every so often, her fingers strayed to her face as if checking the heavy coat of makeup remained in place. *That's okay, Noelle,* Jake thought. *Keep your little secret, I'll figure it out later when you think you've fooled everyone.* He leaned back and sipped his wine. The oaky taste of chardonnay teased his taste buds with hints of citrus and sage.

Nick asked him a question and he leaned forward to hear it. He had forgotten the chaos of the Hamilton house. As an only child, Jake's dinners were often a box of pizza eaten off the coffee table in the living room. His mom hadn't been much of a cook. Her nose was usually buried in a lab manual or an obscure microbiology text, his dad working late at the office.

He tried a nod in answer to the question Nick had asked. He had only heard a couple of words and they had been something about work. Nick looked at him expectantly waiting for more. Ruefully, Jake shook his head and sat forward, forcing himself to pay attention. Until now, Nick had been distant, but polite, like a dog circling to check the lay of the land.

"Well, do you?"

"Do I what?"

"Wake up, Jake," Nick muttered impatiently. "Do you think Noelle is safe?"

Jake considered the question. He shrugged. Safe? Define safe. If she insists on taking off on her own and staying out all day, no . . . if she remains unwilling to listen to reason, probably not.

"I can't answer that, Nick. I'm not part of the investigation. I don't have any information." The words sounded lame to his own ears.

Nick eyed him, weighing what he said, trying to look through the cracks to see what Jake wasn't telling him. The conversation stalled. Nick returned to the brunette beside him.

Jake went back to watching Noelle as she winced and checked her face for the hundredth time. Jake's eyes narrowed. Before the evening was over, he was going to find out what she was hiding. Noelle's Uncle Bob asked him a question and he turned away from Noelle. For now, her secrets would remain her own.

20

Noelle snuck another peek at her watch and wished for an end to the evening from hell.

"You must be so pleased that Jake has returned," Aunt Mabel said, sliding off one shoe and rubbing her foot. "Never ignore your feet dear. They are all you have to carry you in your old age. I remember stuffing my feet into shoes much like those. That was the start of all my troubles with bunions. Yes . . ."

Noelle muttered something in reply, half-listening to her great aunt's words. She was having a hard time keeping her eyes off Jake. What was it about those broad shoulders and tight buns that drew her like a magnet? There had to be something wrong with her . . .

"Right, dear?" Aunt Mabel nudged her arm.

Noelle blinked. What had Aunt Mabel just said? Bunions . . . feet, right. She turned back to the regal white-haired woman beside her.

"You'd have to be dead not to look at that young man. The years have turned him into one fine piece of eye candy." Aunt Mabel sighed and nodded, squishing her blocky foot back into its sensible black shoe. "Life is wasted on the young. I remember back when I—"

"Aunt Mabel excuse me. Mom's calling me." Noelle jumped up and escaped before Aunt Mabel could share her memories further. Noelle had always suspected that the aristocratic old gal had a past, but she didn't want to hear what memories the sight of Jake had triggered. Cheeks reddening, she put some distance between herself and her elderly aunt, blushing harder as Jake met her eyes. Aunt Mabel was a sweet old girl, but her hearing aids rarely worked. Her whispered comments had obviously reached Jake's ears.

She checked her watch again. Friends and neighbors were starting to arrive. The living room was filling up. Could she sneak off to her room yet? It was hard enough deceiving her family, without Jake and his all-seeing eyes. Why couldn't he leave her in peace? Was it asking too much?

It was finally happy birthday singing time and her stint in the spotlight was over. Tree trimming took center stage. Noelle half-heartedly offered to help with the clean-up from dinner, but was turned down. She seized the chance to escape and snuck down the hall to her room. Once there, she kicked off her shoes, sighing in bliss as she flexed her toes. Aunt Mabel might be right, she thought smiling faintly. Her feet felt as if they had been released from the rack. She looked up at the sound of a knock on the door.

Jake didn't wait for an answer, she noted in disgust. He opened the door and entered, closing it behind him.

"I saw you escape."

"I didn't escape," Noelle muttered, shoving her feet back into the high heels. "I wanted to take my shoes off for a bit. You have to be good to your feet," she defended.

"Come on, Noelle, this is your big night. What gives?"

"Nothing. Why are you following me?" A good offense was the best defense. He must have figured out that something was wrong. Playing for time, Noelle crossed to the dresser and picked up a brush. She brandished it in front of her like a weapon.

"I don't recall asking you to join me. You're starting to make a habit of showing up where you're not wanted."

"Seriously, Noelle, not wanted? That's not what that kiss said."

"That was a mistake. It won't happen again." She dropped the brush onto the dresser and took a step towards the door, intent on leaving.

Jake didn't move.

"Can you please move. I have things to do."

He shook his head.

"Not until you tell me what you're hiding."

Noelle retreated across the room. She settled into the chair by the window and pretended a sudden interest in the tiny diamond buckle on the heel of her shoe.

"What's the story?" Jake prodded.

"What do you want Jake?" Noelle couldn't pretend polite indifference. Jake's presence had reopened the wound covering the buried hurt from the past. "Why can't you leave me alone?" She had enough on her mind without an intimate conversation with Jake.

"What happened to your face?"

"My face?" Her hand rose to her cheek. "Nothing."

"Don't give me that. I know you didn't walk into a door, and I doubt a soccer ball hit you. What happened?"

Noelle looked away as angry tears welled in her eyes. She was not going to cry in front of Jake.

He stepped forward and gently touched her face, turning her head until her eyes met his.

"What happened?" he repeated softly.

A tear overran her lashes and drifted down her cheek, weaving a path through the makeup. Jake grabbed a box of Kleenex and handed her a tissue. He waited for her to regain control.

She snatched the box from him and blotted at her face, wincing at the thought of looking in the mirror and seeing the damage the tears had wrought. The smudge of makeup on the Kleenex told the tale. She glared at Jake. Fine, let him see for himself.

Jake went into the bathroom and returned with a warm wet facecloth. He watched her wipe her face clean of makeup until only the faintest smudge of mascara remained.

"Satisfied?" she asked, daring him to comment on the damage. She wanted to see the monster-sized bruise for herself. If she guessed right, she had a hell of a black eye.

"What the hell Noelle?" Jake stared at her, paced off a small circle and turned back. "What happened? What were you thinking? You could have—" He shut up.

His face now expressionless, he studied the pale oval of her visage against the black backdrop of the dress. The purple bruising was starkly garish under the overhead light.

"What happened?" he repeated. He already knew. Sometime after slipping past her watchdogs, she had run up against trouble. Watch it, Jake, he told himself. You don't have the right to yell at her for putting herself at risk. You gave that up ten years ago when you let her pass out of your life without a fight. She's someone else's problem now. He frowned. Was there someone else? No one had said anything about a guy waiting in the wings.

Noelle sighed and closed her eyes. She held the facecloth to her cheek.

"You want some ice?"

She shook her head. "You aren't going to go away until I tell you, are you?"

"What do you think?" Jake countered.

"Okay, but don't start yelling again, my head can't take it."

Noelle recounted the events of the afternoon, stumbling a little over the attack with the knife. Jake stayed silent. Finally, he sighed.

"So he found you—worse—he knows exactly where to find you again."

"I know, Jake. I screwed up. I'm sorry."

Jake didn't answer. He was already working the problem. The shooter knew where to find Noelle. If he waited long enough, he would catch her alone. Ryerson said the guy was smart—a cobra. He covered his tracks and never left a print. The gunfire at the store was an act of rage, a sign that the robberies weren't enough anymore. The police had to ramp up Noelle's protection because, right now, Cobra would be trying to figure out a way to get in close and remove an inconvenient witness. Jake rubbed his hand over the stubble of whiskers on his chin.

He reached for his cell phone.

"What are you doing?" Noelle demanded, standing. "Jake, I'm handling this." She grabbed at his arm.

"Yeah. You're doing such a great job that he found you in the middle of downtown Victoria."

"Jake, I am dealing with this. I don't want your help."

"Yeah? Did you think that maybe if you had called Ryerson, we might have gotten the guy?" He knew there wasn't much chance of that, but saying it let him vent his frustration.

Noelle glared at him. "I didn't call because I knew just what would happen. This. They wouldn't have caught him.

He got out of there too fast. The people who helped me didn't even see him. I—"

Someone knocked on the door. It opened it a few inches.

Jim peered around the edge of the door. "Is it safe to come in, or has World War III broken out?"

Jake tossed his hands up in surrender, stepping back to expose Noelle to her father's eyes.

"What the . . ." Jim opened the door wider and stepped into the room. His stunned look flickered between them.

Jake watched the play of expressions cross Jim's face. "Don't look at me. I didn't do it. Ask your thick-skulled daughter why she thinks it's okay to take off alone when she's the only witness to a shooting. Did she happen to think that maybe it wasn't such a clever idea?" Jake had to move. He couldn't stand here doing nothing. He might say something he couldn't take back.

"You don't go anywhere. Do you hear me? I'll be back in a few minutes." He stalked out of the room, passed through the crowded kitchen, and wordlessly let himself out the back door.

21

Jake jerked the door shut behind him, taking care not to slam it. Slamming meant loss of control. Slamming meant he had let Noelle get under his skin. Damn it! Whom was he kidding? She had done that the first time he met her. Ten years later she was still buried so deep he'd need a knife to dig her out. He crossed to the edge of the sundeck. Bloody Noelle, what was she thinking? She wasn't thinking. She didn't think. He sucked in a deep breath of icy air and glared at the twinkle lights woven through the trees. She could have gotten herself killed. The thought crystallized in his gut forming a hard knot in the pit of his stomach.

A gust of wind tossed the tops of the cedar hedging making the twinkle lights dance. The cold washed over his cheeks, cooling his temper. Jake sighed and leaned against the railing, pondering Noelle's ability to make him crazy. It had been a long time since he'd lost his cool like that. He was the one who stayed sane while everyone around him lost it.

What was it about Noelle that sent him so far into orbit? He let go of the wooden railing and flexed his fingers. And what the hell was wrong with him that he let her?

The wind ate through the thick wool of his sweater. He should go in, but he didn't move towards the door. Instead he glanced up at the sky. It glowed with a pale opalescence. No, cold as he was, he wasn't up to confronting the source of his aggravation.

Away from Noelle and the red-hot crackle of energy flowing between them, he could regain his detachment. Out here he could consider the issues, tear the situation apart, and analyze the angles. He raked a hand through his hair and scowled. Who was he trying to kid? As long as Noelle was around there would be no analysis; pure raw heat would rule the day. It had always been like that.

Maybe it was time to call Ryerson and walk away. He pulled his cell phone from his hip pocket and stared at its face. No, not yet. He had promised Lou that he would look out for Noelle. He pocketed the phone. He'd call the local talent and bring them up to date, but first, he'd have a look around. Once he made the call, help would arrive with sirens blaring. If someone *was* watching, they would be gone before the last echo of sirens died away.

A little reconnaissance would let him vent some steam. It would also ensure the search was done properly. While Landings may have a police force, how many cases like this had they ever handled? Ryerson could say he didn't need Jake's help, but tough—he was going to get it.

Jake's gut said someone was out there keeping an eye on the Hamilton house. The fact that the convenience store shooter had followed Noelle downtown, parked in the underground lot and waited for her to return to her car was proof that he knew exactly where to find her. Jake frowned. The Cobra was waiting for another chance. Damn, the guy was probably sitting outside Noelle's house the day before. If Jake had been less fixated on Noelle and more aware of his surroundings, he might have prevented all this.

He pushed away from the rail and crossed the deck to the stairs. Frost painted the cedar boards in a slick coating of ice. His foot skated out from under him. He flailed for a hold on the stair railing and pulled himself up. Great, the hero falls on his ass, breaks his leg, and the bad guy gets away. Cautiously he worked his way down the stairs to the concrete slab at the bottom.

The Hamilton house was part of a 1960's subdivision. Each custom-built home backed onto a narrow lane way. Fences or cedar hedging separated the yards. The milky light of the sky helped him find his way through the yard. He glanced at the sky. If he were in Toronto, he would bet snow would fall by morning. He let himself out the gate onto the lane.

Standing in the shadows he listened to the distant laughter from the house behind him. Was Noelle enjoying the party? Aside from the Hamilton home, the street was quiet—the houses silent sentinels.

The branches at his back exploded. Jake grabbed at his non-existent shoulder holster and jumped backwards. His foot plunged through the ice on a frozen puddle. Cold water filled his shoe.

Woof. A half-grown bloodhound nosed the fence, rattling the links. The dog shook its head and its long ears flopped around its face. Snuffling, it dropped to its haunches and pounded the ground with its tail. Three seconds of inactivity was too long. It bounced up and tried to climb the fence to reach Jake.

Jake shook his head in disgust. He'd forgotten the neighbor's new hound. According to Jim, the dog had a taste for shoes. After snacking on a pair of Jimmy Choo's, it had been exiled to the yard. Cheech, yeah—that was the dog's name—now spent his days patrolling the perimeter, baying at any squirrel that violated the space.

"Hey, boy," Jake said, leaning forward to pat the dog's droopy ears.

The dog's appearance gave him something new to consider. The neighborhood was full of dogs. That was the first thing he had noticed when he'd gotten out of his car. Man's best friend would sound the alarm the minute an intruder set foot on one of the perfectly manicured yards.

If the Cobra was here, he sure as hell wouldn't be on foot.

Jake gave the dog another pat and straightened. Anyone watching the Hamilton house would be inside a car. Jake continued down the laneway. Water from the puddle squished between his toes. He stopped outside another gate and listened before testing the latch with a shake. The chain link rattled, but there was no sign of Rover coming to investigate. Good. He opened the gate and let himself into the yard. Keeping to the shadows, he skirted the house to reach the street. In the darkness of a sprawling cedar, he hunkered down to study the parked cars.

Lou and Jim lived in a close-knit neighborhood that celebrated every season. The houses on the road were done up with so many lights the electric company would be counting their increased revenue well into January. The street, listed in the annual Christmas Light Up magazine, was included on a seasonal tourist map. That meant increased traffic through the area. Who wouldn't want to view the Santa's workshop on the corner? The place looked like a hundred demented elves had run amok with blow up globes and tinsel.

"One of these things is not like the other," Jake muttered, studying the long line of parked cars. Most were covered in a heavy rime of frost. The car he was looking for would have a clear windshield. Methodically he worked his way along the line of cars. He didn't hurry. He had learned the benefit of patience a long time ago.

A flare of red glowed in the dark interior of a battered Buick parked crookedly, halfway down the block. A hand reached through the partially opened driver's side window and flicked a cigarette to the pavement. Bingo. Jake smiled. The old Buick stood out like a partridge in a pear tree.

The pile of butts littering the road was evidence the car had been there for a while. That many cigarettes and the guy's night vision had to be shot.

"Fool," Jake muttered in disgust. First rule of surveillance—right after, don't drink a mega-Grande

Americano at the beginning of the night—don't degrade your night vision by smoking. He smiled. The guy's stupidity was a plus. He was likely cold and bored, smoking to stay awake.

The Buick Town car had seen better days. At some point, someone had cared enough to prime parts of the rusted doors. The front fender, anchored to the chassis with heavy wire, fit Noelle's description of the car.

Jake stepped from the shadows. A quick hit of adrenaline washed over him. It was always like this. Action was a powerful drug.

Moving quickly, he covered the fifty feet to the car. Through the misted glass, he watched the driver swivel in his seat. Maybe the guy wasn't that dumb. Too bad. It would be easier if he were less alert. Whatever. Jake stumbled onto the sidewalk, weaving along the road. Let him think Jake was a partygoer who'd imbibed a few too many eggnogs. Jake stopped level with the rear of the car. He swayed, fumbling in his pockets as if searching for keys. The driver's head swiveled, following his actions.

Jake ducked behind the car. Staying low, he worked his way along the car to the passenger side. The shadowy figure in the car leaned heavily against the door, trying to see through the window. Carefully, Jake took hold of the door handle. One, two, three. He yanked. The door sprang open with a metallic groan. Caught off balance, the driver toppled through the opening. Jake followed him down, jamming his knee into the middle of the man's back.

"Le'me up. Le'me up. I'll call the cops!" The man struggled to throw Jake off.

"Call away, but right now, I'm the only cop you have to worry about," Jake said grimly.

At his words, the man's resistance collapsed. Expertly, Jake patted him down, running his hands over bony arms and legs.

"What's in your left front pocket?" Jake asked, pausing in his search.

"My stash," the man said sullenly.

Satisfied he was unarmed Jake dialed 911.

He summed up the situation to the dispatcher, ending with, "Get Detective Ryerson here. This is his case." He shoved the phone back into his belt clip and turned his attention to the man in front of him. "You and I are going to have a little chat.

"I dunno anything. Let me up. I'm not taking the rap for this," he said, struggling.

Jake dug his knee into his back.

"What's your name?" he said coldly. "Why are you watching the house?"

"Sid, it's Sid. Come on, man, I'll tell you what I know, and you let me go," Sid begged, groaning as the pressure between his shoulder blades increased.

Jake considered the skinny man. Sid's ratty blonde hair hung in tangles to his shoulders. He was nowhere near a match to the description Noelle had given.

"Where's the guy that owns this car?"

"I dunno. He paid me. He gave me this car and crack for later. I was supposed to watch the house and tell him if the girl went out. I was gonna call him. There's a number and a cell phone on the seat." Sid was crying, babbling information like water running through a broken pipe. "I don't want to go back to jail."

Sirens shattered the night and pulsing red and blue lights lit the street. A patrol car slid to a stop. The doors flew open. Two officers erupted from it.

"Get your hands up where I can see them," one ordered.

Jake let the wallet he held in his left hand fall open to reveal his badge.

"I called it in," he said. "Where's Ryerson?"

22

The officer in the rear hung back watching, his hand lingering at his side, then slowly dropping to his hip. He exchanged a quick glance with his partner.

"Ryerson's on route," he said stepping forward to take the proffered identification from Jake's hand.

"Toronto? You're a little out of your jurisdiction, aren't you?" he asked, looking from Jake to the picture and back. He passed the wallet back to Jake.

"Yeah a little. Hand me your cuffs," Jake said.

He took the handcuffs, snapped them onto Sid's bony wrists and pulled the smaller man to his feet. An unmarked police cruiser slid to a stop in front of them. Dan Ryerson climbed out frowning in irritation at the sight of Jake.

"Don't you think you're a little off your beat?" he asked.

"What, you ran my creds?" Jake said. "I'm flattered." Why wouldn't Ryerson do his due diligence and check him out? It was what Jake would have done. He looked at the detective with new respect.

"Yeah," Ryerson said. "What's this?"

"This is how your Cobra is keeping tabs on Noelle. There's a cell phone on the front seat, along with a number to call. This guy's a hired goon, an addict. Careful with his right front pocket."

At a nod from Ryerson, the patrolman gingerly patted down Sid's jacket. He extracted a baggy of dirty grey crystals and a syringe.

"Get him out of here. Book him on possession. I'll see him later." Ryerson turned back to Jake. "What's your part in all of this? You seem pretty involved, considering she's an ex."

Jake met the detective's gaze. Ryerson had done his homework. The guy didn't miss much. In a way, he and Jake were a lot alike. If times were different, they'd probably go out and grab a beer. No, Jake's problem wasn't with the guy's work, it was with the interest he was showing in Noelle.

"Come on," Jake said abruptly. "Let's take a walk. I'll tell you what happened this afternoon. You can have a chat with my ex-wife, and she can tell you that she's invincible and doesn't need help."

Ryerson fell into step beside Jake and listened to his rundown of the afternoon's events. He didn't say anything for a moment and then," I talked to your partner. She said to tell you that holiday means relaxing, not getting involved in an ongoing investigation."

"Is that all she said?"

"Yeah, that, and that you're a pain in the ass when you think you're right."

Jake laughed.

They neared the Hamilton house and found a knot of people gathered on the front lawn watching the activity down the road.

"Looks like a party," Ryerson observed.

"A yearly special. Noelle's annual birthday/Christmas tree decorating party. Big family event." So what if Ryerson interpreted Jake's words to mean he was part of the celebration.

At least Noelle wasn't in the crowd. For once she was showing common sense and staying out of the action.

The crowd shifted. Noelle's brothers hovered at the edge of the front lawn like aggressive bulldogs. None of them looked happy to see Jake.

"What the hell is going on?" Ray demanded.

"Excuse me, sir. Let's take this inside," Ryerson said, stepping past him.

"Jake, what happened?" Nick shoved Ray aside and blocked Jake's path.

Jake saw a glimpse of friendship in Nick's eyes, before Ray pushed past him.

"Now," Ryerson said, walking by Ray as if the former linebacker wasn't there.

Jake smothered a smile. Old Ray was wound up tighter than the bandages on the head of Scrooge's first ghost.

Inside the tree decorating was in full swing. The sound of sirens hadn't interrupted the party. Mind you, the volume inside had likely overwhelmed the shrieking alarms. Louise looked up from where she was admiring the artwork of a toddler. She cast a strained look at Jake and tilted her head towards the kitchen.

"Kitchen," Jake directed Ryerson.

They entered the room at the back of the house. Noelle and Jim were sitting on bar stools at the center island, a half-empty bottle of Chardonnay between them. Noelle looked at Jake and took a gulp of wine. Jim frowned and turned to face the newcomers.

"Jake." He stood abruptly and took a step towards his ex-son-in-law. "What's going on?"

Noelle smiled at the detective, ignoring Jake. "Detective Ryerson, did you find anything?"

"Yes, it looks like we have some new developments." Ryerson greeted her. "Ms. Ryan—"

"Hamilton," Noelle corrected.

Ryerson looked confused.

"It's Hamilton. I'm going back to my maiden name."

"You are?" Jim said. "I thought you said . . ."

Noelle's cheeks reddened under the fresh layer of concealer.

Jake smirked.

Jim grimaced as Noelle tossed back the rest of her wine.

Noelle avoided Jake's glance and directed a dazzling smile at Ryerson. Mesmerized Ryerson smiled back.

Jake gritted his teeth and forced his own lips into a bland smile. So what if Noelle smiled at Ryerson. She could smile at anyone she wanted. The big "D" in the word divorce guaranteed that. "D" like dud or dead or—damn, Jake, get a grip. He was here strictly as a favor to her parents. He had to stop taking everything Noelle did so personally. Think of Julie, he told himself. The on again, mostly off again relationship he had with the Emergency room doctor in Toronto was safe and predictable. He looked at Noelle and subconsciously substituted the word boring. Safe wasn't a word you would use to describe Noelle.

The detective pulled out a chair and sat down next to Noelle. Jim took a step towards the door.

"I'll leave you three to talk."

"Wait, Dad," Noelle said, placing a hand on Jim's arm. "Stay and hear what Detective Ryerson has to say."

Poor Jim. Jake felt a twinge of sympathy. Noelle knew something bad had gone down outside, and she wanted to use Jim as a buffer.

Jim sat and poured himself another glass of wine. He looked like he needed fortification against the storm brewing in his daughter's eyes.

"You know what? We should take this conversation somewhere private," he said.

Somewhere private turned out to be Jim's carpentry shop in the basement. Jim grabbed a broom and swept aside a small pile of cedar shavings.

"Sorry. I didn't get this cleaned up. Come in, have a seat." He looked apologetic. "Maybe I should have taken you some place where there weren't so many sharp objects lying around."

"Funny, Dad," Noelle muttered, brushing past him to lean up against the wall, as far from Jake as she could get.

Jim glanced at his watch.

"Hey, you know what," Noelle leaned forward and nudged Jim's arm. "You go upstairs and help Mom. I'm fine."

"What the hell is going on?" Ray shoved past Jake. He emanated a blend of testosterone and over-protective older brother.

Jake had never hit it off with Ray, and he didn't think that was about to magically change. Ray spread his glares over the group, his chin jutting belligerently, a vein pulsing at his temple.

"Don't think you're cutting me out of this. Whatever is happening with Noelle is my business more than it is his," Ray said, directing an angry glare at Jake. He moved closer to Noelle.

Yup, Jake thought regretfully, there was about as much hope of getting rid of Ray as coaxing a four-hundred-pound gorilla away from a box of bananas.

"Ray, nice of you to join us," Jake said. He crossed his arms over his chest and leaned against the wall. Let the games begin, he thought cynically.

"Don't give me any of your crap, Ryan! You weren't around ten years ago when we had to pick up the pieces. We sure as hell don't need you now."

"Ray!" Noelle cut in.

"The guy needs to know—"

Jake looked from Ray to Noelle. "Something I'm missing?" he asked.

Ray took a step towards Jake. Jake levered himself off the wall.

"Go ahead, Ray. This time I'm ready."

Jim stepped forward, positioning himself between his son and his ex-son-in-law.

"Why are you here anyway?" Ray said, shooting a look of disgust at Jake.

"Ray, your mother and I asked Jake to help. He has certain skills that Noelle can use right now." Jim rubbed his hand over his head. "Either sit down and shut up, or leave."

Ray sent Jake another hostile look and flopped into a battered armchair in the corner of the room. "Oh, I'm not leaving."

Too bad, Jake thought. Ray had been looking for a fight since Jake arrived. Obviously, he blamed Jake for the divorce, but his presence was only making things more difficult.

Jim's forehead creased into a worried frown.

"I need to touch base with my wife and see how things are going. As you probably noticed, we're having a Christmas party. Call me if there's any blood spilt. Jake and Ray don't see eye to eye," he said to Ryerson.

"Let's just get this over with," Noelle said. "Sit down everyone." She waved a hand for the men to take a seat and perched on the arm of the chair beside Ray.

She told her story for the third time. Ryerson listened quietly, occasionally interrupting, asking for more details.

She looked exhausted, Jake thought, studying the faint lines on her forehead and the pallor underlying the cover up. He glanced at Ryerson. The detective's face was a polite mask. Ray resembled an angry gorilla. Too bad old Ray had taken to shaving his head to hide his thinning hairline.

"Well?" Noelle prodded.

It was her turn to look worried.

"We found the car from the parking lot down the street," Jake said. "Police arrested the driver, but it's not the guy from the store."

The detective took over.

"We ran the plates. The car is stolen. At this point, we have no fingerprints, no leads, and no name for the suspect. We have you, and the fact that he's willing to take a chance to get to you. I'm taking you into protective custody until we can guarantee your safety."

"No way!" Noelle shot to her feet.

"You're not taking Noelle into any type of custody. I'll stay with her. Just let someone try and get at her." Ray stood up, looming over his sister, his hands closed in fists at his sides.

Jake started to speak, but stopped as the detective waved them to silence.

"Unless you can think of something else, it's the best option we have." Ryerson said.

"Talk to me, not Jake," Noelle cut in. "This affects me." She waved off Ryerson's attempt at interruption. "I am not sitting here, doing nothing, while you decide what's best for me."

There. Jake hid a smile behind his hand; let the detective chew on that. It wouldn't hurt if he got a glimpse of the real Noelle. He glanced at Ray. He had gone strangely quiet. This was probably the first time Ray had heard the whole story. Until now, he had probably gotten bits and pieces from Jim, and in typical Ray fashion, brushed them off.

Sensing Jake's gaze, Ray looked up. For once, his face was devoid of hostility.

"In a nut shell, you're saying my sister's life depends on this guy not being able to find her," he said.

Ryerson nodded. "So far he's been a few steps ahead of us."

"We need to put her out of circulation, somewhere he won't find her." Ray fished a key ring out of his pocket and dangled it on the end of one thick finger.

Noelle rolled her eyes and returned to her argument. "I am not going into police protection. That's a stupid idea. I have a dog. I'll get an alarm."

Jake shook his head. Judging by the flash of fire in her eyes and the sharp set of her jaw line, the detective was going to have a hard time convincing Noelle of anything. He shrugged. Let someone else fight the battle. He settled his shoulders more comfortably against the wall and breathed in an appreciative breath of freshly sawed wood.

"Noelle, be reasonable," Ryerson cut in.

Jake shook his head. Bad choice of words. If you wanted to send Noelle off the deep end, suggest she was behaving irrationally.

"Do not call me unreasonable. I am not a child. I am perfectly..."

"Hey!" Ray jangled the keys in front of Noelle's nose. "I have an idea. I know a place that will put you out of sight until the cops catch this lunatic."

"Sounds interesting," Ryerson said, leaning back against the workbench. "Continue."

"This is the key to a cabin up at Fulton Hill. You remember the old ski hill that closed down a few years ago? I have a client who wants to sell a property there. He gave me the keys so that I could show it any time. You take the key and go there. You'll be out of sight while the police do their thing." He paused to glare at Jake. "The only problem is, I can't go. I can't leave my wife with the baby due any day."

Silence. Even Noelle was quiet, either speechless at Ray presenting a workable plan, or busy creating a list of reasons it wouldn't work. Jake pondered the suggestion. It might work. Ryerson could set up a decoy and lure the gunman in while Noelle was out of the way. He nodded.

Ryerson spoke up. "It's not a bad idea. We can sneak her out of town in an unmarked car, but she'll need protection." He glanced at Jake. "You'd be the logical choice to ride shotgun, but from what I've seen so far, I might get called up to investigate a homicide."

Noelle flushed and closed her mouth. Jake laughed, earning another glare from Ray.

"Tell me about the cabin," Ryerson continued.

"My client bought it during the seventies hoping to cash in on the ski industry. The guy is super rich. He married a model from Sweden who loved to ski. He figured he'd buy an asset and keep his wife happy at the same time." Ray paused and shook his head. "He poured money into furnishings and upkeep. When the marriage broke up, he threw in the towel. Unfortunately for him, the hill doesn't get much snow. No one uses it in the winter. In the summer, they run the lifts and the mountain bikers go nuts."

"Can you get in there?" Jake asked.

"That's the beauty of it. They just graded the logging road. I was there last week, but you need a four-wheel drive," he added.

"What about power?" Noelle demanded.

"Monster generator in tip top condition. The guy wants to sell the place as a summer cabin. He's even put in a hot tub."

"No one lives up there? No caretaker?" Jake asked.

Ray shook his head. "A guy goes out there once a week, but he's in Florida right now. That's why I went up to check things out. You can hole up there for a few days. In the meantime, the police might actually find the guy." He cast a withering look at the detective.

Noelle shook her head. "I am not running and hiding because some lunatic thinks he can scare me."

"Uh, Noelle." Jake moved away from the wall. Enough already. While they pussyfooted around the obvious, Cobra was making plans. "He's not trying to scare you. He's trying to kill you." Okay, he paused, as the color drained from her cheeks, maybe that was a little harsh.

"But we're going to prevent that," Ryerson cut in, sending Jake a chiding look.

Jake shrugged. At least he had gotten the point across. She wasn't arguing any more.

"Who do we send?" the detective continued. "I can't spare anyone right now. The holidays have left us tight for staff." He appeared to be considering the problem. "I could go," he said.

Jake's head snapped up and he met Ryerson's eyes. They held an unholy gleam of amusement.

"I'll go," Jake said abruptly. "I remember the place. We used to ski there."

"This is crazy," Noelle cut in. "I am not going anywhere. I'm going to stay right here." She crossed her arms across her chest unaware of how the gesture lifted her breasts, drawing attention to the lush curves.

Jake was all too aware of those curves and he gritted his teeth at Ryerson's look of appreciation. It was time to put an end to this farce. Ryerson wasn't going to help Noelle across the street. It would be like letting the wolf carry Red Riding Hood's basket!

"I'll go," he repeated." I've done this kind of work before, and I know the area."

23

"No way!" Noelle closed her mouth, took a deep breath and tried again, this time, aiming to keep her voice at a level that wouldn't shatter glass. "I am not . . ." No one was listening.

"We'll move her out tonight. Get a four-wheel drive unmarked vehicle here, and we'll head out." Jake's orders came rapid fire. "We'll need food and clothes. We'll go before he figures out what to do next."

Noelle stared at him. "Do you really think I am going anywhere with you? Uh-uh, not happening." She shook her head emphasizing the words.

Ryerson ignored her, concentrating on the plan Jake was outlining. Ray was drawing a map on a piece of scrap paper, occasionally nodding in agreement, or shaking his head. Together the three men were sketching out a framework that would get Noelle to a place of safety.

"Ray, tell them…"

Ray waved his hand impatiently cutting her off. He appeared to have gotten over his misgivings about Jake.

"Right, I'll tell the folks," Ray announced getting to his feet.

"No, you won't," Noelle cut in. "You are not going upstairs with this idiotic scheme. This is the stupidest plan I have ever heard. I don't believe this." She paced across the room.

The door opened and Jim slipped through. Noelle didn't like the worried frown on his face. He tried to catch the attention of the detective, while avoiding eye contact with her.

"What's the matter?" Noelle demanded.

"Detective, there's an officer at the door wanting to speak with you." Jim stepped back to allow Ryerson past.

Ray waved his father to a seat. "Here's the plan," he said and filled him in on what they had cobbled together.

"It should work," Jake said. "Noelle will be safe away from here, provided everyone keeps quiet about her whereabouts. We'll get her out while the party's in full swing. It's the perfect cover. People will be coming and going all evening."

"I'll go talk to Lou and get a few coolers of food put together. The camping stuff is in the garage. Grab whatever you need." Jim stood up, looking pleased to have something useful to do.

"Dad." Noelle stretched out a hand to stop him. "This is silly. I'm not going across the road with Jake, much less to some deserted cabin. Have you all gone crazy?"

"Yes, you are. You go with him, or you spend a few days in custody, and protective custody doesn't mean a five-star hotel." Ryerson reentered the room. "This guy is wacko. The one we arrested is terrified of him. He told us everything we asked, plus more. In fact, he's demanding we keep him in jail out of the Cobra's reach. That's what the shooter is calling himself. He likes the name the media leaked."

Noelle collapsed into the chair. Great. Sentenced to hard time with Jake. Happy holidays.

"Is there cell phone reception up there?" Ryerson asked.

"Yeah," Ray nodded. "Pretty good too. I wouldn't be surprised if the owner paid to put in a tower." He added a final scribble to the map he was drawing.

"Here." Ray held out the paper. "These are the directions to the cabin. It's in good shape. As I said, there's a generator, as well as a big store of firewood. The interior is nice. The owner's wife thought it was a cute little getaway and she had lots of money to work with. They're selling it fully furnished."

"We're not buying it, Ray," Noelle said sharply. She snatched the paper from his hand. She may have been outmaneuvered, but she wasn't giving up. She glanced at Jake. He wore a mocking smile. Why shouldn't he be smug? He had always read her like a book. She clenched her teeth to keep from growling.

Ryerson took the map and studied the crude drawing.

"This is pretty isolated. You're sure no one else is up there?"

Ray shook his head. "Not now. In the summer people go up, but right now, just the guy that does the caretaking. Like I said, he's away."

Ryerson frowned and tapped the paper against his palm. He reached up to the buckle on the holster at his shoulder. "I take it you're not carrying?"

"I didn't think I'd need to," Jake said.

Ryerson unbuckled the holster and handed it and the revolver nestled in it to Jake. "Here, just in case. You never know when you might need one. I guess I don't need to ask if you know how to use it."

Jake took the proffered dull black Glock22, holding the cool metal in his hand, feeling the familiar weight. No, he didn't need instructions.

Noelle smoothed the fabric of her dress over her thighs, glaring at nothing. It looked like the meeting of the "good old boys club" was about to end. Goodie, now that they'd saved the damsel in distress, the high fives were about to commence.

"Excuse me, I'm going to go put some clothes together," she said, brushing past the knot of men. She closed the door behind her. Had they even noticed her leave? They were arguing over check in times, for god's sake. Her feet thudded up the wooden stairs. She relaxed the tight fists her hands had curled into, frowning at the eight crescent-shaped divots her nails had left. Bloody Jake, where did he get off messing up her nice tidy life?

At the top of the stairs she turned left and stalked down the hall to the bedroom she had used the night before. Lou was there, staring at a pile of clothes stacked in a box on the bed. She turned at the sound of Noelle's footsteps.

"I packed your clothes into this box along with some extra things you might need. I don't know how long you'll be up there, so I guessed at what you should take." She didn't look directly at Noelle. "I put in ski pants and things like that. The weather reports are calling for snow."

She closed the box. "Nick and I put together some of his clothes for Jake." Lou smiled wryly. "I don't know how Jake feels about the skate boarder look, but it will have to do. I didn't know what else to pack, or how long it will be for . . ." Her voice trailed away and came back stronger. "Noelle, promise me you won't take any chances. You'll listen to Jake." She held up her hand to stop Noelle's reply. "He does this kind of thing for a living. I know things ended badly for you two, but maybe time together will give you some closure. Promise me that you'll trust him." She paused. "You're the only daughter I have. Take care of yourself." She wrapped Noelle in a tight hug before pulling away and offering up a watery smile.

"I'll tell your Dad that everything here is ready." Lou hurried from the room.

Noelle watched her go and prayed for the strength to keep her hands off Jake. She grimaced. Right now, strangling sounded like her only option.

***

The man seated in the corner cradled a hot coffee cup between his hands. The heat burned his fingers, but he ignored the discomfort. Instead he watched the pay phone on the back wall of the fast food restaurant. If it rang, his plan was successful. If not, he would fall back on his contingency plan. His thin lips curled in a smile. The drug addict had been easy pickings. Drugs were all the payment needed. The guy hadn't even checked to see if the goods were real. A little pressure and the scrawny little man was too terrified to do anything but what he was told.

He took a sip of the burning coffee and pushed a French fry through the pool of ketchup on his cheeseburger wrapper. Any minute, the phone would ring with a report on the girl. The girl, the man frowned. He should have that wrapped up in no time. The cops couldn't protect her. He was too smart for them. He was the Cobra. He could do things they couldn't do. He could move faster than they could. It was a game and he was the master.

The door opened and two uniformed officers entered. Standing by the cashier, they ran assessing eyes over the room checking each of the occupants. He looked up curiously, raising his eyes from the real estate pamphlets covering the table. He checked his watch and glanced towards the bathrooms before returning to the papers. He looked like any bored husband waiting for his wife to appear so they could continue their search for the perfect house. The second cup of coffee in front of him reinforced his disguise.

Yes, he was smarter than they were. The officers walked through the restaurant, checked the phone and spoke with the servers. Of course, no one had used the phone. He was so much smarter than they were. The officers left. His question was answered. The girl's house was under observation. It was time to move to phase two.

.

24

Noelle watched the bedroom door close behind Lou. How had her master plan gotten so royally fouled up? Everything had been going well, right up until Jake got involved. Good old Jake. His intervention had turned her bedroom into a cell—a prison. Good analogy, Noelle mused. For the next unknown length of time she was sentenced to hard time in prison with a warder who was her last choice on earth. Noelle kicked the end of the bed and stubbed her toe.

"Ow, damn, bloody . . ." She hopped up and down, venting her anger before collapsing onto the bed to nurse her injured foot.

Why me? I'm a good person. All I did was buy junk food. Is that so bad?" She scowled at the twinkling lights outside the window. "This is all Jake's fault. If he hadn't shown up, I would never have let Maria convince me to go to Zumba. I would never have been near that store."

She studied the pile of bags by the door. Everything was taken care of—bags packed, food, equipment, everything they might need. No one had asked her what she wanted, or what she thought. She chewed on her lower lip. It didn't matter. It wasn't as if she had choices in what to bring. Everything she owned was currently surrounded by yards of yellow tape. Like it or not, she *was* dependent on everyone else.

"Noelle, the truck's here." Jim rapped lightly on the door but didn't come in.

Noelle stood up. This was it then, time to cross the final line. From here on, it was her and Jake. A scary thought considering she had kept their past swept up in a neat little pile for the past ten years. Face it, Noelle. You walked out of the hospital and told yourself it was all for the best. You used your family to build a wall of protection and didn't have the guts to face Jake and tell him about the near miss he had survived. He would have been down on his knees sending up hallelujahs. She sighed. Would he though? She'd never know. Spending time alone with Jake was going to be unbearable.

The room was cold, the heat registers closed, redirecting the warm air to rooms used on a daily basis. Jim and Lou hadn't expected company, and no one had thought to open them up.

She rubbed her hands over her arms. It was time to stop whining and blaming Jake. The real reason this was happening was the shooting. If she wanted to live to identify the guy in court, she had to get out of here and let the police find him.

The door opened. Ray reached through to grab the pile of bags beside it. He hesitated.

"This is for the best, you know," he said. "I wouldn't let you go anywhere with Jake if I didn't think he could do the job. For God's sake, Noelle, I was there that night. I remember the miscarriage. I took you to the hospital. Do you think I would ever let that bastard hurt you again?"

"I know, Ray." Noelle grabbed him in a tight hug, standing on tiptoes to kiss his cheek. "This is the only way," she said.

Ray didn't answer. He turned abruptly and left the room. He'd violated his code of manhood by showing emotion.

The hallway was empty. No reprieve there. A cacophony of voices rose from the living room. Jim entered the hall and stopped at the sight of Noelle.

"We haven't told anyone anything," he said answering her unspoken question. "Everyone is in the living room with the tree. Those relatives of your mother's sure can eat." He shook his head in mock outrage. "The police think you and Jake can hide your exit in all the confusion." He smiled wryly. "Wouldn't you know it; this *would* be the year everyone shows up for the open house? Good thing we laid in lots of food and drink."

His eyes were full of doubt. "You know—" he started.

"Dad, I know it's for the best. I'll be fine." She gave his arm a little shake. "Don't worry about me. Worry about Jake."

"Noelle be nice. He's trying to help," Jim said.

She shook her head and laughed. "Don't worry, I'll be nice," she repeated. "Now take me to the warden, I mean Jake."

The kitchen was empty except for Ryerson and Jake. They looked up as she entered. Jake was leaning against the counter. He watched her expressionlessly. She turned to Ryerson waiting for him to speak. Poor Jake—he looked worried, Noelle decided with a dash of satisfaction. As if guessing her thoughts, he crossed his arms across his chest and scowled.

Noelle perched on the edge of a bar stool—perched as much as the skirt of the black dress would let her. The move slicked the clingy fabric against her hips and breasts. Jake's eyes dropped to her chest. Oops. She started to tug the low-cut neck to a more modest level and stopped. Let him weep. Jake had always loved her body. That had never been an issue. She took a deep breath and watched him swallow convulsively. Noelle raised her eyebrows. Fascinating.

Detective Ryerson cleared his throat. Jake jumped as if she had reached out and goosed one of his tight butt cheeks.

"Are we ready to discuss what we have planned?" Ryerson asked blandly.

"Yeah, go ahead," Jake said. His scowl deepened.

Noelle smiled.

Ryerson's eyebrows lifted as Jake abruptly opened the kitchen window a few more inches.

"It's hot in here," Jake muttered.

He did look hot, poor baby, Noelle thought smugly. His ears were the bright red of Rudolph's nose, and he appeared suddenly fascinated by the display of twinkling lights in the back yard.

"Okay, Noelle," Ryerson said, pulling her attention from Jake. "The truck is loaded. We've packed pretty much all the basics. It has a full tank of gas. You won't need to stop anywhere. Stops make it easier to track you." He waited for her nod before continuing. "There's a lot of activity here, so your departure will blend in. To add to the confusion, we've arranged for a few cars to leave at the same time. That's it. Touch base with me daily. Jake has his cell. Don't use yours. There's no phone line to the cabin. We'll contact you if there are any developments."

Lou swept into the kitchen holding Noelle's jacket and shoes in one hand, a black woolen beret in the other.

"Mom, I'm not wearing those shoes. They're four-inch heels. I'll kill myself before I get across the street!" Noelle eyed the sleek black pumps.

"It has to look like you're leaving the party, not heading into the wilderness," Ryerson cut in, taking the shoes and coat from Lou and handing them to Noelle. "There's boots in the truck. And this," he took the oversized hat, "will hide your hair." He gently tugged the oversized hat onto her head, casually brushing her bangs to one side.

Jake moved abruptly, pushing past Ryerson and grabbing the coat. "Put this on, Noelle. We're leaving. Jim, you ready?"

Jim dangled his car keys, "Ready."

The front door bell peeled. More guests. Lou threw up her hands in surrender. She grabbed Noelle in one last tight hug. Releasing her, she disappeared to greet the newcomers.

"Truck's out front." Jake grabbed her arm and steered her toward the door. Noelle followed silently. She forced a smile as she passed a family friend in the hall. No one noticed their departure. Why would they? It was probably the party of the century. She cursed under her breath.

"You say something?" Jake asked, glancing away from the arriving guests.

"No," she said.

A car was pulling into the driveway. Up the road an engine started. Headlights cut the darkness. The driver, head down against the wind, scraped diligently at the frost on the windshield. Jake draped a muscular arm around her shoulders, hugging her up against his rock, solid body.

"It's show time. Pretend we're a couple," he whispered. His breath tickled her ear. A shiver of awareness passed through her.

The walk to the car took her mind off Jake. The sidewalk was slick with ice, and she was happy to concentrate on staying upright. Jake opened the door and boosted her into the passenger seat before climbing in on the driver's side. The door slammed. Silence formed a cocoon around them.

.

25

"You ready?"

Noelle jumped at the sound of Jake's voice.

"Ready?" she repeated. "Are you? We don't have to do this."

"What's the alternative—lockdown somewhere? Believe me, a few nights at a deluxe cabin is a hell of a lot better than three square meals a day at a local jail."

Nights. That's what she was worried about. A few nights sharing a cabin with Jake. Who knew what might happen. *I can't do this.* The thought sent shock waves through her. From this second on, it was her and Jake ... alone. No buffers. No neat social Band-Aids to cover the wounds they'd left on each other. The closed space of the cab was torture. Every breath she took filled her lungs with the fresh woodsy scent of Jake's aftershave and the unadulterated scent of Jake. Can you smell pheromones? Stop it, Noelle. You're a moth fluttering around a candle flame, one wingspan away from combustion. She inhaled another tangy breath of aftershave. No, not a candle—a bon fire—a raging inferno. If she kept this up, she was going to get scorched.

The heat blasting through the vents of the dashboard wasn't helping her internal temperature. It turned the cab into a furnace. Noelle reached for the woolen hat covering her head, but Jake stopped her, grabbing her wrist gently. Where his fingers touched, her arm burned.

"No, leave it on. We don't know who might be watching. Let's make sure we don't have any unwanted company before you take it off."

"You think this is my fault, don't you?" she demanded.

"If you had stuck with the program we wouldn't be in this mess."

Noelle looked away. She had that coming. She had made herself an easy target.

"If you'd followed instructions the local police might have done their job and made an arrest," Jake continued.

She gritted her teeth against a harsh reply and leaned forward opening the window a few inches to let the icy air pour through.

"You haven't changed. You still jump before you think."

"What gives you the right to lecture me on what I should have done?" she demanded.

Jake put the truck in reverse and backed out of the driveway. "I get to tell you my opinion because I investigate crimes and save the butts of people like you for a living."

"I didn't ask for your help," she said tightly.

"No, you didn't, but when your Mom called and begged me to keep you safe, I couldn't just throw you to the wolves."

"You're going the wrong way, the highway's that way," Noelle muttered, pointing back behind them.

"We're going to tour the neighborhood and make sure we're alone. Relax and look at the Christmas lights. When I'm sure we're clear, we'll head up island," he answered.

Noelle leaned back in her seat. Relax, right. As if that were possible. She looked over at Jake. He was anything but relaxed. His eyes moved constantly, flitting from mirror to mirror, watching traffic, checking for signs of someone following them.

"You really think someone might be tailing us?" she asked.

"It doesn't hurt to be cautious."

Noelle flushed, but she didn't rise to the dig. She deserved it after the events of the day.

"We should make it to the cabin in a couple of hours." He glanced over at her. "Still got a headache?"

"It's fine. I took something before we left."

She picked at the fringe on the scarf Louise had insisted on wrapping around her neck before they left the house. Jake was different. He looked the same, except for the tiny lines around his eyes. They only added to his attraction. It was his eyes that had changed. There was a cynical glint to their deep blue depths, a hint of ice, as if he were on the outside looking in, a spectator watching life go by. The Jake she remembered had burned hotter. That Jake would have yelled at her for screwing things up and forcing them into this situation. She watched him from beneath her lashes. This Jake was tough and hard, willing to risk himself to protect her.

Sensing her gaze, Jake glanced over at her. "Want me to turn up the heat?"

"God, no," she muttered. She undid the top two buttons on her coat. She was hot enough. What was with her tonight? One minute she wanted to hit him, the next, she was looking at him like an alley cat, wanting . . . She stared into the side mirror and watched the traffic.

"I think we're clear. If you see a car more than once, or someone following without turning off, tell me," he said. "We should have the roads to ourselves. They're calling for low temperatures and snow. I hope we get to the cabin before it starts to dump."

"Do we have chains?" Noelle asked, happy to take her mind off Jake and focus on something more mundane, like getting caught in a blizzard. There was nothing like a good old-fashioned snowstorm to cool you down.

"We have chains," he said. "Why does Ray need this four-by-four anyway. He's a realtor. Or is this the wife's car?"

Noelle ignored the comment. Ray and Jake had never seen eye to eye, and that wasn't likely to change.

Jake relented. "This truck is more than capable of getting us up there, but I'm worried about the road to the cabin."

The truck hit a patch of black ice and slid. Noelle's stomach dropped.

"Damn, hold on!"

Jake fought to control the skid as the truck slid towards the tree-lined boulevard. Noelle dug her fingers into the armrest and braced herself for the impact. She closed her eyes.

"Breath, Elle. You can open your eyes."

Noelle cautiously opened her eyes and let go of the armrest.

"Still hate driving in snow?" Jake asked.

Noelle laughed shakily, straightening in her seat. "Yeah, and I don't think that's about to change—look."

A delicate earthbound snowflake touched the windshield and melted to a drop of water.

"Great, after all that rain the roads will be a skating rink." He shrugged. "We'll make it. Trust me. This truck is up to the task."

Noelle didn't answer. Trust me . . . Elle . . . How many times had he said those words to her when they were together?

More snowflakes were falling, bouncing off the windshield, melting against the warmth of the glass.

"I was hoping the snow would hold off until we got over the Malahat summit," Jake muttered.

The Malahat. Noelle sighed. The portion of highway between Victoria and Duncan was mountainous terrain split by a four-lane highway. In summer the view was photo op spectacular, in winter the road treacherous.

"If it's snowing heavily the highways department might close the road. What do we do if that happens?"

"I guess I'll flash my badge."

"Will that work?" Noelle asked.

Jake shrugged. "I can probably talk us through."

Noelle nodded.

"You want some hot chocolate? Your Mom packed a thermos. It's in the back." Jake pointed a thumb at the pack tucked behind his seat.

Noelle twisted to drag it onto the front seat between them. She found the thermos and a couple of cups and pulled them free.

"Want some?" she asked.

Jake shook his head. They were starting the long climb out of town and the snow was falling heavily, gathering in powdery drifts.

"It's been snowing here for a while," he commented.

Noelle poured a mug of chocolate and settled back in her seat. She took a sip of the hot, sweet drink. She hated driving in snow. Snow belonged on the mountains. People should stay home and off the roads when it snowed. A tractor-trailer shuddered by on the left, shooting a spray of dirty slush over their windshield.

"Damn." Jake fought his way out of another skid. "The roads are ice under this snow. It's like driving on glass."

"I guess he thinks the weight of his rig will keep him on the road," Noelle observed.

"Yeah, fine for him, but I saw enough fatal accidents when I worked traffic to know that's not true. If he doesn't slow down, he'll end up in a ditch before the night's over."

Look." Noelle nudged his arm. Ahead, amber lights flashed. "They're closing the highway."

Jake rolled down his window and inched towards the roadblock. Highway crews were swinging a heavy yellow barrier bar across the road. Two police cars buttressed by a sanding truck, a snowplow and two highways pickup trucks with flashing yellow warning lights, blocked the lane.

The unlucky officer assigned to check traffic approached Jake's window. His eyes were the only thing visible in his face. He had tied down the earflaps on his hat and wrapped a scarf over his chin as protection from the wind.

"Evening, sir, we're closing the highway due to severe winter conditions up ahead." He stepped back and considered the heavy three-quarter-ton four-wheel-drive truck. "Are you carrying chains?" he asked, rubbing his gloved hands together as he spoke.

"Chains, sand, shovels, you name it," Jake answered.

Across the road, the highway crew unloaded fluorescent striped barriers from the back of their truck.

The officer looked from the truck to the sky. "I'll tell you what. Since you have a four-wheel-drive and chains, I won't stop you from carrying on, but take it slow. The roads are better after the summit, but by morning they'll be impassible."

Jake nodded. "Thanks, we'll keep going. I'm used to this weather."

The officer stepped back and waved them through. In the side mirror, Noelle saw him step up to the car in line behind them.

Jake inched past the highways trucks and glanced down at Noelle.

"This is good," he said. "With the road closed, we should be safe for a while."

He shifted into low and started the steep crawl to the summit of the Malahat. Far below, the Saanich inlet lay invisible under the stormy sky. Behind them the barrier dropped into place and the last car turned back.

Zero visibility forced the highway to two lanes. The cars coming towards them, inched past like turtles putting one deliberate foot in front of the other. Wind buffeted snow against the glass. The flakes reflected the light of the headlights leaving Noelle feeling as if she was traveling through a swirling tunnel. Beside her Jake raised a hand and rubbed his eyes.

"We could turn back," Noelle said, wishing it were an option. Her knuckles were white just sitting in the passenger seat.

He flashed a grin at her. "This is nothing. You should see the 401 in Toronto during a white out."

"Yeah, but the highway in Toronto doesn't have cliffs that will send you to the bottom of the Saanich Inlet if you mess up," she retorted. The quick grin reminded her of the old Jake, the Jake who had wormed his way into her heart and then broken it. She looked away.

The truck lurched and broke through an uneven drift of snow. The wheels spun, lost traction and slid. Noelle held her breath. The knobby treads caught hold and the truck jumped ahead. Noelle let out a quiet sigh of relief. They passed the sign marking the summit.

"All right, only three hundred and fifty-six meters to the bottom," Jake said.

Far ahead, Noelle caught a glimpse of red taillights.

"There's our buddy the semi-trailer," she said.

"Yeah," Jake shook his head. "Doesn't look like he decided to slow down."

As they watched, the truck's brake lights swayed. The heavy tractor-trailer swung across the highway. Jake slowed to barely creeping.

"Hold tight, it's a skating rink. Shit, that truck's going in the ditch," Jake called out.

As he spoke the semi's back end swung overtaking its front. Sideways the semi slid off the road and came to rest in the deep snow at the shoulder.

"Should we stop and help him?" Noelle asked doubtfully.

The driver's side door of the truck swung open and the driver jumped down into knee-deep snow. He looked up at Jake and Noelle and waved them onwards.

"No, he'll call for help, or hike to the gas station up the road. He's fine. This isn't the arctic. Besides if we stop, we'll get stuck. That guy is an idiot. He was driving way too fast." There was no pity in Jake's voice.

Noelle glanced over at him, but didn't answer. He was right, but she felt guilty not stopping. They carried on in silence.

The side of the highway was littered with empty cars. The semi driver wasn't the only one to discover too late how treacherous the ice under the snow was. The snow continued falling like sugar through a sieve.

"I'm worried about the road to the cabin." Noelle half-turned in her seat, tucking one long leg up beneath her. "It's not that great of a road at the best of times."

"Ray said it was graded in the fall. He figures that it's in better shape than it used to be. Let's play it by ear and see what happens," Jake said absently. "Look there's Duncan."

"Are we going to stop?"

"No, better to push on. Who knows how much snow we're going to run into."

Noelle watched the town's brightly colored Christmas lights recede in the rearview mirror. Good-bye civilization. From now on it was Jake and her. And the blizzard . . . don't forget the storm of the century heading their way. The fluffy snowflakes layering the edge of the windshield already threatened to overwhelm the wipers.

"Brr. Everyone's tucked up by their fireplaces tonight."

"Everyone except for them," Jake said, pointing towards the yellow flashing lights that marked the sand trucks and snowplows struggling to clear the roads.

Noelle let go of the armrest and flexed her fingers. Her hands were stiff from the death grip she had assumed at the summit. She was surprised there weren't claw marks in the leather. The descent had been scary enough to make her consider going back to Victoria and taking her chances with the guy from the store. Her eyes burned courtesy of the unblinking stare she had held for the last hour of the drive.

With Duncan behind them, visibility vanished, the highway whited out by the storm. Noelle leaned forward trying to see the road through the snowflakes.

"Can you see?" she demanded.

"Nope." Jake grimaced. He flicked the windshield wipers to high speed.

Snow drifts formed heavy ruts in the lane. The truck's tires slipped and spun, leaving them fish-tailing over the road. Noelle resumed her death grip on the armrest.

"Shit, hold on," Jake called out.

His arm stretched in front of her forming a bar across her chest as the truck spun in a 360-degree turn. They plunged towards the ditch. Whump! Noelle's' head slammed against her headrest. Jake grunted and released his hold on her. She sagged against her seat belt as they came to a stop, leaving them resting at a 45-degree angle, the truck's nose buried in a snowdrift.

26

"You okay?" Jake asked unbuckling his seat belt and turning to run assessing eyes over Noelle.

"Yeah," she said, pushing herself back in the seat. "I think so."

Smiling crookedly, he leaned over to open his door. The slide had left the truck nose down, the deep snow burying the bottom of Noelle's window.

"Sorry, Elle. It doesn't look good. I'll check out the damage." As he spoke, he braced his feet against the bottom of his door and pushed. The door swung open and he climbed through the gap.

Noelle unbuckled her seatbelt and slid over the seat to the open driver's side door.

"How bad?" she asked.

"I can't tell yet. I'm going to check out the front end."

"Jake, look. There's a snow plow."

The flashing lights of the advancing plow spun a yellow glow over the snow. The driver slowed to a stop, opening his window half-way to the gusting snow.

"Need a hand?" he called down. He didn't wait for an answer before continuing, "Although, I oughta leave you in the ditch. Damn four-by-fours." He rolled up the window and a minute later, the cab light blinked on. "Let's get this done. The road won't plow itself while I fish you out of the ditch."

"Thanks," Jake called. He waded through the thigh-deep snow and climbed out of the ditch onto the side of the road.

The driver was a big man, his muscle long since turned to flab. He hoisted himself from the cab grunting under the effort of climbing down from the plow.

"Damn four-by-fours," he repeated. "You guys think you can outdrive the conditions just cuz you've got knobby tires." He slammed his door and plodded through the snow to stand above Jake's truck.

"Thanks for stopping," Jake said. "Jake Ryan." He introduced himself.

"Bricknell." The driver nodded. "Alright, let's get this done," he repeated, slapping his heavily insulated gloves together. "You're lucky. If you were going faster, you woulda buried the nose in the ditch."

"It's solid ice under the snow," Jake answered levelly.

"Take the end of this chain," Bricknell ordered, bending to free up the coils of heavy cable draped over the bumper. "Put it through the tow hook on the back of the truck."

Jake grabbed the end of the chain and played it out, dragging it through the snow behind him. He slid down the side of the ditch to the back end of the truck and looped the heavy links around the truck's frame, setting the hook in the tow bar built into the undercarriage.

"Got that done yet?" the other man called.

Jake gave him a thumbs up.

Bricknell leaned back against the plow and surveyed Jake and the snowbound truck. He wrestled with the pocket of his heavy jacket and unearthed a battered cigarette package.

"Smoke?" he offered.

"No, I'm good, thanks," Jake answered, a hint of impatience underlying the politeness in his voice.

"Suit yourself." Bricknell shook a cigarette free and settled into a more comfortable position against the shelter of the plow. He bit down on the end of the cigarette, lit it, and inhaled a lungful.

"You know," he said, "You can't out drive the conditions. You folks with the fancy SUVs and pickup trucks think you can drive hell-bent like you always do when it snows. You think four-wheel means better traction. It doesn't. It means you end up in the ditch faster."

"Thanks for stopping. Maybe we could—"

Bricknell ignored the interruption. "You boys gotta practice defensive driving. I remember . . ."

Irritation settled over Jake's face. Noelle, listening from the vantage point of the open door, let out a snort of laughter. It was nice to see someone give Jake a dressing down.

Bricknell stopped mid-sentence and looked at the truck. He straightened from his lounging position and directed a tobacco-stained smile towards Noelle. Jake turned and scowled.

Noelle frowned. Now, what was Jake's problem?

"You must be cold, ma'am," the driver called. "We'll get you out of that ditch and back on your way." He tossed his half-smoked cigarette into the snow.

"Yeah, you must be cold, Noelle. Maybe you want to climb back into the truck and stay warm," Jake said pointedly. He looked as if he were smothering a grin.

Noelle followed the direction of his gaze and found that the skirt of the tight black dress had ridden up her hips. An inch higher, and the men would have no doubt as to the color of her thong panties. She scooted back inside and wrestled the door closed. She wasn't cold, the heat in her cheeks left her toasty warm.

Bricknell stomped back to his truck and climbed in. A heavy clunk marked the release of the parking brake. The plow inched forward dragging the four-by-four out of the ditch. In moments, the truck was back on semi-solid road. Jake freed the chain from the truck's frame and gathered it up. He was looping it over the hook on the plow's bumper when Bricknell joined him.

Bricknell thumped him on the shoulder and pegged a thumb towards the truck. He directed a smirking smile at Noelle.

"Now, you slow down, eh. You'll get where you want in one piece that way and so will the lady. I can see why you'd want to hurry." He nodded knowingly and smacked Jake on the shoulder again before swaggering back to the plow.

Jake shook his head and returned to the truck. Climbing in he brushed the snow from his shoulders and sleeves. The flakes melted in tiny puddles on the heated leather seat.

Jake looked at the long length of leg left uncovered by Noelle's dress and smiled. He dropped a frozen hand to her knee. Noelle gasped.

"The plow driver liked your legs. He figures we ended up in the ditch because I was driving too fast so that we could get where we were going faster." Jake shook his head and started the truck forward.

Noelle's mouth dropped. Red-faced, she tried to tug the dress down, but the tight sheath didn't budge.

"That perv," she sputtered.

"Well, he liked what he saw."

She hit him.

"Hey, what was that for? You can't fault the man for good taste," he protested.

Noelle subsided into her seat, feeling inexplicably happy. Oh, oh, she knew that feeling. Jake's backhanded compliment introduced another chink in her carefully built armor. She shook her head. Things were getting complicated.

"What's the matter?" Jake asked, the humor gone from his voice.

"This whole mess . . . Jake, we're stuck in that cabin for who knows how long and we can hardly hold a conversation without fighting. You can't walk back into my life as if nothing happened. I don't trust you, and I don't know what to do about it."

"Nothing," he said so quietly she almost didn't hear him.

"Nothing?"

"Yeah, we act like we're two strangers stuck together. If I can do it after what you did to me, then you can too."

"What I did to you? What are you talking about?" Noelle demanded.

"This isn't the time."

She had wronged *him*?

"And just what did I do to you?" she asked.

"Look, this is ancient history. Right now, we have to drop out of sight so the police can do their job. Consider me the hired help if it makes you feel better."

Silence dropped over them. The bitterness in Jake's voice chilled her. What right did he have to be angry? She's the one who'd had the miscarriage. She was the one alone in the hospital while he chased a puck around the ice with his friends. The lights of Nanaimo passed but Noelle was oblivious to their festive display.

Outside the city limits traffic dwindled to nothing. Once again Jake had both hands on the wheel fighting to keep the truck on the road. Snow swirled over them closing off the world. Noelle stared into the white, concentrating on finding a sign that would mark the way to the closed ski hill.

"There." She pointed. She had almost missed the marker in the heavily falling snow.

Jake slowed. The truck slid past the fork in the road. He backed up and forced the wheel to the left, moving them from the semi-safety of the more travelled highway. The tires spun as the truck fishtailed over the heaps of plowed snow onto what in summertime was a gravel road. Jake switched the engine off.

"I'm putting the chains on. We need the extra traction."

"You want help?"

"No, they're easy to put on, not like those stupid cables you used to have." He slammed the door.

Noelle smiled. She had forgotten the cables they had bought for her ancient Honda. The cabled chains had been anything but easy to put on. In fact, if she remembered correctly, putting them on entailed Jake lying on his back cursing as the slippery plastic-coated metal cord slipped through his fingers. Once in place, the chains stayed clipped for twenty feet before spontaneously releasing.

Her smile changed to a frown as she considered the winter wasteland in front of them. Already snow weighed down the boughs of the fir and cedar trees, burying small saplings under a blanket of white. The only difference between the road and the scenery on either side of it was the graded surface was a flat thoroughfare, two cars wide. Once they started the climb to the cabin, it would be easy to figure out where the road ended. It would be right outside her window.

Jake climbed back into the truck. Shivering, he leaned forward and cranked up the heat.

"It's bloody cold out, and I don't think it's going to stop snowing anytime soon," he said.

"Chains go on okay?"

"Yeah, heavy duty ones. Only the best for good old Ray."

Noelle didn't bother answering. Jake released the parking brake and they started forward.

Someone had taken the time to put up new signage marking the way to the cabins. They followed the road markers, stopping occasionally so Jake could bang the snow from the face of a sign. He kept the truck in the center of the road, away from the steep drop at the edge. Around them the thick snow was undisturbed. They were truly alone.

They swung around another curve and buildings emerged from the white—empty ski chalets awaiting a season that never came. Their hideout was at the end of the road—an A-frame cabin with a steeply-pitched blue tin roof.

"This is it," Jake announced. He climbed out and pulled on his coat, ducking his head against a blanket of snowflakes.

Trudging to the back of the truck, he opened the canopy and grabbed Noelle's boots. He returned to drop them on the seat beside her.

Noelle picked up the boots. They looked a little big, but nothing she couldn't fix with a couple of extra pairs of socks. She kicked off the black heels and pulled the boots on, delighting in the warmth of the thick fleece lining. Tugging up the collar on her coat, she buttoned it to the top, climbed out of the truck and sank thigh-deep into a drift of snow.

"Damn," she said.

"What?" Jake called. He had already tromped a path to the front of the cabin.

"Leave it to me to find a snow drift as soon as I get out of the truck," she answered. She heard his quiet laugh and smiled.

"Here, you take the key. There's a flashlight somewhere in the truck." Jake appeared beside her. "You want a lift to the porch?" He flashed a wicked grin.

"No, I'm fine," Noelle said, backing away.

Jake's smile faded. "Suit yourself." He pulled open the back door of the truck and began a search for the flashlight.

27

"Stupid," muttered Noelle.

Jake was trying to open a truce and she stomped all over his white flag. She ducked her head and plodded up the path he had cleared to the cabin. The blowing snow stung her cheeks and swirled over her eyes.

"Stop," she muttered. "Focus on the building in front of you, not the man behind you."

Right. Great idea. Concentrate on the blizzard. Mother Nature had decided a straightforward snowstorm wasn't good enough. The old witch had cackled, tacked on gale force winds, and stalled a low-pressure system on top of them.

Reaching the shelter of the covered porch, Noelle shoved her hands deeper into the pockets of her coat and sagged against the rough boards covering the wall. The roof's overhang formed a vague windbreak that wouldn't last. Already the swirling snow was collapsing in drifting piles. By morning the drifts would cover the entire porch. She narrowed her eyes against the wind and examined the blurry outline of the truck.

Come on, Jake. How long does it take to find one little light? She shivered. The wind bit through her coat with a cold that left her bones aching. Obviously, the flashlight had pulled a Houdini. It was Noelle against the elements until it decided to be found. She stomped her feet and looked up at the pearly glow of the sky. Its light bleached the shadows grey, almost banishing the need for artificial illumination.

Inside the cabin was a different story. She wrapped her fingers around the heavy ring of keys Jake had handed her. The interior of the cabin was as black as a lump of coal. She dragged her hand over the glass of one of the long windows framing the door and peered through the opening she had made. A swirl of snowflakes breathed down the nape of her neck. She shivered and rolled her shoulders before trapping her frozen fingers in her armpits.

"Hurry up, Jake," she muttered, turning back to check his progress. It didn't look like the flashlight was coming out of hiding any time soon. She looked back at the snowy window.

Until she had the flashlight in hand and Jake beside her, she wasn't stepping through the door. Who knew what type of critter had found its way into the building. Ray's definition of cozy and hers were a billion miles apart. She kicked at a drift of snow that threatened to swallow the doorstep. The act rewarded her with a boot full of fluffy powder that rapidly melted into icy water. She stomped the rest of the drift away from the door.

Once the snow was beaten back, she stuck the key in the lock and turned it. Nope, until there was light, that door was staying closed. Ray had once said that a hotel she was considering was a five-star resort. Noelle had spent the night sleeping in the bathtub to avoid the bedbugs. No way was she taking Ray's word for what they'd find inside.

"Damn, Jake, hurry up!" she muttered. She had to pee. Please let there be indoor plumbing. She tugged at the hem of her dress, trying to make it cover more skin. The dress, although a sexy little number for clubbing, was an epic fail as a snowsuit.

A pained expletive from Jake brought her eyes back to the truck. Under the light of the interior lamp, he was stretched across the rear seat digging under the driver's seat. Their nosedive into the ditch had tossed anything loose onto the floor of the truck.

Hmm. Noelle considered Jake's position. His stretch created a gap between his coat and the waistband of his jeans exposing a hand span of bare flesh. As she watched, he rolled onto his side. The gap widened. Noelle swallowed, imagining his washboard abs playing peek-a-boo with the edge of his sweater. Down girl. She tore her eyes away and plowed another restless circle around the porch.

What was the matter with her? Show her a bit of bare skin and the arctic outflow surrounding her vanished. When she got back to civilization she was calling Maria's accountant friend. She needed a real date. She could count on one hand the number of relationships she'd had since Jake had left. Three. She frowned and shook her head. No, that wasn't right. The occasional dinners with her old university professor didn't count. The guy was eighty if a day. She was definitely calling the accountant.

Her eyes strayed back towards Jake. What able-bodied woman wouldn't get hot at the sight of him? Broad shoulders, tight butt . . . the guy moved in ways that would make any girl turn around for a second or third look. No, she decided sourly, Jake had gotten better with age.

Stop it, she commanded herself. This is Jake. Remember Jake? The guy who ran out on you while you were in the hospital? No, she hadn't told him about the baby. She had never given him the chance to be there for her. What was the matter with her? Why was she making excuses for him? She made another circle of the porch, narrowing her eyes against the falling snow. Her face stung from the cold lash of the wind. Maybe time together was a good thing. She could get over him. She snorted. Yeah, she was succeeding so well with that. Marooned in an isolated cabin, hunted by a crazed killer, and the thought of Jake and his washboard abs was making her drool all over the freshly fallen snow.

"Got it," Jake called, wiggling backwards across the seat.

He climbed to his feet, and groaned, stretching to work out the kinks left by the twists he'd performed rescuing the light. His sweater parted ways with the top of his jeans, offering her another vague glimpse of ab muscles. She gulped.

"Now we need to find the generator."

"Ray said it was in a shed at the side of the cabin," Noelle answered, pointing at a snow-covered building fifty feet from the truck.

Jake played the flashlight beam over the snow and located the shed's door.

"I'll see if I can get the generator up and running so we can get out of this wind."

Noelle perched a hip against the porch railing, and unbuttoned the top two buttons of her coat. Right, up and running . . . the icy wind would have to substitute for a cold shower.

"They're trusting sorts up here," Jake called. "There's not even a lock on the door."

She smiled at the disgust in his voice.

"You've been hanging out in the big city too long. Probably half the people in Landings don't lock their doors," she said.

She heard his snort of disapproval as he cleared the snow from the opening and pulled the door open.

"Yeah, it's here." The beam of light moved deeper into the shed.

Noelle turned and looked back at the truck. Its lights reflected off the swirling flakes, illuminating the wall of the cabin. One thing Ray had gotten right—the cabin was a well-tended flower in a bed of weeds. Nearby buildings were boarded up and abandoned, slowly falling to ruin. It was sad. Global warming had made snow fall sporadic.

Instead of adapting to their new reality, the cabin owners had given up. Summer would be a great time for the hill. Nearby lakes stocked with trout and a network of logging roads and trails made it heaven for outdoor lovers.

The roar of the generator broke the stillness. The machine chugged raggedly and settled down to a quiet purr. Ray had gotten that right too, she conceded. She had half-expected the generator to be seized up and rusted out. Ray's idea of mechanical maintenance was driving to a local garage and popping the hood.

Jake emerged from the shed. He gave her a wave before turning back to close the door. Noelle watched him walk towards her as a tingle of awareness crawled up her spine.

28

"Everything okay?" Noelle asked, trying to ignore the thump, thump, thump of her heart.

"Good." Jake gave a quick nod. "That's the biggest generator I've ever seen. We'll have lots of power. Have you looked inside?"

"I was waiting for a light." She shivered. "I'm so cold I would climb into an igloo to get warm." She turned the doorknob and with one foot pushed the door open leaning back from the gap.

Jake looked at her and rolled his eyes. Reaching past her, he flipped the light switch up. Incandescent light flooded a wide-open room topped with polished wooden beams. Discreet rows of recessed lighting reflected off the hues of wood grains. A bank of floor to ceiling windows lined the back wall behind a massive fireplace of smooth river rock stretching to the ceiling. In front of the hearth was an intricately designed wrought iron screen.

Noelle stepped through the door and kicked off her boots. Beneath her wet feet, the planks of hardwood were smooth and cold. She crossed the room to stand beside the fireplace, stretching one hand to run her fingers over the smooth rock.

"Wow," she said.

"It looks straight out of a log cabin magazine published in Sweden. A little clichéd, don't you think," Jake said, eying the artfully arranged antique snowshoes hanging above the carved log mantle.

"When you have the kind of money this guy does, you can pick any design theme you want."

Jake shrugged.

"Come on," Noelle said. "You have to be a little impressed."

"I'd be more impressed if it had a big screen TV with a hockey game on."

It was Noelle's turn to shake her head in disgust. She turned back to the room, greedily absorbing other details like the overstuffed leather couch and armchairs grouped around a low coffee table created from a vintage steamer trunk. She stepped onto the thick Persian rug resting beneath the furniture and sighed in appreciation.

Off the living area an antique cherry wood table gleamed dully. The cushioned pads of the chairs surrounding it were the same blue and white French provincial motif as the throw pillows nestled on the couch. A granite-topped island invited guests to pull up a stool and watch the cook work. Cabinets, skillfully antiqued by what had to be a master craftsman, provided a backdrop for gleaming stainless steel appliances that made the kitchen a chef's dream.

"Look at this place," Noelle demanded, turning to find Jake right behind her. Her breath caught in her throat. She hadn't heard him move.

"Yeah, must be nice to have money to throw away on a cabin you don't use." He turned away and disappeared out the front door reappearing with an armful of wood. He dumped it in a wooden box beside the fireplace.

"You stay here. I'll get the rest of the stuff from the truck. You can't be too warm in that dress," he said.

Noelle shook her head in disgust. Marooned with Scrooge and his bah humbug attitude. She continued her investigation.

There wasn't much left to discover. The kitchen opened onto a short hallway leading to the master bedroom. A picture window backed a built-in reading nook against one wall. Across from the window a king-sized sleigh-styled bed was covered with a luxurious black faux fur quilt, piled high with white linen pillows.

Noelle passed through the room to investigate the en-suite bathroom. She pushed the door open, stepping into a room that made her eyes widen in awe. So this is how the one percent lived. Decadence and opulence wrapped in earthy tones of wood and stone. On a sunny day, the exterior wall, created of wood framed panes of glass, would reveal a vista of trees and sky. Tonight, with the wind pelting the snow against the glass, it was a swirling barrier of white backlit by the exterior lights. A massive shower took up one wall, its floor to ceiling glass doors and multiple shower heads hinting at long steamy trysts.

Rough-hewn beams spread like branches above the tiny river rocks cobbling the shower floor. Near the window, a giant free-standing bathtub waited. Scented candles were clustered in every nook.

No wonder Ray was so smug when he'd suggested the cabin. Its isolation and luxury were things Ray and Beth would appreciate. He probably wasn't working hard at selling the place. Now she knew why Ray and his realtor wife worked so many weekends.

She retraced her steps to the living room. One bedroom, one bed. Flip for who slept where? The other option ... her stomach fluttered.

"Here, let me help you with that," she said stepping forward to grab the end of the cooler Jake was manhandling through the door. She helped carry it to the kitchen. "You've been busy."

"Yeah. Your Mom must figure we'll be here a while. Food, clothes, who knows what else. That's it though, the truck's empty."

I can't get over this place."

Jake smiled. "Ray said he thought it would be a good spot to hide out. Only a few people know it exists. He and Beth come up here now and then."

"Yeah, that would be Ray. He's probably not even trying to sell it."

"Probably not much of a market for luxury cabins on abandoned ski hills," Jake said.

He leaned down to kick off his boots. Already, the snow had obliterated his tracks to and from the truck.

Noelle stepped over to the wall of windows and stared out at the blowing snow. "In an hour, it will be as if we never came this way."

Jake nodded. "It probably already is. If he's out there, he'll have a hard time finding us in this weather." Jake hung his jacket on a wooden coat stand by the door. "Ryerson is going to keep us informed of any developments."

"There's a fire already laid," Noelle said, moving towards the fireplace.

"Looks like Ray was a boy scout." Jake struck a long wooden match and touched it to the kindling.

"That's a realtor for you, always staging in case of a sale."

"Hope there aren't any birds' nests in the chimney," Jake muttered.

"They wouldn't dare. This place is immaculate," Noelle replied.

"Yeah, the generator is brand new. Lucky for us, some people have more money than brains." The kindling caught and flame curled around the twist of paper tucked into the wood.

Noelle lugged the cooler into the kitchen and flipped it open—packages of vegetables and meats, boxes of pre-prepared appetizers, milk and juice.

She glanced up. "She didn't leave anything out. We have everything we need to eat a well-balanced meal every day for a week. There's enough to feed an army. How long are we going to be here?" She opened the fridge and began loading the contents into it.

Jake looked up from the blaze he had started in the hearth. "Depends on how successful Ryerson's plan is."

"And just what is that plan?" Noelle left the kitchen area to perch on the arm of the couch.

"He's got a policewoman staying at your place. She looks like you. With luck, she'll lure Cobra out of his lair. We'll know in a few days." Jake shrugged and stood up. "Maybe we'll get lucky."

Get lucky. The words hung between them. Noelle was silent for a moment, dwelling on the meaning of the phrase. Her cheeks burned.

Jake mistook her silence for worry. "Don't worry. Your folks are safe. She'll stay at your place, and the house will be under surveillance at all times. I think the plan has a good chance of working. Consider this a holiday—a break from bunny costumes." He slanted a sideways look at her.

"Hah, you are so funny." Noelle stood up.

"Hey, I aim to please," Jake called to her back.

The words were an echo from the past. Her cheeks were on fire. She scuttled back to the kitchen and the boxes. At least there, she could focus on something other than Jake's tight butt in his worn jeans.

The next box held fruit and wine. She shook her head in exasperation. Louise appeared to have covered all the food groups. She dug further into the box and unearthed a container of chocolate-covered cherries. Yup, all the food groups. She tossed the empty carton to one side and went back for another.

The next held clothes for her. She carried it into the bedroom, glad to be away from Jake. She pulled out yoga pants, t-shirts and sweaters, stashing them in the drawers of the armoire in the corner of the room. Jeans and a hooded-sweatshirt came next, with underwear at the bottom of the box. She pulled out a handful of thong underwear, price tags dangled from the lacy strings. Nice touch, she thought sourly. Was this a joke? She dug deeper and unearthed a diaphanous nightgown. Funny, ha, ha. These things were brand new. No way would they fit her comfortably built mother.

Jake appeared in the doorway, a frosty beer bottle in one hand.

"Where do you want . . ?" His voice trailed off at the sight of the sexy nightwear. "That's nice. You going to model it for me?"

She balled it up and stuffed it in the drawer.

"Not likely. Where did this stuff come from?"

"Your brother said he had some stuff you could have. Nice touch. Nick is still playing the field, huh? Don't get all bent. He said he had some things to put in your box." His eyebrows rose comically. "I didn't know Nick was a salesman for Victoria's secret. You can't fault his taste though." Jake picked up a tiny wisp of panty and dangled it from the end of one finger.

Noelle snatched it back and threw it into the drawer. She dumped in the rest of the box's contents, slammed the drawer shut, and grabbed Jake's arm, yanking him from the room. They retreated to the living room, to find the fireplace already warming the cabin. Good, she could blame its heat for the color in her cheeks.

Jake settled onto the sofa and took a sip of his beer.

"I think you can say we are effectively snowed in. It doesn't look like it's going to stop any time soon," he said.

Glad of the topic change, Noelle held her palms out to the flames. The bedroom was freezing in comparison to the rest of the cabin. Even with extra sleeping bags, she was going to have icicles forming on her nose. She scanned the walls for a thermostat. Nothing.

Silence stretched between them. Even during the rockiest times of their brief marriage, they had never lacked for words.

"All settled?" Jake asked as he drained the last mouthful of beer and stood up. He couldn't stand the quiet. Pretending to ignore her, he moved to the kitchen and dropped the bottle into the recycling box. That was better. A little space made him less aware of her perfume and the long length of leg revealed by the black dress. That gap had driven him crazy on the trip to the cabin. His fingers itched to touch her skin, to see if it was as silky-smooth as it looked. He stirred restlessly, his jeans feeling a size too tight.

He had to stop thinking about Noelle. He couldn't help it though. She had changed. He had watched her at the party. She looked happy, with no brittle edges; just a calm confidence. She had taken charge of those wild little boys of Ray's and settled them to coloring. She'd left them trying to outdo each other in the attempt to please her. It was the same with the older men. She made them all feel like they were special, as if she were interested in talking about the big bad winter of '65. She had moved about the room touching everyone but him.

He wandered over to the long bank of windows and stared at the falling snow. Time stretched in front of him.

"Jake?"

He glanced back at her.

"We need to make a truce. This is as hard on you as it is me. You didn't come to the island to get stuck babysitting me." She shrugged. "Maybe I should have let them take me into protective custody." She frowned and shook her head. "No, couldn't do it, so we're stuck together. I am grateful for your help. I'm sorry I didn't listen to you."

He wondered how long she had been rehearsing that little speech. So this was her olive branch, a truce. Did she consider this a war? He knew she didn't want him around, but he hadn't realized that he had any effect other than annoying her. The fact that she needed to declare a truce meant maybe she wasn't as immune to him as she pretended. Fine, he'd take her truce and see where it led. He extended his hand in acceptance. Her hand trembled in his grasp.

Noelle pulled away.

"Okay," she muttered. "I'm going to bed. I'll see you in the morning."

***

He parked the plumbing van in front of the house and studied the surrounding houses from beneath the brim of his ball cap. His mouth twisted into a smirk as he noted the absence of any surveillance.

The police thought their decoy had worked. They didn't realize he was a step ahead of them. They were no closer to finding him than they had been a year ago. After he took care of the witness, things would be back to normal. A pity about the girl, but things had to be kept neat and tidy.

He picked up the clip board someone had so obligingly left on the passenger seat. The van was pathetically easy to steal. A quick switch with another van's license plates and he was ready to get the job done without the bother of the police.

He slid out and cast a last check for prying eyes. In his experience, no one took note of tradesmen. Like an invisible army, they scurried around under everybody's nose, rarely remembered.

This was the time of day when people were at work. As expected the house in front of him was quiet and empty. An answering machine had picked up his earlier call. He grimaced as he traversed the pile of snow left by the plow. The weather complicated things, but he would win out. He always did.

He rang the bell and waited, his ears tuned for the sound of approaching footsteps. Nothing.

With the ease of experience, he let himself into a foyer decorated for Christmas. A soft chime marked the opening of the door. Typical. The owners had an alarm, but chose not to use it. People spent money on monitored systems, yet never turned them on. The steady tick of a grandfather clock was loud in the silence.

He scowled at his surroundings. People never realized how easy they made things. He wasn't here to rob them though. He was here to find out where they had stashed the girl.

They would have written down the information he needed. They always did. Call it efficient, or call it stupid. None of them were as smart as he was.

It took him less than three minutes to find what he was looking for. The paper, with a map neatly showing the way to the cabin, was tacked to a board beside the phone, the contact and file number for the police beside it.

He pocketed the directions and left the house the way he had entered. Aside from the missing map, it was as if he had never been there.

29

Cold air trickled through a gap in the sleeping bag. Noelle grumbled, tucked the bag in closer, and tried to move away from the frosty zipper. Her chilled limbs were ice against her own skin, and she swore the tip of her nose was frozen. She rolled over seeking the elusive pocket of warmth that had evaded her all night. Giving up, she opened her eyes and stared at the uncovered window. The world outside was silent, absent of bird calls, traffic sounds and even the familiar pitter-patter of rain on the roof. Dull light proved it was morning, but morning when? Was it too early to crawl out of her ice bunker and huddle by the fire?

What type of lunatic spent money decorating, but didn't heat the place? No, she knew what kind of lunatic. The erotic textbooks, body oils and scented candles told her exactly what type. Who needed a furnace when you generated your own heat? The faux-fur-lined handcuffs were a dead giveaway that the seller and his soon-to-be ex, had their own fifty shades going on. What would Jake—no don't go there. Jake didn't need to know anything about the diverse tastes of their host.

She crawled out of the sleeping bag, stifling a gasp as her bare feet hit the cold floor. A ripple of goose bumps marched up her arms. Shivering, she stumbled to the dresser and unearthed a matching thong and lacy bra— sophisticated underwear to hide beneath bulky sweaters and leggings. Sexy though, she thought catching a glimpse of her reflection in the mirror. Another shiver made her hastily pull the sweater and leggings over the lingerie.

Warmth—for the first time since she had left the living room, she began to thaw out. Flopping onto the bed, she thrust her feet into a pair of fleecy ski socks. Her gaze fell on the silky nightgown at the end of the bed. She may as well have slept naked for all the warmth it had generated. Tonight, she'd sleep in her clothes. The room had been warm enough, until she'd shut the door. That's when the sub-arctic front rolled in.

She opened the bedroom door and stepped into the tropics. Heat wrapped her chilled limbs. At the sound of the door, Jake looked up from where he crouched by the fireplace feeding a log to the greedy flames.

From the smile on his face he knew the fireplace was the cabin's sole heat source.

"Have a good sleep?" he asked.

"You knew that the bedroom didn't have a heater, didn't you?" she accused.

Jake shrugged. "You could have slept out here with me."

Noelle huffed. "Yeah, right," she muttered.

"You were the one that wanted the door between us. I was willing to take a chance with my virtue and sleep in the same room as you."

Noelle rubbed her hands over her arms and moved to stand in front of the fire. Her muscles were stiff and achy, and her temper short. She glared at Jake, noting his sleep-rumpled hair. He had the disheveled look of a man who had slept well.

"Tonight, you take the bedroom," she said. "I'll sleep on the couch. It's only fair we share." No way was she going back in there to freeze.

"You look cold."

She glanced at him sharply. Was he trying not to laugh?

"You knew that room was going to be an igloo. That's why you offered to take the couch."

Jake shrugged. "Ray told me in no uncertain terms to sleep on the couch."

He strolled into the kitchen and returned with a big mug of coffee. He silently offered it to her.

She melted towards it, holding the cup between her hands, absorbing the heat of the heavy clay mug. Taking a sip, she closed her eyes and savored the taste on her tongue. Perfection, just the way she liked it. He remembered how she took her coffee. The thought warmed her.

Sinking onto the couch, Noelle pushed Jake's sleeping bag to the side. She imagined she felt the lingering warmth of his body. Did he still sleep naked? The thought popped unbidden into her mind. Knock it off, she told herself.

Jake dropped down onto the couch beside her and took a sip of his coffee.

"It's still snowing. Doesn't look like it's going to let up soon."

"You've been out?" she asked. She thought he had just crawled out of bed.

"I shoveled the walk and moved the truck. No one's here, but us." He shook his head. "Doesn't look like anyone has been near any of the cabins in a long time. It's bizarre that someone would pay so much money to keep it up. The guy must be some kind of hermit."

Right—*keep it up*. Noelle almost choked on her coffee. Judging from the owners' reading material and other paraphernalia, truer words were never spoken.

When Noelle didn't answer, Jake continued, "I walked up the road. The snow is three feet deep in spots. If it warms up, it'll be a mess."

She nodded. West Coast snow melted fast. Sometimes a fluke storm dumped a ton of snow, and a day or two later, rain moved in.

"What do you want for breakfast?" Jake asked.

Noelle moved to stand up.

"No, you sit." He waved her back down. "I'll do breakfast. You can do supper. We'll split on the dishes."

She sank back onto the sofa. Jake cooking? She couldn't wait to see this.

In minutes, the scent of frying bacon filled the cabin. She sniffed appreciatively, and lured by the mouth-watering aroma, moved to sit on a stool at the kitchen island, where she watched Jake chop vegetables and scramble eggs.

"I could get used to this," she said.

"You should see me do Italian. Gino's take out, the house special pie. For ten bucks, they'll deliver a bottle of red wine."

"Breakfast." Jake announced, heaping two plates with bacon and eggs. The toaster popped. He buttered toast and slid the slices onto the edge of the plates.

"You look surprised? I really can cook. What's so amazing about that?"

"You never cooked," Noelle said, stealing a slice of bacon and nibbling on the end.

"Never?"

"Never." She shook her head.

"I must have." He frowned, thinking back. He didn't remember cooking. "I wasn't that bad?"

She didn't answer; she just met his gaze, her eyebrows slightly raised.

Her lack of reply told the story. But he liked cooking. He even watched cooking shows. In fact, he couldn't remember not being interested in food. Had he really been that self-absorbed? He was young—twenty-one was young. He hadn't even known who he was at that age. As a kid, he never had to cook. His mom had all the take-out places neatly printed on a paper beside the phone. When she wasn't working on some obscure research project, or his dad was home from one of his endless business trips, she cooked. Tacos, fajitas, nachos—no wonder he loved Mexican food.

"I was a jerk," he said.

"No." Noelle said. "Not really. We were just always running in different directions. I had school and you had work and hockey. Then you were trying to get into policing, while I was buried under a load of case studies and judicial opinions." She shrugged. "It was both of our faults. We shouldn't have gotten married. We were way too young and selfish."

The words hung between them. Jake was silent, uncomfortable with the direction the conversation had taken.

"Let's eat. It's getting cold," he said.

They sat on the stools at the breakfast bar to eat. Noelle picked at her food, nibbling on a piece of toast. From the looks of things, talk of the past had robbed her of her appetite.

She pushed her food around on her plate until Jake couldn't stand it any longer. He stood abruptly, and cleared his plate away, starting to run water for the cleaning up.

"Do you have snow pants?" Jake asked.

"Yes. Why?"

"I don't want to sit around. Let's go for a walk, or, if you want, I saw some cross-country skis in the shed. We could try those."

"I don't know how to cross country ski."

"It's easy. You downhill ski. It's like that."

The kitchen cleanup was quick. Noelle closeted herself in the frigid bedroom, yanked on ski pants, and wrapped a scarf around her neck. She found Jake dressed in ski clothes, stamping snow from his boots.

"Try these on." He held out a pair of dust covered cross-country ski boots.

She eyed them doubtfully. They looked like a fit. What was she worrying about? She had downhill skied for years; cross-country couldn't be any harder. At least it would stop the memories for a while. She grabbed the boots and sat down to lace them up.

30

"All right. I'm done. I admit it. I can't keep up," Noelle called, collapsing in the snow laughing. Her arms were rubber and sweat trickled down her back.

Jake heard her call and skied back, propelling himself forward smoothly, his arms and legs moving in perfect harmony. He slid to a stop beside her and looked down with a grin.

"You can't be tired. Your friend Maria told me that you were a lean mean machine. That I should be careful or you might kick my butt."

Noelle laughed. "She did, did she? Maria's protecting me. Nick must have been filling her in on ancient history."

"I figured she was warning me off. She kept telling me how you worked out a lot."

Noelle rolled her eyes. Just what else had Maria shared with Jake?

Jake bent down to adjust his ski and continued, "She also said that you were delicate, and that I should be kind."

Noelle snorted. "Maria has a master's degree in psychology and an over-active imagination. I'm just fine, Jake."

"You are that."

Noelle smiled. "I didn't think cross-country skiing was so much work."

"You did great. I should have warned you not to try stopping the way you do when downhill skiing."

The first hill they traversed had left her in a pile at the bottom. She had crossed the long skinny skis and momentum had rolled her down the hill like a giant snowball.

"You're a good teacher. Thanks for the lesson," she said.

He shrugged and dropped to sit beside her. The sky was full of endless snowflakes. Fluffy powder covered their jackets and cushioned their make-shift seat.

"It's so beautiful. It could snow forever if it stayed like this."

"Had enough skiing?" Jake asked.

"No, I thought we might go another mile or two."

He laughed. "It's harder than downhill. Everyone thinks it's easy, but it's a workout. I ski a lot. We head into the back country and camp if a few of us are off at the same time."

Jake continued talking, telling her funny stories about his work and life back east. In turn Noelle described the daily thrills and chills of working with a roomful of six-year-olds.

As the sweat cooled on her body, Noelle began to shiver. She was cold, but didn't want the moment to end.

"You're freezing. We should head back," Jake said standing.

"Yeah." Noelle nodded regretfully. "It's because I was working three times as hard as you were."

"No, you're getting the hang of it. We'll make a back-country skier out of you in no time."

Noelle didn't answer. By the time she was a competent back country skier, Jake would be back working the mean streets of Toronto. She gathered up her poles and stepped into her skis.

On the way to the cabin she concentrated on moving her arms and legs in sync with the forward motion of the skis. It was good to be outside breathing fresh air after the stuffiness of the classroom. Christmas was a few days away. Would she be home for it? The thought hit her with a suffocating weight. In the brief year she and Jake shared they hadn't lasted until Christmas.

Their tracks to the cabin were already buried under fresh snow.

"I'm just going to take a run to the edge of the village," Jake said.

"Who do you think is up here," Noelle asked. "We barely made it up here."

"I don't know." Jake shrugged. "It's better to keep your eyes open."

Noelle watched him go and then bent to unfasten the bindings on her skis. She kicked them off and leaned them up against the cabin wall. She sat down on the step to wait for Jake.

He returned and in unspoken agreement they grabbed their snow boots from the cabin. Neither one of them was ready to return to the ghosts of their earlier conversation.

"Should we put the skis in the shed?" Noelle asked.

"We may as well. It's better for the bindings."

Noelle picked up her skis and followed him to the shed behind the cabin. As she waited for him to stack the skis, she scooped up a handful of powdery snow. It broke apart in her hands as she tried to pack it into a snowball. The ski resorts would be happy this year. It had been a long time since they had received a major snowfall right before Christmas.

She imagined relaxing at a ski resort—a blazing fire, a glass of wine and a handsome attentive man... She studied the snow she had packed in her glove. No, don't do it. Jake's broad back was a tempting target. He wasn't paying any attention to what she was doing. Should she? Growing up with a bunch of brothers had taught her that the first two rules of throwing a snowball were aim well and run fast.

The snowball left her hand with uncanny accuracy. It arced cleanly through the air and hit the patch of bare skin at the base of Jake's neck. The loosely packed ball exploded in a cascade of white finding a dozen paths to the warm skin below. She didn't wait for Jake's roar of surprise. She bolted for the safety of the cabin.

Jake leapt in pursuit like a football player on a touchdown run. His long strides ate up the ground.

Noelle glanced back. He was gaining.

"Humph." Her toe caught a tree root and she sprawled face first. Jake landed beside her pinning her down. She squirmed away from the handful of snow he waved over her neck.

"No, Jake. Don't!" she gasped, trying to contain her laughter. She snatched a palm full of snow and rolled to face him, catching him in the face with the loose snowball. Snow clung to his eyebrows and rough growth of whiskers. It dropped off speckling Noelle's exposed skin, making her gasp at the sudden cold.

Jake settled his weight more firmly pinning her in place. He captured her hands in one of his holding them above her head. His eyebrows slanted upward as he lifted a fresh ball of powder.

"So you want to play rough," he said, threatening her with the snowball careless of the bits that broke free powdering her cheeks.

"No, Jake, get off." She shifted her hips to dislodge him, suddenly conscious of the solid warmth of his body. She stopped, realizing the more she struggled the more intimate the contact. The laugh froze on her lips.

"Jake?"

The handful of snow fell from his glove. He stared into her eyes. Slowly, he reached to touch her cheek, tracing its curve.

"You have snow on your face," he said.

He pulled his gloves off. His fingers were warm against the cold of her skin. Melting snow trickled down the neck of her jacket. Jake's fingers followed its path, leaving fire in their wake. He dipped his head and captured her lips in a slow hot kiss. His tongue traced the outline of her lips and he nibbled gently at the delicate skin. She pressed towards him. He released his hold on her hands. Noelle wrapped her arms around his neck pulling him down.

She ran her hands over his head, fingers raking through the dark curls as she met the onslaught of his kisses. Her touch followed the curve of his face, feeling the growth of his beard beneath her fingertips.

She felt the slow slide of the zipper on her jacket, and rocked closer. Far away, a voice told her to stop. It was too late. His hands trailed past the edge of her sweater, finding the hot skin waiting beneath, tracing the curve of her waist to her aching breasts. His fingers swirled over the crests, stroking and molding the peaks. Her nipples puckered into hard pebbles.

She moaned, then gasped as a pile of snow hit the back of Jake's head. Frosty flakes powdered her chest. She leapt to her feet.

Jake cursed, sat up and started shaking the snow from his head and collar. A Magpie perched on the swaying branch of the fir tree above began a raucous scold.

Noelle started to laugh.

"Nothing like a cold shower, eh?" she said, pulling the zipper on her jacket up, shivering at the wetness of her clothes beneath. That's what you got for rolling around in snow banks. What was wrong with her? More and more, she was forgetting the past and wanting Jake. She couldn't trust him, but damn, he was so appealing. She was a big girl. Why pretend nothing had happened, or might happen? Why keep fighting it?

She stood up, feigning an interest in brushing off the clinging snow, while searching for a way to ease the tension between them. She spied a pair of garden shears under the eaves by the woodpile. She and Jake were stranded here, but there was no reason that they had to skip Christmas. In front of them was an inexhaustible supply of fir and cedar, and their pick of trees.

"Did you see an axe in there?" she asked.

"Noelle. I'm sorry." He looked alarmed at the sight of the garden shears she was holding.

"Don't worry you're safe. We're going to go and find a Christmas tree."

"A tree?" He looked as if he doubted her sanity.

"Yes, a tree. It's Christmas in a couple of days. I refuse to miss it because of some lunatic. We're going to celebrate," she announced, plowing through the snow to the entrance of the shed. She peered dubiously into the gloom.

Jake moved to stand behind her. Apparently satisfied that Noelle's clippers weren't a threat to his manhood, he leaned in and inhaled the scent of her herbal shampoo. He lifted her hair and nuzzled the back of her neck.

"No, Jake." She gently swatted away his hands. "Work. Find an axe."

Reluctantly, he stepped back. He reached around her and recovered the axe he had used that morning.

"At your command," he flashed her a mock salute.

"Come on then," Noelle said, leading them towards the edge of the trees.

They spent the rest of the morning searching for the perfect tree, arguing over the requirements for perfection as they climbed over fallen logs and under low-lying branches. They finally agreed on a small Douglas fir. Jake chopped it down, and together, they dragged it back to the cabin.

"So now that we have the tree, what do you suggest we do with it? Jake asked.

"This is a ski cabin. It's used for winter vacations. There has to be a box of decorations somewhere."

"That would be true if we were dealing with normal people. You'll probably find a box of hand cuffs decorated with holly, and red and green glow-in-the-dark condoms," Jake muttered.

Noelle looked at him.

"What?" Jake shrugged. "It's hard to miss the sex toys in the bathroom."

Noelle laughed, and opened the door to the cabin. She stomped the snow from her boots and stood them on the rubber mat by the door. She headed for the bedroom and its closet full of boxes.

The neatly stacked boxes were labeled with black marker—linens, tools—she wasn't opening that one—ski clothes, Xmas.

"Found it," she called, freeing the box from the pile and dragging it into the living room.

"You've got to be kidding," Jake said, leaning over to flip open the top of the box. Nestled inside was a tree stand, strings of lights and decorations.

"See, it's meant to be." Noelle began rooting through the box. "These are pretty." She held up a set of delicate crystal snowflakes."

"I'll get the wine," Jake muttered, heading for the kitchen.

31

Noelle tilted her head to the side surveying the Christmas decorations she had placed on the mantle. Her head wasn't really in the decorating game. Lucky for her, the exquisite hand-carved decorations could be dropped onto a dollar store Christmas tablecloth and still look like a million dollars. She leaned forward and straightened a pewter Santa nestled in the branches of a fir bough and stole another glance at Jake. He had retreated to the kitchen and was once more staring out the window. Ten minutes ago, they had been laughing over a box of hideous Santa garden gnomes, but now he was quiet and unapproachable.

At least the decorating had offered a brief distraction, along with some festive charm. Branches of fir and cedar draped the mantle in shades of green. The air was rife with a woodsy scent. The candles sheltered in the branches cast a soft glow over the room. The lights on the tree twinkled off tiny crystal stars.

Jake had already stacked the boxes neatly back in the closet. At first, he had *"humbugged"* their attempts at decorating, but she had soon seen through his Ebenezer act. Deep down, Jake was more Bob Cratchit than Scrooge.

Decorating helped her forget that the cabin wasn't a holiday adventure, that there was a reason for their seclusion. Watching Jake pretend to scoff had supplied some much-needed laughter. That part of their relationship hadn't changed. They had always shared the same zany sense of humor.

Yeah, they had shared that right up until their last fight. Noelle settled onto the arm of the couch and stared at the newly decorated hearth. It was hard to forget that day. She had started the day feeling tired and crampy, and put it down to the stress of final exams and early pregnancy. She hadn't told Jake about the baby. She was still trying to sort out her own feelings. How could she possibly know how the free-spirited Jake would take the news? Besides, they had been fighting again, arguing over money, friends, school and life direction. A baby could be the last straw in their fragile relationship.

The big reveal was to have taken place that evening, but when she'd arrived home, she'd found Jake airing his sweaty hockey gear in the middle of the living room and the remains of his dinner—spaghetti Bolognese—splattering the kitchen counters and cabinets. She'd lost it. After another screaming fight, Jake had gathered his gear and stomped out. Noelle had thrown herself into a frenzy of crying and cleaning. An hour later, she was in hospital, blaming Jake.

From there, things snow-balled. She'd announced that she never wanted to see Jake again. True to her word, she never wavered and her brothers helped make it happen. Jim and Louise had balked at denying Jake the right to know, but Noelle was so overwrought, they followed her wishes. Noelle had gone from the hospital to her parents' house. Ray had told Jake that Noelle had "sprained her ankle kicking Jake to the curb." He had strongly suggested Jake was no longer welcome anywhere near her. Noelle had spoken to Jake once—telling him they were through and to take whatever he wanted and get out. Luck had sent Jake to police training school within the week. From there he had left the province permanently.

Thinking of that time left a sick feeling in her stomach. It was all so stupid. Why hadn't she told Jake then and there? She knew why. They were each so entrenched in their argument, neither one would open the lines of communication or admit fault.

Yeah, the truth was it was easy to blame Jake but she was just as bad. As an only girl in a bevy of boys, she had learned to be a diva early. On top of that, everything came easy to her. Marriage was hard. It needed to be worked at. The miscarriage was the first time in her life something was out of her control.

It was ironic. She had spent the last ten years pretending she hated Jake, but it was all a big lie. She had named her dog after him, telling herself it was a funny way of getting back at him. But she had never gotten over him. He was the match to her candle. One spark and she was on fire. It was torture being so close to him, pretending polite companionship. She didn't want companionship. She wanted flaming passion. She wanted him with the same wild abandon she always had. Today proved that. The sad thing was the only reason he was here was to do her parents a favor. She was a job—a little pro bono work.

Jake moved away from the window and pulled his phone from his hip pocket. He checked the connectivity display for the hundredth time. One bar—Ryerson had said that reception might be spotty—but the satellite phone should stay in range. Fat chance. He shoved the phone back in his pocket.

What the hell was he doing here? He was getting way too comfortable, *way* too focused on Noelle. The heavy snow wound him up tighter than a rookie the first day on the job. No, it wasn't the snow's fault. It was Noelle's. She was killing him. How had he gotten himself into this? The more time he spent with her, the more he wanted to kiss her, tumble her to the floor and explore the curves beneath her baggy sweater. The day had been picture-perfect, and perfect had never been a word to describe what they shared.

He moved from the window to the fridge, opened it, and stared blindly at its contents. Pushing the door closed, he paced the length of the kitchen. He felt like he was standing at the edge of a sheer drop. One look into the mossy depths of Noelle's green eyes, and he was falling. Only this time, there would be no recovery when he hit bottom. Nope. The drifting snow outside, and the cozy atmosphere inside, were making him forget his purpose for being here.

If it weren't for the cold shower supplied by the bird, who knew what might have happened. Noelle's silky skin beneath his hands, the scent of her perfume—he shook his head. So much for telling himself that he could spend time with Noelle and treat it like a job. One tiny test to his self-control, and he lost it. He'd thought he could play with fire and he'd gotten burned . . . again.

What was wrong with him? Since he had returned to Landings, Noelle had taken over his thoughts. It had started out a game. Matching wits with her had upped the sexual tension. Then, he had kissed her, and like a fool, instead of running, he had hung around. Then she had declared a truce—now he was an addict searching for that last fatal fix. How was he going to keep his hands off her?

"Jake?"

He jumped at the feel of her hand on his arm.

"What are you doing?"

"Looking for something to eat." He turned abruptly. "I'm going out."

Brushing past her he crossed the cabin, pulled on his boots and grabbed his jacket. The door slammed behind him, leaving Noelle stunned and staring.

Okay . . . Now what? Every time she thought they were beginning to make progress, something like this happened to spoil the moment. Was Jake feeling the same cabin fever she was?

Maybe he had the right idea. Keeping busy would use up some of the empty time. She'd grab a quick shower and see what she could make for supper. Great, she was becoming her mother. If you can't solve a problem, feed it. It was amazing Louise didn't weigh 300 pounds—but then again—Louise seldom ate the awe-inspiring food that she created. She didn't let Jim eat much of it either.

With her shower completed and still no sign of Jake, Noelle returned to the kitchen. Opening the fridge, she retrieved two steaks, seasoned them and set to work making a salad. That done, she leaned against the counter watching the falling snow and succumbing to the memories.

Spending time with Jake made her see the past differently. It let her touch the memory of the baby and her feelings of loss. She knew Jake wasn't to blame for the miscarriage. The doctor said sometimes nature just takes its course. There was nothing anyone could have done to prevent it. It was her own guilt over her ambivalence to the pregnancy that had made her look for a scapegoat. Jake had fit the bill. She had wanted him gone and burned the bridges behind him. She shook her head in self-disgust. She hadn't been fair, but should she tell him now? Would he want to know? If she told him, would he hate her for keeping it from him?

She heard the door open and close, and turned to greet Jake, glad for the distraction. Her memories weren't good company. She didn't want to be alone with them.

Jake kicked off his boots and dropped an armful of wood onto the growing pile by the fireplace. Wet snow clung to his hair and lashes.

"Where did you go?" Noelle asked.

"I walked down the road." He shrugged. "I don't do snowbound well."

"With you—" he didn't finish the sentence. He didn't need to. Noelle knew what he meant. She had the same sense of waiting, the feeling that every moment they spent together added another link to the chain between them.

Jake slouched out of his jacket and hung it on a peg by the door.

"Are you hungry?" she asked.

Jake's gaze dropped to her chest. After her shower, Noelle had changed into a thin knit sweater and jeans. The cold air let in by his arrival raised the hairs on her arms, and pebbled her nipples into tight buds.

"Hungry?" Jake repeated dazedly. He groaned. "Uh, sure, I'm going to grab a shower. The hot water heater should have warmed the tank by now." He bolted from the room.

32

Now what? Noelle tossed her hands up and scowled at the bathroom door. Jake was making her crazy. One minute he was rolling around in a snow bank with her, teasing her with sizzling kisses and fiery touches, the next, he couldn't stand to be in the same room. She blew out a sigh of disgust and rubbed her hands over her arms. The cabin was cold. Even with a fire roaring in the hearth, the temperature demanded action. It was time to dig out the heavy "granny-style" sweater she'd found at the bottom of the clothes box.

Still contemplating Jake, she shook her head. First hot, then cold. What did he want from her? What did *she* want?

If the temperature in the main cabin was wintery, the bedroom was an arctic outflow, cold enough to grow icicles. She found the sweater shoved to the back of the dresser drawer. Eureka. As she turned to pull it on, she faced her image in the full-length mirror. She blinked, looked again, and laughed. The thin sweater she had tugged on after her shower was sheer enough to expose the effects of the cold air on her breasts. Maybe Jake's frosty walks were his version of a cold shower. She scowled. Maybe she should try a frosty walk. It might wear off her sexual tension and stop her from dwelling on Jake. Although, in her defense, it was natural to be aware of the person you were sharing a small cabin in the words with, all alone, just the two of them . . . Stop. She told herself firmly.

She laid the sweater on the bed. Maybe she should test her suspicions. She nibbled her bottom lip, and stared down at the heavy cable-knit cardigan. It was definitely a granny sweater. If she put it on Jake's libido would be safe. On the other hand, maybe she should stop taking the safe route. Maybe she should rattle Jake's cage. It wasn't as though it could complicate things further. Her feelings for him were a mess. She would need a hundred years to sort them out, but his reappearance had energized her like nothing else could. It had always been that way. With Jake, she lost her perspective. With Jake, she took risks. That's why they had rushed headlong into marriage.

No, passion was never the problem. Sharing their lives was where they'd fallen short. If she were sane, she would strap on the sweater, button each of the big wooden buttons to the neck and add an armful of wood to the grate. Relationships were messy, they hurt, but she didn't want to do the smart thing. Out there in the snow, the feel of Jake's body against hers was so right. If the cold shower courtesy of the magpie hadn't shocked them to their senses, she would have risked hypothermia and made love to him then and there.

The sound of water running in the shower made Noelle's heart beat faster. Jake was in there, all alone, the warm rain slicking down his skin, stroking his— Stop it! Get a handle on yourself, girl. Making snow angels or seducing Jake in the exotic shower built for two were not options. Then why did the thought make her blood run hot?

She had made the Jake mistake before. But… they were different now—changed. She looked at the door to the bathroom. What if she took a risk, lived dangerously? Then again, what if she were reading this all wrong? What if this afternoon was nothing but Jake's response to a warm body?

No, it was Christmas, a time for miracles. Maybe that's what this mess was all about. It was a Christmas miracle meant to give them another chance. Right. Stress was turning her brain to mush. A Christmas miracle—who was she supposed to be—little Virginia? *Dear Santa, I know you're real. Can I have a second chance? Please wrap a ribbon around Jake and leave him on my pillow.* Did she *want* another chance? If one was offered, would she have the nerve to take it?

Turning her back on the sweater, she returned to the main part of the cabin. Everything was conspiring to push them together—the robbery, Jake's visit, the attack, this beautiful cabin—maybe it was all part of some deeper equation? Even the food packed neatly in boxes, set the stage for seduction. Bananas, chocolate, red chili peppers—how many tins of smoked oysters did two people need? It was as though the packer had googled foods with aphrodisiac properties.

Noelle opened the fridge door and looked inside. A bottle of white wine was chilling on the rack. She hadn't bought that brand in years. The wine, popular when she and Jake were together, was the wine served at their wedding reception, and the wine they'd shared on their first date. She pulled the bottle out, turning it in her hands, feeling the chill against her fingers. Coincidences—she set the bottle on the counter and rubbed her hands against the legs of her jeans—way too many coincidences.

She looked at the Christmas tree in the corner, the greenery on the mantle, and the subdued lighting. She couldn't plan a better seduction if she tried.

The water was still running in the shower. What was she going to do—flip on the lights, put the wine back in the fridge and pull on the bulky sweater or...? She grabbed the corkscrew, the wine and two crystal glasses and carried them to the coffee table by the fireplace. Quickly, before she lost her nerve, she dimmed the lights and lit more candles. There—she surveyed the room—the mood was set.

Now, for her part in the seduction. Back to the bedroom. She pulled out her ponytail holder, grabbed a brush, and coaxed her hair into a mass of sexy, tousled curls. Did she look come-hither enough? It would have to do. Beneath the thin sweater was a silky camisole. She opened a few buttons and checked the result in the mirror. No, it was all or nothing. With fumbling fingers, she undid the buttons. The sweater hung open, playing peek-a-boo with the silk beneath it. She took a deep breath and watched her breasts strain against the fabric. She smiled. Jake didn't stand a chance.

Dumping the contents of her purse onto the bed, she unearthed perfume and misted herself in a light floral scent.

She was rusty in the seductress department. She did a final check in the mirror. She had dated a few times after Jake, but no one measured up to her memories of him. The relationships had fallen apart after the big moment. Worse, she had felt a sense of relief when they did.

She hurried back to the living area before she could chicken out. Now what? Any second Jake would open the door. Should she pose? Where—the couch? She didn't want to look too obvious. The door to the bathroom opened and her jaw dropped.

Jake was gorgeous, no not gorgeous—beguiling, smoldering. He made her heart race and her palms sweat. He was wearing jeans; his feet still bare from the shower. His broad shoulders tapered to a narrow waist, the scattering of hair on his chest pointing a V to the unbuttoned waistband of his jeans. Come hither, Noelle. Where does this lead? She gulped. Who was seducing whom? She forced her eyes up to meet his gaze.

"Did the generator die?" Jake asked, looking back at the light shining in the bathroom.

"No . . . I thought we should conserve power." There. She had come up with a perfectly logical reason for the subdued lighting.

Jake headed for the suitcase he had left by the door. He tossed his dirty clothes in and grabbed a t-shirt. Standing by the fire, he pulled it over his head. His chest was muscular, the muscles taut. As he moved his pecs rippled and his biceps flexed. The flickering flames lit the hard planes of his stomach. Noelle licked her lips and moved jerkily to perch on the edge of the couch.

Jake looked from the wine back to Noelle. His eyebrows raised in silent question.

"Would you like a glass of wine?" she asked brightly, lifting the bottle in invitation. Not waiting for an answer, she poured two glasses, thrusting Jake's glass into his hands. She took a big swig, choking on the smokiness of the chardonnay. Cautiously, she took another sip.

"I made supper," she added. "Are you hungry?" Nice, Noelle, put it all out there. She was hungry. Who wouldn't be when faced with a half-naked Jake. The man was eye candy. He would tempt the biggest teetotaler to guzzle a mug of 151 Rum. Her cheeks heated to blast oven temperatures. "For food," she clarified, digging herself in deeper.

Jake considered her question. Hungry for food? No. Something else . . . he winced at the tightness of his jeans. Noelle and her mixed messages. He was going to need another cold shower. She had unbuttoned her sweater, revealing the silky shirt beneath it. His fingers itched to touch it, to feel the softness of the warm silk. He could see the outline of her nipples through the thin fabric. He moved warily in his seat. His groin ached. He watched her take another gulp of wine, draining her glass.

She set the glass on the table and leaned back against the overstuffed pillows, her finger idly curling a disheveled lock of hair. She looked relaxed, not keyed up and uncomfortable the way he was feeling.

"I thought it would be nice to sit and talk. You can tell me about Toronto," Noelle said.

Jake sat on the couch, carefully keeping his distance. Talk, yeah, talk was good. Conversation would keep his mind off Noelle and the soft allure of the curves beneath the silk. He changed position and gritted his teeth.

"Why did you become a teacher?" he demanded abruptly.

Noelle frowned. "I'd rather talk about you."

"We can, but I want to know what happened, what made you change your mind."

Noelle sighed and reached for her empty glass.

Jake leaned forward, filling it up, topping his up at the same time. He waited. He'd wanted to ask this question from the moment he'd seen her wearing the ridiculous bunny suit.

"I wasn't cut out for law. I didn't like the person I'd become, so I made the switch." She shrugged and continued, telling Jake about her decision.

As he listened to the musical cadence of her voice, Jake started to relax. This was new. Noelle and he had never sat and talked. Their lives had rolled out at a frenetic pace— school, hockey, friends, work. If they weren't on the move, they were beneath the covers, under the spell of their smoldering attraction. No wonder they had drifted apart. Sex was great, but you had to like each other to stay together. Hell, she hadn't even liked him enough to say a proper good-bye. She had sent her goon of a brother to get rid of him. He'd made a great first impression on the police instructors when he'd shown up for training sporting a black eye. Good old Ray, it must be killing him that Noelle was here with Jake now.

Noelle paused and took a drink—liquid courage?—and then hurried on. That was interesting. He studied her expression. What wasn't she telling him? What was she holding back? That's all right. She was entitled to her secrets.

He refilled their glasses again. Noelle finished speaking and relaxed against the cushions, her feet curled beneath her. She looked cold. He stood and tossed a fresh log onto the fire. When he sat down, he sat beside her. He tucked his arm around her, drawing her in. Her thin shirt couldn't possibly provide her with any warmth. He eyed the blanket draped over the back of the couch. No, this was better. Body heat was best for hypothermia. He knew that. He was an experienced outdoorsman.

"So, what about Toronto?" she asked, reminding him that it was his turn to share.

As he spoke, Noelle nestled against Jake's muscular body, savoring his heat. She breathed in the fresh scent of his soap, and the underlying masculine smell that was all his own. If she reached out, she could touch the golden hairs speckling his forearms. She laid her hand on his arm. He stilled, then abruptly carried on. Noelle cuddled closer, positioning her head under his chin, her breast nudging his arm.

Jake rested his chin on top of her head and wrapped his arms around her.

"Flowers," he said.

"Flowers?" she asked puzzled.

"You smell like flowers in a sunny garden on a hot summer day." He slid his hand down her arm. His fingers circled her wrist. Her blood pulsed beneath his hand. He bent his head and tipped her lips up to meet his.

This time, Noelle was ready for the kiss. She felt the power of the link between them as her lips met his in eager anticipation. She pulled him closer, her fingers sliding over the stubble on his jaw, thrilling at the rough rasp against her skin. Her breasts squashed flat against his chest, the friction, starting a delicious itch deep inside of her.

The kiss intensified and pulled her in, claiming her senses. She forgot why Jake and she wouldn't work. All she remembered was how good they were together. His mouth trailed tiny, nibbling kisses over her cheeks and down her neck, leaving fire in their wake. Impatient for more, she held his head still. His tongue teased her lips. Her mouth opened. The kisses no longer teased. They demanded. They left her breathless and wanting.

His hand brushed her ribcage as softly as a butterfly, slowly, deliberately, moving upward. She sighing as his palm curved over her breast. The thin silk of the camisole magnified the warmth of his touch, leaving a heat so hot she thought she would combust.

She pressed against his hand, wanting more, moaning as his fingers shaped her nipples through the cloth. She struggled to shed her sweater. Discarded, it slipped to the floor. Jake pulled her down on top of him. Grinding slowly against him, she ran her fingers over his face, discovering the changes in the planes and angles of his cheeks. His lips left hers, roaming down her neck. Her head fell back, opening her up to the warmth of his mouth.

He found the boundary of the silk camisole and shoved it up, the friction exquisite torture on her sensitive skin. His palms molded her breasts, his fingers teased her nipples. Impatient to be rid of the silk barrier between them, she sat up, lifting her arms over her head. Jake peeled the camisole over her head and pulled her back down.

"Wait," he said. "I want to feel you touch me." He sat up, impatiently yanking his t-shirt off.

Noelle laughed and straddled him, rocking her pelvis against his need. She ran her hands over the ridges of muscle lining his chest, brushing her fingers over his skin. Jake planted her more firmly against himself, as her hands edged downward to the waistband of his jeans. He caught his breath, and lifted his eyes to hers in unspoken question. Noelle nodded and pressed closer.

His hands shaped her butt, and stroked upwards to her breasts. He bent his head and licked and kissed until Noelle hummed with pleasure.

The kisses stopped. Noelle moaned in protest and tried to pull him back.

"Shh, love," Jake whispered.

He left her for a moment, wiggling out of his jeans and dropping them on the floor. His reached for the button on her jeans and helped her kick them free. The torment of his bare skin on hers was more then she could stand.

"I want you," she whispered. "Now."

She ached. She had to feel him deep inside. She pushed against him, feeling his need against her own.

"Are you safe?" he murmured.

Her nod swept away the barriers. He pulled her in, his body hard and urgent, seeking entrance. Noelle gasped, arching her back, pulling him deep, welcoming him back. The world dissolved. There was only the moment, only them and their desperate need for each other.

Afterwards, Noelle clung to him powerless to move away. Her skin was damp and glowing. She lifted her face to meet his kiss, languidly tracing a finger over his muscular chest. The crackle of the flames in the hearth was loud in the silence of the room. She closed her eyes and drifted to sleep snuggled close to Jake, feeling the rise and fall of his chest and the soft thud of his heart beneath her cheek.

33

Noelle's nose was cold, but the rest of her was blissfully warm. The hollow of Jake's shoulder was the perfect resting place for her head, the cocoon of his body wrapping her in its heat. She curled closer. Sometime during the night, one of them had reached up to pull the blanket down on top of them. She stretched, idly trailing a finger along the flat planes of his stomach.

"I wouldn't do that." Jake's voice rumbled against her ear. "Not unless you're willing to face the repercussions." His mouth slanted upward in a wicked grin as he propped himself up on one elbow.

Noelle laughed and pressed closer.

"And just what would those be?" she asked.

"I warned you," he growled, ducking his head and capturing her lips in a soul-stealing kiss.

This time, they made love slowly, exploring the changes, remembering the spots that sent each other crazy with desire. The slow touching fueled their passion, awakening the blazing hunger between them.

Exhausted, they collapsed together, their sweat-soaked limbs intertwined, hearts beating staccato. Jake brushed a curl back from Noelle's forehead and kissed her brow, before resting his chin on her head.

She turned her face into his shoulder. The moment should have been perfect, a homecoming, but the past's secrets hung heavily over her.

"Jake," she began softly and stopped. No, this wasn't the time. Later. There would be lots of time to tell him later.

"I'm really hungry," she said instead. Her stomach growled fiercely, backing up her words.

"Again? I don't think I can."

"No." She swatted him. "For food." Using his ears as handles, she pulled his head down, and kissed him deeply before rolling away, wrapping herself in the blanket. She stood, shivering as her feet hit the floor.

"Hey," Jake protested, grabbing for an edge of the blanket. Noelle slipped out of his reach. He sat up and fumbled for his discarded jeans. "Want to share a shower?" he asked hopefully.

Noelle laughed. Her face glowed with happiness. "We'd never get out."

"That was my point."

"Down, boy. You make breakfast. I'm going to grab a quick shower."

"It's better to conserve water and shower with a friend," he said hopefully.

"Nope, that would mean no breakfast, and I am starving."

She wrapped the blanket tighter and dodged away from his grasping fingers. Holding the blanket, she sauntered to the bathroom, leaving Jake to get dressed.

Regretfully, he moved off the couch to pull on his jeans and the discarded t-shirt from the night before.

He grinned, looking at the *Get Lucky* slogan emblazoning the front of the shirt. The beer brand labeled shirt was compliments of Noelle's brother, Nick. Nick had supplied Jake with the clothes for their escape. It figured that all the shirts bore some sort of advertising logo. Nick worked for a marketing company that promoted the beer industry. Grabbing socks from his bag, Jake covered his cold feet and crouched by the hearth to rebuild the fire.

"Breakfast," he muttered to the empty room. He had to admit he was hungry too. He checked the contents of the fridge. The steaks meant for supper were still marinating on the top shelf. He pulled them out—steak and eggs it was.

Noelle emerged from the bathroom, flushed from her hot shower. The aroma of frying steak and sizzling eggs wafted to her, along with the all-powerful scent of freshly brewed coffee. Strolling to the kitchen, she pulled up one of the tall stools, and perched at the breakfast bar to watch Jake work.

"Well, good morning." Jake's voice was deep and sexy. "Did you sleep well?"

"Hmmm. The best." Noelle smiled, accepting the steaming mug of coffee he handed her.

"It stopped snowing," Jake offered, nodding towards the window.

"No," Noelle protested. "It's too soon."

Jake nodded. "Yeah, I was looking forward to being snowed in with you."

Noelle sighed. Snowed in meant safety from lunatics who shot other people. Snowed in meant just Jake and her, free from the pressures of the outside world. Any moment the phone might ring ending their time together.

"What are you thinking?" Jake asked.

Noelle shook her head and looked away.

"Noelle." Jake stepped towards her.

The phone rang. Cursing, Jake pulled it from his pocket.

"Yeah," he growled, listened for a moment and grunted a good bye. He hung up and dropped the phone onto the counter.

"What?" Noelle asked. Good news or bad? She couldn't tell from Jake's face.

"That was Ryerson. He says the guy's gone to ground. If we're lucky, he's headed somewhere else. Sometimes when things get too hot in one place, they move away and start fresh elsewhere."

He gave her a reassuring smile that didn't match the troubled look in his eyes.

"What aren't you telling me?"

"Nothing. That's all he said. I promise. Scout's honor." He solemnly held up four fingers.

"You weren't a scout, and that's the Vulcan sign of peace."

Jake laughed and changed the subject. "After breakfast, let's ski some of the old trails, get a bit of fresh air. You up for it?"

Right. What Jake really meant was "Don't freak out."

He wanted to make sure that they were still alone. Fine by her. It meant more time together, more time to explore what was happening between them.

"Don't you think that you're overdoing the protective cop thing a bit? I mean, first off, he would have to know where we are, and secondly, he would have to be driving a snow plow."

"You're probably right," Jake agreed. "But we should stay alert."

They dished up breakfast and ate in companionable silence. Sunlight lit the long row of windows along the cabin wall. Outside, the pale blue sky was studded with long wispy clouds. The thick copse of trees lining the road drooped under the weight of piled snow. Already the sun was melting that snow. The trees were shaking off their burdens, dropping miniature bombs of white to detonate on the surface below.

After cleaning up, they changed into outdoor gear and met by the cabin door.

"Do you want to ski the old road?" Jake asked.

"Whatever you like," Noelle said. "Go easy on me. I'm still stiff from yesterday."

Jake raised his eyebrows and grinned.

"No, don't even go there," Noelle said laughing. "I meant from skiing."

Jake laughed and passed her jacket to her.

She zipped it up, nestled a hat over her ears, and stepped onto the porch. The touch of sun on her face felt good.

"If it warms up, it's going to be a fast melt," she observed, taking the cross-country boots and skis Jake offered.

Fastening the bindings, she tugged on her gloves, grabbed her ski poles, and dug in, following Jake towards the old road leading away from the village.

Snow had turned the dilapidated collection of cabins into a sparkling winter wonderland. Jake stopped to let Noelle catch up. He had fallen back into what Noelle called his "alert mode," scanning the buildings, studying the unbroken landscape of snow. He was edgy, worried about something he wasn't telling her. What had Ryerson told him?

"What did Detective Ryerson really say?" she demanded.

Jake shrugged. "What I told you." He didn't make eye contact.

An awkward silence fell over them. Noelle changed the subject.

"Do you remember the last time we skied here?" she asked.

"Which part? Where the axle broke, or making fifty trips back and forth to drag everything to the cabin. Or was it the part where too many people showed up and we had to sleep in the lean-to?"

"I forgot all that," Noelle said and laughed. "Anyway, the sleeping arrangements turned out fine."

"Remind me of what happened," Jake said, making a grab for her.

She laughed again and ducked away, skiing away from the empty village.

They picked their way along the road, listening to the raucous calls of the jays and magpies flitting through the trees.

"This is one thing I miss about the island," Jake murmured. "One day there's a massive snowfall, the next it's back to grass. That doesn't happen back east. There it's cold for months."

He bent, pretending to adjust the binding on his skis as his eyes swept the empty buildings and the long outcropping of untouched snow. He hadn't told Noelle

Ryerson's real news. Yes, Ryerson said the guy had failed to take the bait, but what Jake omitted was that Louise had misplaced the map to the cabin. Jim and Louise thought it may have become mixed in with papers meant for recycling and been sent out with the garbage. Jake on the other hand, remembered watching Louise tack the map to the corkboard on the night they left. Two tacks—one in each top corner.

Jake shook his head, trying to clear away his worry. Ryerson was a smart guy. Once traffic was moving again, he would have men watching the road to the cabin. Until that happened, the road would remain impassable until plowed.

"Jake," Noelle called.

He turned and found he had outdistanced her, leaving her behind on the trail.

"Sorry." He stopped and let her catch up. She was flushed and panting. "I forgot you were a beginner."

"I thought that you were trying to ditch me!"

"Never. Let's take a break. Here," he said, bending to clear the snow from a fallen log. He stepped out of his skis.

Noelle collapsed gratefully into the space beside him.

"I didn't think you were going to stop. Didn't you hear me calling?" she asked, pulling off her hat and shaking her hair loose. She took off her gloves and bundled the hair back into a ponytail, before looking up at him again.

"What's up? You're awfully quiet."

He shook his head. "Nothing, you were doing such a fabulous job of skiing that I forgot you were a beginner," he lied, leaning over to catch her lips in a kiss.

Her lips were warm on his and he pulled her closer. Would he ever get enough of her? He held her tightly, as if his grip could keep her safe. He knew better. So far, he had been powerless to protect her. With this break in the weather, the bad guy would be on the move. The missing map made Jake's warning radar ping. He hadn't stayed alive all these years by ignoring its caution. Something bad was headed their way.

"Come on." Reluctantly, Jake let her go and stood up. "Let's ski a bit more and then go find something to eat."

After all, they were safe for today. Once the snow started to melt and the roads cleared, that's when trouble would find them.

As they skied, the wind chased away the clouds. Towering evergreens sloughed off their blankets of snow and stretched for the bright blue sky. In front of them, the trail was an unmarked easel, the tracks of their skis the brush strokes.

In unspoken agreement, they set aside their worries. They spent the day exploring the trails, dined al fresco under the cloudless sky, and made love in front of the fireplace. As the sun drooped in the sky, they took a final ski run to the top of the ridge. Noelle was cold and impossibly happy. The thought of Jake and a roaring fire was more potent than the sweetest wine. She was done fighting her attraction to him.

"I'm going to ski down and check the road again," Jake announced. "You okay skiing back on your own?"

"Of course," Noelle said, slowly. "But that will be the third time you've patrolled the road today. What aren't you telling me?"

"I don't know…. Nothing. I'm just antsy. Until they get this guy, I'm not going to relax."

Fair enough. Noelle nodded. She understood that.

"Well, I'm going to light all the candles and fill that massive bath tub. Don't be long," she said with a saucy wink. A hot bath sounded good. It would sooth her tired muscles. The last couple of days had awoken some she forgot she had.

"With that image in my head? I'll be right behind you," Jake said, pulling her close for a cold kiss. He planted his poles in the snow and struck off strongly for the road.

Noelle watched him fade into the gathering twilight. She understood his disquiet. It seemed their dream world was coming to an end.

34

Noelle huffed out a breath of frosty air and made another careful turn. She was starting to get the hang of cross country skiing, enjoying the skating action Jake had taught her. It was getting colder. Dark clouds scudded across the face of the moon. The wind was picking up, ruffling the branches, blowing snow over their earlier tracks.

As she neared the cabin, her imagination kicked into overdrive. Jake's tension was contagious. She approached the porch, peering around the clearing, running her eyes over the snow, trying to pick out changes, anything new or different since they had left. Slowly she climbed the stairs and reached a hand to turn the doorknob. She pushed the door open with her foot and stepped back, poised to run when the boogeyman man jumped out. No, not the boogeyman man; a living, breathing crazy man with a knife. Nothing happened.

The cabin was as they left it, the fire burned to embers, the room icy.

Leaving her gloves on, she gathered bits of kindling and bent to gently blow on the cinders, fanning the flame back to life. Once satisfied the flame had caught, she fed the fire some larger pieces of wood and sat back on her heels. No matter which way she looked at it, it always came back to this. If she and Jake were to have a future, they had to return to their past. She had to tell Jake why she had run away from their marriage. She had to tell him about the miscarriage. He had the right to know, but would he understand how emotionally distraught she had been? Would he get her need to turn into herself and hide away?

It was the past. Ten years was a long time. She tried to ignore the ache of disquiet curling around her heart. She felt cold inside and out. Only by telling Jake would she find the answer to the question of their future.

Jake eyed the untouched snow running through the village. He had intentionally avoided the road leading to the cabins, knowing that the unbroken powder would offer the best warning of an intruder. He'd seen nothing—not a tire track, foot print, or man-made rut of any kind—so why was he twitching at shadows? Hell, he'd thought he'd heard the sound of a car engine earlier. Sure, he'd convinced himself it was the distant sound of a passing airplane, but the memory of the noise kept intruding on his thoughts.

Tomorrow he would call Ryerson and find a new spot to stash Noelle. It was up to Ryerson to keep Noelle safe. Until they found this nut bar, Jake couldn't afford to let down his guard. Right, no more giving into temptation. He looked up and blinked away a few falling snowflakes. Okay, maybe he could afford to be tempted for a little longer. It looked like mother nature was going to wallop them with more snow. As long as the snow kept falling, they were likely safe.

He reached the cabin, kicked off his skis, and leaned them against the wall. Taking a last look back at the tree line, he strained to see any movement in the shadows. Nothing. He shook his head, trying to ignore the creeping feeling between his shoulder blades.

Noelle heard the cabin door open and close. She dropped the pre-packaged tray of appetizers she was holding and turned to greet Jake.

"What?" she said, her heart sinking at his expression. "Did you find something?"

"Nothing. I don't know—I guess I'm feeling spooked."

"Welcome to my world. I've been feeling that way since the shooting. I have gotten so uptight—" She stopped. No way was she going to tell him that she thought she'd heard the sound of a car engine when they had been skiing the upper logging road. He'd think she'd finally snapped.

Turning back to the fridge, she spied the untouched salad. Maybe tonight they would have the chance to eat supper.

Jake slipped his arms around her waist and laid his cold cheek against hers.

"You're freezing. Get away from me." She laughed and struggled to escape.

"Not so fast. I need warming up." He hugged her closer, playfully tugging her shirt loose from her pants and laying his cold hands on her bare stomach.

"Jake, stop it." She laughed and turned to face him.

"Uh huh, trapped, just where I want you." His lips captured hers. His hands shaped her butt, pulling her up against him.

Noelle couldn't stop herself. She rocked against him, leaning into the kiss. A soft moan escaped her. She forgot the icy hands on her warm midriff. She was melting. It was happening again, the Jake spell. They couldn't be in a room for two minutes without wanting each other. She wanted him right now, right here. Her hands framed his face as she deepened the kiss.

Jake's hands spanned her waist and he lifted her, sitting her on the counter, stepping between her legs. His fingers traced the top of her jeans, pausing at the button. She sucked in her breath. He smiled, slowly working the button free. He kissed her belly button, his tongue swirling over her skin. Gripping the zipper pull with his thumb and finger, he nudged it down. Noelle gasped. She was going to implode. Her breath caught.

Jake's cell rang. Their eyes met and he turned away swearing as he yanked the phone from his pocket. Noelle slid off the countertop, zipping and buttoning her jeans.

"Hey, I don't agree with you. My wi— ex-wife's safety is the only thing that matters." Jake shook his head. "No, that's not . . . Hello? Damn." Jake threw the phone onto the counter.

"What?"

"No signal. Bloody Ryerson. I told him I wanted you out of here tomorrow."

"Why?"

Jake shook his head. "Something's not right."

The sexy playmate of a moment ago was gone.

"You want me to pack?"

"No. The weather's taken a turn for the worse. It's snowing again, and the roads are closed. He said nothing is getting through. They can't send a chopper in this mess either. He thinks we're safe for now."

"But you don't?" Noelle asked.

"I don't know." Jake tossed his hands in the air and turned away. "I'm going to grab a shower," he said.

Noelle nodded silently. When he came back, they had to talk. It was time they set the past free, otherwise she would always feel guilty, as if she were hiding something. "Okay. I'll throw these in the oven."

"You could join me. We could pick up where we left off." He caught her hand and pulled her to him, placing a teasing kiss on her lips.

Noelle leaned into it, losing herself to the moment.

"Well?"

Mutely she shook her head. She wanted to—wow, how she wanted to—but they had to talk first.

"Okay, but you don't know what you're missing." Jake winked at her and sauntered towards the bathroom, doing a slow striptease on route.

Noelle leaned up against the counter.

"Be still, my foolish heart," she muttered. It took every ounce of her self-control to not rip off her clothes and plunge into the shower with him, but she had promised herself that she would start again fresh, this time with no secrets.

She opened the oven door and picked up the salad. Shaking her head, she dropped the bowl back onto the counter and grabbed the tray of appetizers. Jake would scramble the brain of a nun.

She curled up in one of the overstuffed easy chairs to wait and fell asleep, waking when he gave her shoulder a gentle shake.

"Hey, dinner's ready." His voice was low and seductive.

"I sat down and was out like a light. It must be all the fresh air and exercise," Noelle said stretching.

Jake raised his eyebrows and they both laughed.

After dinner, they settled onto the couch, cuddling close, watching the flames. Jake's hand stroked her hair.

"I can't get enough of you," he whispered in her ear.

His lips trailed over her neck leaving kisses that demanded more. As he pulled her closer, the kisses deepened. Need and want overwhelmed her senses. Tomorrow—they could talk tomorrow. She reached up pulling him down. His lips tugged at the delicate skin of her earlobe, passing over her neck, bringing goose bumps in their wake.

"Now, Jake," she gasped.

Impatiently they tugged at each clothes needing to feel only skin between them.

Later, they curled under the blanket, too sated to stir from the embrace. Jake moved first. He rolled over, a smile tugging up the corners of his lips.

"Jake," Noelle said. She pushed herself up on her elbows and stared at his face, memorizing every plane of his features. "We have to talk."

Jake sighed and sat up. He nodded slowly.

"I guess we have to do the autopsy before we bury the past."

Noelle scrunched her nose in disgust. "Yuck. You couldn't come up with a better adage than that?"

He shrugged. "I'm a cop. Sue me."

He pulled her into his arms and tucked her head under his chin. He wanted to stay like this, but she was right. They had to talk. Their past had fixated him all afternoon. He had to know what had gone so wrong between them that she could walk away without a backward look.

"Why the restraining order?" he asked. He sat up and reached down to grab his jeans and t-shirt from the floor.

He sensed this was a conversation that would go better with clothes. "I don't get it. What the hell happened?" He sat back down facing her.

Noelle moved more slowly, wrapping the blanket around herself before reaching for her scattered clothing.

She had been dreading this moment since she had felt the first stirrings of closeness between them. Was she ready to revive that time and expose it to the light? It was easier to leave it tucked away in its closed box where she didn't have to think about the loss. Stalling, she fastened the last button on her sweater and wrapped the blanket around her shoulders.

Jake watched her, trying to analyze her changing expressions. A growing sense of uneasiness gripped him. This was bad. Whatever she was going to say, he wasn't sure he was ready to hear. He waited.

Noelle sat on the edge of the coffee table. She needed distance between them. Telling him meant tearing down ten years of walls. Could she trust him? She raked her fingers through her hair, starting when he gently took her hands in his.

"Noelle." His voice commanded her to meet his eyes. "You're scaring me. I just want to know how we went so wrong."

His fingers were strong and warm.

"I love you," he said.

Her eyes jerked to meet his gaze. She couldn't answer.

"Wow," Jake said, dropping her hands and moving back. "I never saw myself as a one-night stand kind of guy." He half-smiled.

Noelle stood and moved away from him. Stopping in front of the fire place, she looked back. His hair was disheveled from their lovemaking, his eyes worried. Her heart ached. Would he still love her when she told him about the baby, how she blamed him, but never let him share her grief? Would he care that she had never told him about the life they had created? Her hands clenched, her knuckles whitening.

She had to make him understand how grief and guilt had made her crazy, how she had pushed everyone away, that she had thought she was losing her mind. Her doctor had blamed stress and hormones. He'd sent her to an amazing life coach, who helped her make the changes that made her who she was today. The only thing she had never done was admit that their failed marriage wasn't all Jake's fault. It was easier to place the blame on him than admit that she was as selfish and immature as she called him.

She flashed another glance at him. Surely, he remembered how they had been. Would he understand? Would he forgive? She shivered. She knew the answer to that because she hadn't forgiven. She had nursed her anger for ten years.

She took a deep breath. This was getting her nowhere. He had a right to know. She had to tell him. What happened after that they would deal with together. She tried to crush the tiny seed of doubt sprouting within.

She didn't know how to begin, so she said it bluntly. "Ten years ago when we split up, I was pregnant. No, let me finish." She held a hand up to stop him from speaking. She had to let this all out. She told him baldly with no embellishments, letting out all her anger and the depth of her blame for him. Finally, she was silent.

Jake stood up. He took a step towards her before catching himself.

"How could you? I had the right to know. This was important. You acted like it was all about you. You punted me to the curb as if my feelings counted for nothing."

He shook his head as if to clear his thoughts.

Noelle stood quietly, tears creeping down her face.

"I'm sorry." She reached out to him, her hands suspended between them.

Jake stepped back avoiding her touch as a wintry façade fell over his face. Her hands dropped to her side.

The lights flickered and the distant rumble of the generator faded to silence, leaving only the faint sputter of the coals.

35

The loss of power plunged the room into darkness. Without the faint electrical hum of the generator, it was quiet, so quiet Noelle imagined she could hear the candle wicks sputtering in their pools of wax. Jake was positioned in front of the fireplace, his face limned by the light of the flames. As Noelle watched, his expression hardened into a mask of hurt and disappointment. His eyes, twin chunks of ice stared at her in accusation.

His coldness stabbed her. Slowly her hopeful heart began a free fall back to earth. Her worst fears crystallized into sharp reality.

"Jake?" Noelle began hesitantly.

He held up a hand.

"You have to say something. You have to talk to me."

"Now you want to talk… now… I'm going to check the generator," he muttered and crossed to the door.

He yanked on his boots, tore his jacket from the hook and turned to face her.

Noelle took a step towards him.

"Jake, you don't understand."

"What's to understand? You didn't want me so you sent your brother to warn me off."

"No, Jake. I didn't." It was Noelle's turn not to understand.

"Just don't, okay." Jake shook his head sharply and turned away. He left slamming the door behind him.

Noelle wrapped her arms across her chest. A chill ran through her. She wanted to run after him, to make him understand why she had acted the way she had. She listened for the sound of his returning steps. Nothing. Slowly her rigid control slipped. She sank onto the couch as a strangled sob ripped from her throat. What a fool she was. Oh god. Jake! She buried her face in her hands. How could she have thought he wouldn't care?

She hadn't given him the chance to comfort her over the loss of their baby. She had pushed him away and immersed herself in grief and hurt, angry he wasn't there when she needed him. Instead of letting him in, she blamed him for not caring. Deep down she believed the miscarriage was her fault, caused by something she had done or failed to do. She had succeeded at everything she had ever tried, but when it came to something so fundamental, she failed. The doctors said the pregnancy wasn't viable. It was doomed from the beginning. Needing someone to focus her grief and anger on, she picked Jake as a scapegoat.

She collapsed into the soft cushions of the couch, curled into the spot where they had lain and held the blanket to her face. The scent of his aftershave lingered on the wool. She cried until exhausted she fell asleep. When she woke, the cabin was dark and empty.

"Jake?" No answer. She peered down at the illuminated face on her watch. Nine o'clock. She'd been asleep for two hours. Jake should be back.

She struggled to sit up, wrapping the blanket around herself for warmth. Using the light on her watch as a lamp, she stumbled to the fireplace and rekindled the flames. Where was he? By now he should have fixed the generator and returned.

The ends of her fingers were cold and numb. She held her hands out to the heat watching as the fire licked greedily at the logs. New life. A new beginning. Somehow she had to make Jake understand why she had done what she did. Her grief and guilt had made her lash out at the very person she should have gone to for comfort.

She frowned at the dull gleam of her watch, and crossed the room to the window overlooking the porch. It was snowing again, the sky opalescent with clouds covering what had earlier been a full moon. Jake wouldn't leave her here alone no matter how angry he was. Once he committed to something he didn't quit. He might hate her, but he would protect her to his last breath. Fresh tears leaked from her eyes. She should have remembered that.

Angrily she brushed the tears away. Enough crying. It was time to woman up and make him see that what they had together was worth more than the sum of their past. Jake was out there licking his wounds, convincing himself that the past was insurmountable. She had to stop him before he built the walls around his heart so thick she couldn't get through them.

She stepped into her boots and tucked the legs of her jeans deep inside. Together she and Jake could fix this. She would make him see that. Pulling on her jacket, she turned and picked the flashlight up from the table beside the door. She frowned. Jake would have taken the flashlight if he'd planned to be gone long.

Now she was really worried. A sick feeling burned in

the pit of her stomach. The Jake she remembered didn't play games. He would have come back to the cabin and told her exactly what he thought of what she had done. He couldn't have changed that much.

She opened the door to a gust of snow-laden wind. It blasted through the open jacket raising a swath of goose bumps over her chilled skin. Juggling the flashlight, she struggled to unite the two halves of the zipper. Yanking the pull to the top, she flipped the hood over her head and tied the string tightly under her chin. Face to the wind, she squinted out at the dark. Against the silver sky snowflakes swarmed like millions of dull white butterflies, looping, lifting and plunging to earth, chased by a wind that scooped them up and tossed them out again. The ski village vanished behind a blanket of white.

Cold pierced the opening around her face, stinging her skin like icy needles. She gripped the neck of her jacket and held the hood closer. The towering wall of cedar trees at the edge of the clearing was a blurry smudge on the horizon. She crossed the porch and struggled down the stairs.

"Jake!" she called shining her light over the snow.

The wind snatched her words and tossed them back in her face. Cupping her hands, she shouted again before stopping at the base of the stairs to search for tracks. The wind had scoured the snow clean. She stepped thigh-deep into a drift and plowed through it calling his name.

Turning back, she looked at the faint light emanating from the cabin fighting the urge to turn tail and run for its safety. No, she had to find Jake.

"Jake, answer me," she yelled.

Above her head, a disgruntled raven launched itself from the high branches of an overhanging tree. The bird soared towards the forest sending a cascade of snow down on her head. Noelle shook off it off and thrust her cold hands into her armpits.

Where are you Jake?" she muttered, half-angry, half-worried. It appeared he'd sprouted wings and, like the angry bird, vanished into the night.

36

Blowing snow stung her face making her eyes water, flash freezing the tears on her skin. Lifting her arm, she shielded her eyes and squinted in the direction of the generator shed. Wandering around in a blizzard wasn't the smartest idea she'd ever had, but what else was she going to do—sit on the couch and wait for Jake to come to her? No, she had to go to him.

The generator shed had vanished in a sea of grey. It was out there, a stone's throw from the cabin, but the shifting wind offered only tantalizing glimpses of it. She took a step forward and stopped. Snow storms were dangerous. You only needed to watch a few wilderness movies to know you shouldn't set foot into a blizzard unless you had a rope tied around your waist with someone belaying you on the other end. Right, well—she was fresh out of rope and there was no one lining up to hold it anyway.

Finding Jake should be easy. He wouldn't be out wandering aimlessly in the blizzard. No, he would be hunkered down waiting for the storm to abate. That's what she should be doing, not stumbling around risking frost bite.

Her toe caught the edge of a buried root and she tumbled forward. The deep snow made the fall more of a slow-motion face plant, but she dropped her flashlight and ended up shoulder deep in powder. Cursing she fumbled for the light, shaking the snow off before turning it back on. This really was a stupid idea. She should go back to the cabin and wait.

Yes. Go back, thaw out and let Jake have time to cool off. She hesitated. No, allowing Jake time to think would let him rebuild his defenses. It would bring a return of the Jake who had first appeared on her front porch—charming and funny with a cold light in his eyes that said, "Let's play, but keep your distance." The Jake of the last few days was the Jake she wanted.

She shone her light towards the shed. She'd start there. Jake had shown her the generator on the first day. He'd pointed out the propane holding tank and drilled her on how to restart the engine if the power went out.

The door to the shed was partially open. Drifting snow sifted through the gap and buried the low step. The shed looked abandoned. She shivered. There was no way Jake was inside, but she had to check. She pushed the door open and panned her light over the empty room. Jake had removed the generator cover and leaned it against the wall. A screwdriver rested on the oily guts of the motor.

Noelle pushed the door closed stopping the wind. Worry warred with her frustration. People didn't vanish off the face of the earth. Jake had gone looking for tools. There was a fully-stocked workshop nearby. Find that and she'd find Jake.

She pulled the door open and stepped back into the blowing snow. Visibility was dropping by the minute. Wistfully, she looked back at the cabin. A few minutes of warmth would melt the cold from her skin. It would also melt her resolve. It was too easy to stay inside where it was warm and dry, too easy to be a coward and hide out until the upheaval melted. She'd done that before and look how things turned out—ten years of misunderstanding. No, she had to keep going. Grimacing she tucked her chin into her collar and stepped away from the shelter of the shed.

The wind whipped through the trees, slashing the branches and littering the snow with chunks of greenery. She could distinguish only a few feet in any direction.

"Welcome to my snow globe," she muttered, thinking of the Christmas ornament sitting on her desk at school. This must be how Mr. Snowman felt when one of her students rocked his world.

"Jake," she called. Her voice vanished in the void.

She should have paid more attention when Jake told her about the workshop, but she'd been distracted by the coldness of his nose on the warm skin of her neck. He'd called the shop a handyman's fantasy. The owner had collected every tool known to man, hanging them carefully on the wall like relics from a big game hunt. Jake figured the aging owner used the shop as a hideout from his trophy wife. Aside from the bounty of tools, the shop boasted a wood burning stove and a fully-stocked bar hidden in a cabinet marked solvents. The only thing missing was a big screen television. Maybe that's where Jake was, waiting out the storm with the key to the solvent cabinet for company.

She swung the beam of her light one way and then the other. Where would you build your refuge if you were an uber-rich businessman with a disgruntled wife? At the edge of the tree line she decided. He would want to be as far from the cabin as he could get. She picked her way over the uneven ground trying to avoid another tumble. Her jeans were soaked, her legs numb.

Jake wouldn't just walk away. Ten years ago, he'd camped out in front of her parent's house demanding to see her. He'd called, banged on the door and waylaid Louise in the parking lot of the grocery store. It had taken a *Dear Jake* letter backed by a restraining order to make him leave her alone. Ray had delivered the letter. What else had he handed out? Jake and Ray had never gotten along, but now both were openly hostile. No, Jake wouldn't just walk away. He would come back and tell her his opinion of what she had done.

She waded through a snowbank, wincing as snow filled her boots. Her fingers locked around the flashlight in a death grip. The light was useless, its glow eaten up by the whiteness of the swirling snow, but knowing it was on made her feel better.

At last she stumbled into the wall of a cedar shed. Dark chocolate siding stretched to a peaked roof framed by carved wooden beams painted white. Long flower boxes ran the length of the walls on either side of the door. Above the entrance a whimsical carving of an old man's face stared solemnly down at her.

"Jake?" she called, shoving her shoulder against the door. It swung open a hands-width and stopped. Inside the shed was inky blackness.

"Jake, are you in there?"

She pushed the door again, trying to shift it. Dropping to her knees, she aimed the light through the gap. She'd found him. Jake lay on his left side facing the door.

"Jake!"

She thrust her hand through the crack and touched her frozen fingers to his face. His skin was marble cold. Sliding her hand to the neck of his jacket she felt for the thud of his pulse. Her breath escaped in a sigh of relief.

"Dammit, Jake. Why couldn't you fall away from the door?" she muttered.

Positioned flat against the wall of the shed, she stretched her arm through the crack. Somehow she had to roll him onto his back. That would give her enough space to slide through the gap. She flattened herself against the wall and stretched . . . a little more . . . damn. She straightened and changed positions. She couldn't get the leverage she needed to reach his shoulder. Turning her head to one side with her breasts squashed against the shed, she tried again. This time she touched his shoulder. She pushed hard. Jake flopped limply onto his back.

Noelle flung her body at the door. It moved and stopped. She pushed harder. It inched further. Dropping to her butt, she braced her hands against the doorframe and pushed with her legs. Jake groaned and rolled away.

She squirmed through the opening catching her belt loop on a nail. The nail tore loose, scraping her hip. She winced and wriggled the rest of the way through.

Kneeling by Jake's side she ran her fingers over his head, checking for injury. She found an egg-sized lump behind his left ear. Her hands dropped to her thighs and she rocked back on her heels looking down at his face. His eyelashes were dark smudges against the pallor of his cheeks.

He moaned and moved his head. His eyelids fluttered and he lapsed back to stillness.

Noelle touched his cheek and bent to brush her lips across his forehead. He was alive—she shook his shoulders and his head flopped to one side—but he was out cold. She glanced around the shadowed workshop. She had to get him back to the cabin. Here the temperature was only a few degrees warmer than outside. The icy wind blowing through the open window above the workbench wasn't helping. Snow had drifted in layering the surface in an uneven pile.

Climbing up on the bench, Noelle slammed the window shut and rammed the lock into place. As she turned a gust of wind caught the door, swinging it back against Jake. Her heart hammered in her throat. Jumping down she ran to the door and shoved it closed. Hands resting against the wooden planks, she held it shut, half-expecting it to burst open in her face. The door stayed fastened and slowly her heart rate returned to normal speed.

Turning around she checked the room, eying the racks of tools hung tidily on the wall, the neatly swept floor. There was nothing to explain the unconscious Jake or the bump on his head.

Jake had come to the shop for tools to fix the generator. He hadn't opened the window. He had no reason to. She ran the flashlight beam over the floor again. A tool belt lay next to his right arm. He'd come in, grabbed the tool belt, and turned to leave. An open window would have been a warning to him. It would have spelled danger. Jake was smart and armed. Ryerson had given him a revolver... and that revolver was back at the cabin where Jake had left it. He'd been thinking of the past not the present.

She looked at the work bench. Everything was swept to one side, suggesting an escape route out. Noelle's heart thudded in her chest. Someone had been here hiding. That person had attacked Jake as he turned to leave. With Jake down in front of the door and no way of knowing if Jake was alone, his attacker had chosen the window as a quick escape. She looked around the room expecting to see someone lurking in the shadows.

She drew in a slow deep breath. She'd known they had company since she'd heard the sound of the engine that afternoon. She should have told Jake. He'd been edgy all day. Maybe he had heard it too. She should have believed in herself instead of second-guessing herself. Now all that didn't matter. She had to get help. Jake's attacker may have retreated but he was still out there. With Jake unconscious, it was up to her to get help. Without it, Jake would freeze.

She ran her hands over his pockets searching for his phone. Tugging it loose, she checked the service signal. Two bars. Jake said service was patchy. Seeing the indicator at the half-way mark was reassuring. She found Ryerson's number, pressed call, and waited. Someone picked up.

"This is Ryerson. I'm out of the office at the moment. Leave a message, and I will return your call."

"Dan, it's Noelle. We need help. Jake's hurt . . . Hello?" She pulled the phone away from her ear, swearing as the device powered down and the screen went blank. She dropped it onto the floor. She was on her own.

"Jake . . . Jake!" she called, shaking his shoulders, hoping he'd magically wake up. His eyelids fluttered. Her heart jumped. He snored and lapsed back into dream land. She touched his face. His skin was colder. How long was he laying here?

They'd picked the ski hill for its isolation. The blizzard was a bonus, making the roads impassable. The last-minute decision meant only Ryerson, Ray and her parents knew the plan. There was no way anyone could predict they were here unless that person had inside knowledge. What happened? What hadn't Jake told her?

"What the hell Jake? Why didn't you warn me?" she asked the unconscious Jake. "Did you think I'd panic? Dammit Jake. You should have told me what was going on."

She turned away from him and stared blankly at the tools hung neatly on the wall as she considered her options. She had to get the gun. She had to find someplace to hide Jake until help arrived. When Jake failed to check in, Ryerson would come looking for them. Her partial message would get him moving. Until then she needed a place to stash Jake.

Climbing to her feet, she searched the shop, hunting for a spot he'd be safe. She found a niche against the back wall where a pile of canvas tarps was stacked under an open counter. The tarps would provide camouflage and insulation. Pushing the pile to one side she hurried back to Jake, dropping down to kneel beside him. She shoved her arms under his armpits and pulled. Grunting, she managed to move him forward a few inches. This wasn't going to work. She needed something to slide him with.

Lowering him to the ground she returned to the pile and pulled a tarp off the top. She shook it open and pushed and rolled Jake onto it, aligning him on his back. Wrapping the corners of the tarp around her fingers. She dragged him across the room. Her back collided with the wall. Gasping in relief she sank to her knees. Sweat pooled in the small of her back. Her breath escaped in harsh rasps. She flexed her back and rolled her shoulders before checking his pulse one more time. It was slow and steady beneath her fingertips.

"Jake, I'm not leaving you. I'll be back. I love you."

There she'd said it. He might not have heard her, but if something happened she had told him how she felt. She kissed his lips and picked up the flashlight, turning it off. She didn't need the light. It would act as a beacon. She made her way to the door of the shed.

37

Noelle struggled through another snowbank. She wanted to stop, curl up and rest, but she kept going, dragging one foot forward and then the other. The adrenalin that had first fueled her was gone, robbed by a wrong turn that left her stranded on a logging road. Retracing her steps had been a killer uphill butt-burning workout. Now her legs were blocks of wet cement, heavy with no substance. Bouts of shivering racked her as her muscles worked overtime to generate body heat. On the plus side, the bad weather didn't play favorites. The wind would scour away her tracks, and with those gone, Jake's attacker wouldn't know she'd found him. He'd concentrate his hunt on her. That would keep Jake safe.

She forced her way through another thigh-deep drift. On the surface the snow looked flat. In reality the ground beneath was riddled with holes, roots and logs. A blast of wind buffeted her tossing her hair in her face. She shoved it out of her eyes and stopped again, trying to get her bearings. She had left her hood down in order to hear a warning of danger, but with the wind screaming in her ears and her heart pounding a continuous drum roll, Jake's attacker could have popped up and yelled boo before she knew he was there.

The broad wall of an empty cabin loomed before her. She leaned against it catching her breath, looking out at the shifting outline of another outbuilding. Being in the open made her vulnerable. She had to keep moving. Ignoring the burning cramp in her side she bolted across the clearing. Collapsing against the wall of the building she faced the road in front of her.

Travel was easier on the road, but it left her exposed. Safer to stick to the tree line. It offered an escape route. She slid down a shallow gulley to the edge of the trees. Snow crept up her thighs. It soaked her jeans and packed her boots. Her skin was so cold, she no longer felt the sting of twigs lash her legs. She flopped under the hanging branches of an ancient Douglas fir across from their cabin.

She was ready to drop. Bracing her hands on her knees, she sucked in a few deep breaths. Sweat trickled down her back, chilling to slush beneath her shirt. Her goal was so close—the cabin—with the discarded revolver laying on the table by the couch. The memory of how it had ended up there conjured a tired smile—Jake and his slow strip tease, tempting, tantalizing . . . The shoulder harness with the dull black Glock was the first thing off. Once she got her hands on the gun, could she use it? Did she have the guts? She was scared enough. She didn't have to fire it. She could wave it around and pretend she'd have no problem pulling the trigger.

A flicker of light illuminated the window, remnants of the fire she had left roaring on the grate. Inside it would be warm and welcoming. She could find dry clothes, grab blankets and get back to Jake. Instead of moving she remained tucked in the shadows beneath the branches. The opalescent white of the sky reflected off the shifting snowflakes leaving the night as bright as midday. Was the Cobra in there? She had no doubt that he was the one hunting them. With Jake down, he'd be looking for her. She stared at the door—the only way in, the only way out.

She couldn't look away. Move Noelle. She tried to make herself stand, but it was too much work. Slowly the burning ache drained from her legs, her breathing eased. A sense of calm invaded her. She stared at the cabin until her vision blurred.

Something changed. In the empty space in front of her was a new shadow. She straightened, staring hard at the spot. Move again she urged silently. Show me you're real, not my imagination.

A man climbed the stairs. At the door, he hesitated turning to look back at the trees. His eyes skimmed past her and a wave of déjà vu slammed her. She was back in the convenience store as cold eyes swept the end of the aisle. She froze, even though this deep in the shadows she knew she was invisible. He twisted the knob and pushed open the door.

Her eyes fixed on the opening as she slid from her hiding place. Her knuckles scraped the tree's rough bark drawing blood, but her hand was too cold to feel the pain. Returning to the cabin was now impossible. She had to get back to Jake.

Could she get to the skis? No. The boots were in the cabin. Besides, she couldn't leave Jake alone and defenseless. And then there was the fact she couldn't navigate her way out of a paper bag. She'd be lost in about a minute. She'd probably fall off a cliff and break her leg.

There was also the little matter of the blizzard. As for the truck—useless—snow buried it to its wheel wells.

Breaking glass drew her gaze back to the cabin. A round of cursing reached her. She smiled grimly. Did he think she was hiding there waiting for him to find her? The smile faded. Would he go after Jake? The door banged open bouncing off the wall. He'd helped himself to a flashlight. He lifted it, sweeping the beam over the clearing. Muted light brushed the toes of her boots.

He lurched off the deck slipping on a patch of buried ice. Another round of cursing followed. At the bottom of the stairs, he turned towards the shop. Noelle's heart sank. He was going after Jake.

She had to distract him. Sliding out from under the branches, she fumbled for the flashlight she had stashed in her pocket. Her distraction had to get his attention without getting herself killed.

No more time. He had made his decision. He was heading for the shop. Taking a deep breath Noelle pushed away from the tree. She switched on the light and ran. Heavy snow clawed her legs bogging her down, slowing her racing steps to a turtle plod.

Shooting a quick look over her shoulder she saw his light swing towards her. She ran harder, rounded a corner and collided with a rotting pile of firewood. It clattered to the ground. *Cr-a-ack!* A shot punctuated the fall of logs. The trunk of a nearby sapling blew apart. Shredded moss and bark stung her face. She threw herself to one side. Another wild shot. Closer. A branch above disintegrated. Bits of cedar rained down. She flinched and crawled faster. Bare branches closed over her head. She extinguished the light.

Her lungs burned, her legs shook. No time to rest. She pushed herself up. A quick look back showed he was still coming, tracking her by the path of broken snow she'd left behind. Panicked she threw herself at the thick brush, tearing through the dead wet foliage. Sharp branches poked her. Soggy foliage slicked her face. She hurled herself through a drift draped in branches and surfaced in a cold shower of snow. Shaking her head, she cleared the freezing powder from her eyes and pushed her hair back. The deep snow hampered her. Hidden roots caught her feet. She fell again and again. The weight of her body broke through the buried ice of a creek and her boots filled with freezing slush. Her feet were popsicles, the fake fur on the boots weighed down by balls of snow.

She looked back. The light was still coming. She tripped and rolled down a slope. At the peak of the hill, the light wavered.

Come on, come on, she thought fiercely, what are you waiting for? Extending her arm, she flicked on the light and dived for the base of a tree, turning the lamp off as she fell.

The light above swiveled towards her. She burrowed into the tree. Cold ate through her clothes. She couldn't feel where the wet denim touched her thighs.

She crept past the trunk and spotted a woodshed at the edge of the clearing. The shed was windowless, with a heavy bolt on the door. Could she trap him inside? Snow climbed halfway up the door of the abandoned shed. Noelle kicked it away and grabbed the bolt, sliding it open. The cold metal stung her fingers and stuck to her hand. Letting go, she pulled open the door and risked turning the flashlight on, shining the beam over a small pile of wood and a metal jerry can. A glimmer of hope rose up. Could she lure him in and lock him inside?

He'd have to think she was hiding there. Her hands shook as she pulled off her jacket. Cold. She was so cold. She gasped under the bone-deep cut of the wind. With fumbling fingers, she stacked the can on top of the wood and draped her jacket over top, propping the sleeves up as though she were kneeling. Was it good enough? She took another look with the light. Maybe.

She left the door cracked open, caught on a pile of snow. She wanted it to look as though she had dashed inside, desperate to hide. This was a one-shot deal. Oh my god, the gun. He could shoot his way out. How many bullets did his gun hold? She shivered. Her teeth chattered. It didn't matter. She didn't have another plan. This one had to work.

If it didn't, she'd die from exposure. That brought a hysterical giggle to her lips. She clasped her hands over her mouth stifling it. The warm breath on her fingers thawed them and she held them against her cold cheeks, praying for a miracle.

The bobbing light edged nearer. She waited, leaning into the shadows, grateful for the darkness of her jeans and sweater.

His heavy breathing filled her ears. She was sure he'd hear the pounding of her heart and be warned. He was so close. If he looked up or turned the light towards her, he would see her. He stopped and shone his light at the trampled snow and partially open door. Wary of a trap, he twisted looking back at the surrounding area.

He reached into his pocket, pulled out the revolver and toed open the door. Extending his gun hand in front of him he stepped towards the opening. His flashlight flickered and died.

"*Mierda!*" he cursed, striking the light with the butt of the gun. It shone briefly and went out. "Piece of cheap crap!" He threw the broken torch against the wall of the shed and looked at the door.

Noelle was up on the balls of her feet ready to move. She had one chance. Had Cobra seen the shape before the light died?

"Step inside," she willed. "Just one step."

Slowly his foot lifted over the threshold. One more step and he was in the shed.

Noelle threw herself at the door, slamming it shut and shooting the bolt through its housing. She hurled herself to one side.

Gunshots splintered the wood.

"Open the door! I'll let you go!" He kicked the door and it bulged on its hinges.

Noelle rolled to her feet. She had to barricade the door so that even if he shot the lock off, he couldn't get out. The clearing was riddled with logs and stumps. She dragged them over, piling them in front of the door.

"Damn you, you bitch!" he shouted. "I'll get out of here, and when I do, I'll find you."

Snow shuddered off the roof, settling into piles beneath the eaves. The shed was built of two by fours and thick cedar shakes. If the door held, there was no way he could break free. She had him caged.

Gradually, the kicks lessened, but the violent stream of cursing flowed on.

"I'll find you. If not you, maybe that little kid, the one with the drum set. Maybe I start there. Maybe I . . ."

Noelle didn't wait to hear more. She ran for the cabin, cutting through the bush and up the slope. She needed warm dry clothes. She couldn't help Jake if she died from exposure. Inside the fire was still burning on the grate. She tossed an armful of wood onto it and whirled in the direction of the bedroom. Broken glass crunched under foot. The decorations she had worked so hard at, littered the ground. The Christmas tree had borne the brunt of the gunman's rage. She picked her way through the destruction tearing off her wet clothes on route. Kicking off her jeans she pulled on dry clothes, grabbing a thick woolen turtleneck and the granny sweater. The warmth made her want to weep.

Back in the great room, she stood by the fire wincing as the sting of blood returned to her fingers. She had to get back to Jake. By now he would be seriously hypothermic.

She needed light. Blindly she fumbled through the debris, searching for the box of matches that had sat on the mantle. Shards of glass pricked her fingers. She ignored the pain and finally unearthed the cardboard box of matchsticks.

With shaking hands, she lit every candle she could find. The act forced back the shadows. Her heart rate started to slow. She was thinking clearly again. First warm blankets and clothes, then food. She'd take them back to Jake and somehow find a way out of here. Piling everything onto a blanket, she ransacked Jake's suitcase, throwing sweaters, socks and more blankets onto it. Exhaustion made her movements jerky and uncoordinated. She staggered towards the door, dragging her blanketed bundle.

Bang! The door crashed against the wall, the force shaking the cabin. Snow and wind poured through the gap. The candles flared and sputtered. Noelle dropped the blanket and spun towards the sound.

"You thought you were so smart." The Cobra stepped through the opening. "Your man is dead. You will join him soon."

Noelle screamed and darted to one side. Cobra was a big man, but fast on his feet. Leaping forward, he caught hold of her sweater and yanked her backwards. He grabbed her hair, tangling his fingers through it. Pain filled her eyes with tears and forced her up on her toes to relieve the pressure. Powerless she moved where he pulled her.

He laughed.

"You should have taken my offer. I would have made it fast. Now, we play a bit first."

His nails bit into her scalp. He jerked her head around, forcing her to look at him. He smiled. "On your knees," he ordered.

Noelle gave up, her knees buckling.

"Enough, *chica*? So weak you are." He let go of her hair.

She collapsed, her hands reaching out, clinging to his jacket.

He fumbled at the belt of his jeans, cursing his frozen fingers.

Noelle buried her fingers in his jacket. One—two—three—she pushed him backwards and then, with his weight off balance, pulled him towards her. Setting her jaw and tucking in her chin, she snapped her head up driving her crown upwards in a vicious head butt. Stars filled her eyes. Roaring in pain he reeled back as blood poured from his nose.

Noelle started for the door. Cobra recovered, sweeping out his arm, catching the back of her sweater. She fought but he was stronger. His hands closed around her throat choking her. She raked her nails over his face. The pressure on her neck increased. She gasped once, twice. Darkness closed over her. An image of Jake's face filled her mind, the picture whitening and dissolving to nothing.

Her attacker released the pressure and let her flop to the floor. He prodded her with his foot and bent to check for signs of life. Satisfied there were none, he moved to the candlelit mantle, picked up a burning candle and tossed it onto the couch. He dropped two more onto the carpet. Smiling down at her, he moved to the fireplace, kicking the logs off the grate and propping the door open. A fire needed oxygen to burn. The wind would feed the flames. The evidence would be gone. Once again, he had pulled off the perfect crime. He lifted his hand to his bloody nose. The bitch broke his nose.

A few minutes later an engine roared to life. The sound faded into the distance. Flames greedily licked the carpet, gobbling up the festive greenery, engulfing the broken Christmas tree. The only noise was the roar of the blaze and the howl of wind through the treetops.

38

Jake stirred and opened his eyes to darkness. What the hell? He sat, banging his forehead on a low wooden roof. Damn. His head hurt. He lifted a hand and discovered an egg-sized bump behind his ear. Guess that explained the headache, but where was he?

He slid his hand to the front pocket of his jeans and pulled out a disposable lighter. He didn't smoke, but like a good boy scout he was always prepared. Thumbing the striker on the lighter, he conjured a tiny flame and illuminated the space around him. He was nestled in a pile of tarps tucked into the space beneath a work bench.

Okay. He looked around. How did he get here? He remembered someone behind him and then a voice—after that—nothing. He shook his head and winced. How long had he been out here? Noelle! He lurched forward, and staggered to his feet. The sudden motion made his head swim. He grabbed the edge of the bench to stay upright.

Huffing in a few deep breaths, he forced his legs forward pushing himself to reach the door. Sweat trickled down his face. His head pounded as if it might split open any second. His stomach heaved. Concussion, he thought blurrily. The blow to his head had rattled his brain.

Grimly he pulled open the door and narrowed his eyes against the lash of snowflakes. The sky was alive with them, pearly white flakes swooping and swirling over the trees. He looked towards the cabin. Above it the sky glowed with a brightness that had nothing to do with the snowstorm. Pushing off from the door frame, he reeled towards the cabin, stumbling to a stop at the base of the porch stairs. The work of pushing through the thigh deep snow left him weak and trembling. He grabbed the railing to keep from falling.

"Noelle," he shouted, throwing his arm up in front of his face to block the heat. "Noelle," he whispered.

Flames roared beyond the open door, popping and snapping, morphing and growing. The light burned his eyes. The stinging smoke bathed them in tears. It was a scene from a nightmare—his nightmare.

He dropped to his knees and climbed the steps crawling into the inferno, hugging the ground. The heat robbed him of breath. He sucked in a searing gasp and inched inside shouting her name. The smoke choked him, blinded him. He fought his way towards the bedroom, glass crunching beneath his palms. He hissed in pain as a shard embedded in his palm. Yanking it free, he rubbed his eyes and blinked, trying to see something through the heavy smoke. Grimly he pushed forward, sweeping his hands over the floor in front of him.

Coughing, he tried pulling his t-shirt up over his face, but every time he moved it dropped back down. The fire grabbed hold of the great beams above his head, attacking the heavy wood. Embers fell in a burning rain, each drop starting a new conflagration. His left hand brushed a booted foot.

"Noelle!" he croaked. He ran his hands up her leg and grabbed hold of the waistband on her jeans. He reversed direction dragging her with him. The curtains by the door ignited, flames shooting upwards, gobbling up the expensive fabric, melting away the work of some high-end designer. Tendrils ate at the walls, feeding on paint and drywall. Wind roared through the open door, feeding the fire, whipping the debris into a maelstrom of flying ash and smoke.

Jake bent over Noelle, trying to shelter her from the showers of sparks. He coughed dryly and tried to suck another breath into his painful lungs. How long had Noelle been there? Was she burnt? Was she alive? The freezing lash of the blizzard was welcome. He pulled Noelle through the door and dragged her down the stairs, trying to cushion her in his arms. Exhausted, he couldn't make it to the truck. He collapsed in the shelter of the generator shed and groped for a pulse at the base of her throat. A quick flutter moved under his cold fingers. He dropped his hand lower and felt her chest moving, slowly rising and falling.

"Noelle," he gasped hoarsely. "Can you hear me? Wake up. We have to move." He shook her.

Noelle felt the luxury of cold air on her overheated skin. She took a tortured breath through throat muscles screaming in pain. Slowly she exhaled searing air from her lungs and gasped in a glorious breath free of smoke. A tear crept past her lashes. Gentle hands cupped her face. She faded into a world of darkness unaware of the voice calling her name.

***

"How did you know to get here?" Jake asked pulling the blanket wrapped around his shoulders tighter. He watched the paramedics load Noelle into a helicopter.

Detective Ryerson looked away from the scene. A grimness covered his craggy face. "She called for help after Brenjer knocked you out. She got my answering machine and left a partial message before the phone died." He shook his head and continued, "I don't know what happened after that."

"Huh," Jake said, turning to avoid Ryerson's eyes. He missed the pitying look the detective gave him. He knew what had happened. Noelle had saved his life. Hopefully, he'd been quick enough to make it in time to save hers. The paramedics said she had a lot of bruising around her neck, strangulation marks. That combined with smoke inhalation meant they would have to wait to see what the outcome was. He grimaced, thinking back to what had happened. He was supposed to protect her.

"How do you know who this bastard is?" he asked trying to focus on something other than Noelle's pale still face. "Where is he now? Did you get him?"

The Detective stirred and returned his gaze to Jake. "He left prints at the Hamilton house. First ones we ever found. They matched passport documents. As for where he is, we don't know. We'll get a team in to find out what happened." Ryerson frowned at the smoldering cabin. "Thank God for the snow. The whole hill could have gone up." He ran his fingers through his hair, looking like a disgruntled porcupine.

Jake didn't answer. Instead he looked towards the sound of heavy machinery. "A snowplow at this time of night?" he asked.

"We can't fly out with her. There isn't room. I didn't think you'd want to stay another night. Might get awfully cold."

Jake nodded vaguely, watching the rotors on the helicopter start to spin. A blast of icy pellets stung his face. The chopper rose, bearing Noelle away from him. Jake's face hardened and closed.

Ryerson shook his head and walked away in response to a call from the plow driver.

The lights on the helicopter faded into the night sky. The snow had ended as quickly as it started, and stars were beginning to twinkle. Jake ignored the other men and watched the tiny blinking light. Ryerson stepped in front of him.

"The plow driver says there's a car in the ravine about five kilometers down the road. Must have taken the corner too fast and lost control. We're running the tags, but we think the crash is recent." A look of cold satisfaction covered his face. "Care to guess who might be in it?"

"I don't gamble," Jake said brusquely, his face granite.

"You still have the keys to the truck?" Ryerson asked.

"Yeah. Sorry. I'm not thinking clearly."

"It's okay. We'll get the interview stuff out of the way while the plow finishes. My team is coming in behind them."

They retreated to the shelter of Ray's four-by-four. Ryerson spent the time working, jotting down notes, picking Jake's brain for the few details he remembered.

Finally, silence fell over them. Jake leaned back against the seat and closed his eyes. He stunk of smoke and his hands and face were hot and raw. Was Noelle going to be okay? She had known the Cobra—Brenjer—was out there, but had taken the time to hide him away in the nest of tarps. Ryerson's team had already started putting things together. They had found a woodshed shot full of holes, its door hanging from its hinges.

"She probably saved your life, you know." Ryerson closed the notebook he'd been scribbling in.

Jake grunted. He didn't want to talk about it, especially to the other cop. Ryerson was too astute; he saw too much.

Ryerson climbed out of the truck and slammed the door leaving Jake to brood over what had taken place, to think about Noelle and what they had shared. Could he forgive her for throwing it all away? Was what they had worth fighting for?

Search and Rescue arrived on site, long-lining down to the flipped car, recovering the body of a single male. The case was closed. With Brenjer dead, Noelle was safe.

All Jake had to do was get on an airplane and fly home. He was better on his own. Caring about someone else hurt too much.

EPILOGUE

Noelle closed the book she was pretending to read. The pages were wet and pulpy from an accidental dunking, and she wasn't really reading it anyway. In fact, if someone gave her a spot quiz on the plot, she'd fail it. She sank deeper in the water letting the bubbles swirl up to her chin. So much for a steamy bath curing her Christmas blues. All it had done was turn her into a giant prune. Disgruntled she sat up and yanked the plug on what was supposed to be a relaxing time out. Stacks of scented suds swirled down the drain.

A lock of hair escaped from behind one ear. She shoved it back and her fingers slid over the lump on her temple. She winced. Her head had taken a lot of abuse over the past week—the black eye from her first battle with Brenjer still bloomed on her cheek. More recent was the purple goose egg on her forehead. Couple that with the finger marks around her throat and it looked like she should be celebrating Halloween, not Christmas. Very attractive. She'd be sure to keep out of camera range over the holidays.

Scooping up a fluffy towel, she dried off and donned flannel boxers and a silky camisole, wrapping her housecoat overtop while avoiding her reflection in the mirror. She didn't want to see the haunted look that lingered in her eyes.

She opened the bathroom door and tripped over the furry lump stretched across the threshold. Her elbow clipped the edge of the doorframe, and she hissed with pain.

"Oww. Jackson . . . Must you . . . oww . . ." She rubbed her arm wanting to sit down and bawl like a baby.

Jackson flung her a reproachful look and lumbered to his feet. If there was a problem, his expression said, it was strictly with her.

"Forget it, dog," she muttered, suffering a twinge of guilt. Black labs did wounded dignity well. Jackson took the job of bodyguard seriously. She had barely managed to kick him out of the bathroom, and when she did, his whining and scratching at the door had hardly promoted serenity.

He whined again, nudging her hand. His nose was cool and damp against her skin. Hesitantly he wagged his tail.

"You are so pathetic. I know I went away and left you with those horrible people and they only gave you treats if you stayed on the mat." She ruffled his fur, scratching behind his ears.

Jackson barked and jumped up, planting his paws against her. Evading his sloppy kisses, she felt unhappiness settle deeper over her. She was acting like Ebenezer Scrooge pre the ghostly visits—doling out scraps of attention like pennies. She rubbed Jackson's ears as gloomy introspection buried her.

She had to shake it off. Her own company was bringing her down. Aimlessly she wandered into the living room. In honor of her homecoming, her brothers had decorated a Christmas tree with twinkling blue lights that flashed interminably. She knew she should find the bad bulb and fix the problem, but couldn't summon the energy. A thickness she couldn't blame on strangulation or smoke inhalation rose in her throat. Tears burned her eyes. She blinked them away. She wasn't going to cry. She had promised herself a thousand times that she would move on.

The tears were a leftover from the past week. The doctors said she might suffer some posttraumatic stress-like symptoms. She would rather blame the pathetic excuse for a Christmas tree for her humdrum spirits. The tree would make a snowman cry. Branches down, it was the ugliest ever. If she blamed the tree she wouldn't have to admit what was really bothering her, and she could continue acting like the lovelorn heroine in a gothic romance.

Try to be happy, she told herself firmly. You're out of the hospital in time for Christmas. You could be eating chicken surprise and drinking non-fat eggnog with the nutty old lady in the next bed. The memory brought a weak smile to her face. That could only happen if the nonagenarian hadn't made another escape. She envisioned Mrs. Moore making a getaway on the back of a strategically parked motorcycle, hospital gown flapping in the breeze. The memory of Mrs. Moore's bare sagging bottom was one she wanted to delete.

She bent to pick up a fallen ornament. It was a glass globe she and Jake had collected for their first Christmas— the Christmas that never happened. Memory swamped her—a motorcycle trip to Salt Spring Island—unrelenting rain filling her shoes with muddy water. The weather should have turned the trip into a disaster, but sitting on the back of the bike, her arms wrapped around Jake and her head resting on his back, she had never been happier.

The farmers' market they'd stumbled on was a godsend, giving them an excuse to park the bike in search of dryer ground. They'd walked the cold from their limbs, wandering hand in hand through the booths, breathing in the scents of handmade soaps and organic vegetables, sipping steaming mochas. The weather had chased away most of the tourists leaving the bored vendors willing to bargain.

She hung the glass ball back on the tree. What's done is done. Get on with your life and forget him. Easy to say, harder to practice.

Sinking onto the couch she curled her legs under her and rested her chin on her palms. The radio was set to a blues channel playing Christmas music. A sultry-voiced singer was exhorting Santa to hurry down the chimney. Right. Personally, she wouldn't spend the evening in a vintage gown sitting by a chimney waiting for a fat man in a red velour suit. Her tastes ran more towards built, buffed and oozing with…She crossed her arms over her chest and scowled. Yeah. Christmas Eve. Soft music, eggnog, a crackling fire . . . whom was she kidding?

The glass of eggnog and the platter of cheese and crackers she had left on the table irritated her. No, everything irritated her. The scent of the mulberry candle burning on the mantle and the woodsy tang of juniper and cedar made her think of the cabin. That made her think of Jake. It was a vicious circle—Jake, Christmas, Jake, candlelight, Jake, his body touching hers. Whoa, girl. She reined in her thoughts and let out another gusty sigh. There was no sense in heading off in that direction again.

She stared at the flickering candles and sparkling string of lights draping the mantle. She studied the fire. She gazed at the Christmas tree. Face it, Noelle. You are an idiot. Maybe she should be singing that song, only she wouldn't be waiting for Santa. She would be wishing for Jake.

Jackson sighed and stretched, twitching in his sleep. Was he chasing reindeer in his dreams?

Christmas Eve was here and she couldn't summon up the tiniest bit of enthusiasm. That was why she was alone. She had told so many lies to escape her family's smothering attention, her stocking would be loaded with coal come morning. Not one person could argue with a girl who'd survived strangulation and a bump on the head that should have caused more than a mild concussion. She wasn't up to all the ho ho hos, and the last thing she wanted was company. No, that wasn't true. There was one person whose company she would have taken in a minute, but that wasn't an option. She took a sip of eggnog, wincing as the muscles in her throat worked.

She could blame the fire for that. Smoke inhalation and laryngeal edema were the terms listed on the hospital report. There wouldn't be any lasting effects. When school started in the New Year, she would be ready to go.

She sighed. She was good at lying to herself. Look at the snow job she had pulled convincing herself she was happy for the last ten years. It took less than ten minutes in Jake's company to fall back under his spell. Who wouldn't succumb? The guy could stop traffic better than a red light. No, if she found Jake in her stocking, she would write a thank you letter to Santa.

The real reason she was alone on Christmas Eve was the only person she wanted to share it with, had jumped on a plane to put as much distance between them as possible. He hadn't even tried to see her in the hospital. He hated her. He would never forgive her for failing to tell him about the miscarriage.

She leaned back and watched the flames. Jackson opened his eyes and whined. His ears twitched. Heaving himself up, he padded across the room as a growl rumbled in his throat.

"What's up, boy?"

The sound of footsteps on the porch reached her less sensitive ears. Breathe, she commanded herself. Just breathe. It's over. He's dead. He can't hurt you. It's Ray, or Dad, or one of her other brothers. They were checking on her again. They'd been treating her like an orphaned elf since she had woken up in the hospital.

Standing she tugged the belt of her housecoat tighter, trying to ignore the tremor in her fingertips. Jackson's weight against her legs was reassuring. Having a dog was a deterrent. Yeah, right. She rolled her eyes. Jackson would be all over any would-be intruder. He'd love him to death.

Stop it. Answer the door and send whoever is out there on their way, then you can go back to your pity party. Slowly she walked to the door. Lifting the lacy curtain, she peered out at the tall figure on the other side. She still hadn't replaced the burned-out porch light. Fighting the urge to run and hide beneath her bed, she snapped the deadbolt unlocked and opened the door.

"Noelle." Jake pushed through the opening. "You didn't even check to see who was at the door. God, you need a keeper." He shook his head and yanked off his jacket, and dropped it over the back of a chair.

He crossed his arms and glared at her. For some reason, the look kick-started her heart, sending it skittering in her chest.

"I—" she started.

"What were you thinking? You could have died in that cabin!" He raked a hand through his hair and paced a tight circle around the room before coming back to stand in front of her.

"You could have died. I could have—" He stopped, unable to go on.

"Jake," she whispered, leaning towards him, her hands resting on his arms.

"You smell like flowers after the rain," he said taking a slow deep breath.

He reached out and touched the marks left by Brenjer. They were a dark contrast against her pallor.

"My God, Noelle. I could have lost you." The anger drained from his face. "I made it to the airport, got a standby fare to Toronto, got on the plane, and discovered I couldn't go. Not like this, not without talking to you."

He raked his hand through his hair unaware of the sexy bad boy look it gave him. Sprinkles of rain dotted his hair.

Noelle drank in the sight of him, memorizing every line on his face. If this was the last time she saw him, she was going to be able to recall them forever. She didn't care how much he yelled at her. She wanted to be in his arms.

"Jake, I . . ."

Jake reached out and gathered her into his arms.

"Noelle," he said. The words were muffled against her throat. "I thought I lost you . . . One more minute and the roof would have caved in."

He raised his head. His eyes were haunted with a pain that ripped at her heart.

She burrowed against him. Tears trickled down her face washing away the uncertainty of the past few days.

Jake kissed them away.

"I won't let you walk out of my life again. Ten years ago, I was a fool. My pride let me leave without finding out why we let what we had end. It won't happen again."

Noelle held him, afraid that if she let go he'd disappear. She matched him kiss for kiss as they stumbled to the couch. Curled into his lap, she inhaled the scent of rain and wind. He stroked her hair.

"How are you?" he demanded between soul-stealing kisses.

"I'm fine," she croaked and cleared her throat. "A bit like a bullfrog, but no lasting effects." She shrugged. None of that mattered, not when he was here beside her.

"I was so angry, so worried," he whispered, trailing kisses down her neck.

The kisses sent goose bumps up her spine.

"I didn't know what I felt the most. Never scare me like that again. When I found you, the cabin was engulfed in flames. All I could think was that it was my fault. If I hadn't been so stupid, you wouldn't have been alone." The memory clouded his eyes.

"I'm fine. When I found you in the workshop, I thought you were dead. I tried to hide you in case he came back." A hint of a smile turned her lips up. "I could barely move you."

She traced her fingertips over his mouth and he caught her hand, kissing her palm before releasing it. He pulled away and sat up.

"We have to talk," he said.

He looked so serious. Noelle's heart plunged in her chest. He was leaving. It was over.

"I made it onto the plane and realized I couldn't go." He grinned. "Have you ever tried to get off a fully loaded plane? Security was not amused. They called Ryerson and he vouched for me. Anyway, I holed up at my parent's house to try and think things through. I realized something. I can't live without you. Noelle, will you . . ."

Noelle launched herself at him. The weight of her body rocked him back as his arms closed around her. They kissed until she was breathless.

Jake moved away and fumbled in his pocket. He pulled out a small square box. Carefully loosening the ring inside, he slipped the solitaire over her finger, kissing her hand.

"I love you. Will you marry me again? This time we make it forever."

Noelle eyed the ring glittering on her finger and laughing, brushed away tears of happiness. Forever, she liked the sound of that. Her spirits rose. It was Christmas Eve and miracles happened.

ABOUT THE AUTHOR

Carol Kinnee is a free-lance writer living on the west coast of British Columbia. When's she's not tied to her laptop, she's out exploring what BC has to offer. Currently, she is working on a sequel to her novel, *The Christmas Presence,* Book 2 in the Landings series.

Visit her at her website: carolkinnee.com.

Made in the USA
Lexington, KY
12 May 2018